D0546227

PHILIP K. DICK
FLOW MY TEARS, THE POLICEMAN SAID

Philip K. Dick was born in Chicago in 1928 and lived most of his life in California. He briefly attended the University of California but dropped out before completing any classes. In 1952, he began writing professionally and proceeded to write thirty-six novels and five short-story collections. He won the Hugo Award for best novel in 1962 for *The Man in the High Castle* and the John W. Campbell Memorial Award for best novel of the year in 1974 for *Flow My Tears, the Policeman Said*. Philip K. Dick died on March 2, 1982, in Santa Ana, California, of heart failure following a stroke.

Also by Philip K. Dick
Available from Vintage Books

Confessions of a Crap Artist
The Divine Invasion
The Game-Players of Titan
The Man in the High Castle
Now Wait for Last Year
A Scanner Darkly
The Three Stigmata of Palmer Eldritch
The Transmigration of Timothy Archer
Ubik
The World Jones Made
VALIS

FLOW MY TEARS, THE POLICEMAN SAID

PHILIP K. DICK

FLOW MY TEARS, THE POLICEMAN SAID

VINTAGE BOOKS

A Division of Random House, Inc.

New York

First Vintage Books Edition, July 1993

Copyright © 1974 by Philip K. Dick

All rights reserved under International and Pan-American Copyright
Conventions. Published in the United States by Vintage Books, a division of
Random House, Inc., New York, and distributed in Canada by Random
House of Canada Limited, Toronto. Originally published by Doubleday &
Co., Inc., New York, in 1974.

Library of Congress Cataloging-in-Publication Data
Dick, Philip K.
Flow my tears, the policeman said / Philip K. Dick.—1st Vintage Books ed.
p. cm.
ISBN 0-679-74066-X
I. Title.
PS3554.I3F56   1993
813'.54—dc20   92-50649
CIP

Manufactured in the United States of America
10 9 8 7 6 5 4 3

The love in this novel is for Tessa,
and the love in me is for her, too.
She is my little song.

PART ONE

Flow my tears, fall from your springs!
Exiled forever let me mourn;
Where night's black bird her sad infamy sings,
There let me live forlorn.

1

On Tuesday, October 11, 1988, the *Jason Taverner Show* ran thirty seconds short. A technician, watching through the plastic bubble of the control dome, froze the final credit on the video section, then pointed to Jason Taverner, who had started to leave the stage. The technician tapped his wrist, pointed to his mouth.

Into the boom mike Jason said smoothly, "Keep all those cards and V-letters coming in, folks. And stay tuned now for *The Adventures of Scotty, Dog Extraordinary.*"

The technician smiled; Jason smiled back, and then both the audio and the video clicked off. Their hour-long music and variety program, which held the second highest rating among the year's best TV shows, had come to an end. And it had all gone well.

"Where'd we lose half a minute?" Jason said to his special guest star of the evening, Heather Hart. It puzzled him. He liked to time his own shows.

Heather Hart said, "Baby bunting, it's all right." She put her cool hand across his slightly moist forehead, rubbed the perimeter of his sand-colored hair affectionately.

"Do you realize what power you have?" Al Bliss, their business agent, said to Jason, coming up close—too close as always—to him. "Thirty million people saw you zip up your fly tonight. That's a record of sorts."

"I zip up my fly every week," Jason said. "It's my trademark. Or don't you catch the show?"

"But thirty million," Bliss said, his round, florid face spotted with drops of perspiration. "Think of it. And then there's the residuals."

Jason said crisply, "I'll be dead before the residuals on this show pay off. Thank God."

"You'll probably be dead tonight," Heather said, "with all those fans of yours packed in outside there. Just waiting to rip you into little tiny squares like so many postage stamps."

"Some of them are your fans, Miss Hart," Al Bliss said, in his doglike panting voice.

"God damn them," Heather said harshly. "Why don't they go away? Aren't they breaking some law, loitering or something?"

Jason took hold of her hand and squeezed it forcefully, attracting her frowning attention. He had never understood her dislike for fans; to him they were the lifeblood of his public existence. And to him his public existence, his role as worldwide entertainer, was existence itself, period. "You shouldn't be an entertainer," he said to Heather, "feeling the way you do. Get out of the business. Become a social worker in a forced-labor camp."

"There're people there, too," Heather said grimly.

Two special police guards shouldered their way up to Jason Taverner and Heather. "We've got the corridor as clear as we're going to get it," the fatter of the two cops wheezed. "Let's go now, Mr. Taverner. Before the studio audience can trickle around to the side exits." He signaled to three other special police guards, who at once advanced toward the hot, packed passageway that led, eventually, to the nocturnal street. And out there the parked Rolls flyship in all its costly splendor, its tail rocket idling throbbingly. Like, Jason thought, a mechanical heart. A heart that beat for him alone, for him the star. Well, by extension, it throbbed in response to the needs of Heather, too.

She deserved it: she had sung well, tonight. Almost as well as—Jason grinned inwardly, to himself. Hell, let's face it, he

thought. They don't turn on all those 3-D color TV sets to
see the special guest star. There are a thousand special guest
stars scattered over the surface of earth, and a few in the
Martian colonies.

They turn on, he thought, to see *me*. And I am always
there. Jason Taverner has never and will never disappoint his
fans. However Heather may feel about hers.

"You don't like them," Jason said as they squirmed and
pushed and ducked their way down the steaming, sweat-
smelling corridor, "because you don't like yourself. You se-
cretly think they have bad taste."

"They're dumb," Heather grunted, and cursed quietly as
her flat, large hat flopped from her head and disappeared
forever within the whale's belly of close-pressing fans.

"They're ordinaries," Jason said, his lips at her ear, partly
lost as it was in her great tangle of shiny red hair. The famous
cascade of hair so widely and expertly copied in beauty salons
throughout Terra.

Heather grated, "Don't say that word."

"They're ordinaries," Jason said, "and they're morons.
Because"—he nipped the lobe of her ear—"because that's
what it means to be an ordinary. Right?"

She sighed. "Oh, God, to be in the flyship cruising through
the void. That's what I long for: an infinite void. With no
human voices, no human smells, no human jaws masticating
plastic chewing gum in nine iridescent colors."

"You really do hate them," he said.

"Yes." She nodded briskly. "And so do you." She halted
briefly, turning her head to confront him. "You know your
goddamn voice is gone; you know you're coasting on your
glory days, which you'll never see again." She smiled at him,
then. Warmly. "Are we growing old?" she said, above the
mumbles and squeaks of the fans. "Together? Like man and
wife?"

Jason said, "Sixes don't grow old."

"Oh yes," Heather said. "Oh yes they do." Reaching upward, she touched his wavy brown hair. "How long have you
been tinting it, dearheart? A year? Three?"

"Get in the flyship," he said brusquely, maneuvering her ahead of him, out of the building and onto the pavement of Hollywood Boulevard.

"I'll get in," Heather said, "if you'll sing me a high B natural. Remember when you—"

He thrust her bodily into the flyship, squeezed in after her, turned to help Al Bliss close the door, and then they were up and into the rain-clouded nighttime sky. The great gleaming sky of Los Angeles, as bright as if it were high noon. And that's what it is for you and for me, he thought. For the two of us, in all times to come. It will always be as it is now, because we are sixes. Both of us. Whether *they* know it or not.

And it's not, he thought grimly, enjoying the bleak humor of it. The knowledge which they together had, the knowledge unshared. Because that was the way it was meant to be. And always had . . . even now after it had all turned out so badly. Badly, at least, in the designers' eyes. The great pundits who had guessed and guessed wrong. Forty-five beautiful years ago, when the world was young and droplets of rain still clung to the now-gone Japanese cherry trees in Washington, D.C. And the smell of spring that had hovered over the noble experiment. For a short while, anyhow.

"Let's go to Zürich," he said aloud.

"I'm too tired," Heather said. "Anyhow, that place bores me."

"The house?" He was incredulous. Heather had picked it out for the two of them, and for years there they had gotten away—away especially from the fans that Heather hated so much.

Heather sighed and said, "The house. The Swiss watches. The bread. The cobblestones. The snow on the hills."

"Mountains," he said, feeling aggrieved still. "Well, hell," he said. "I'll go without you."

"And pick up someone else?"

He simply could not understand. "Do you *want* me to take someone else with me?" he demanded.

"You and your magnetism. Your charm. You could get any

girl in the world into that big brass bed with you. Not that you're so much once you get there."

"God," he said with disgust. "That again. Always the same old gripes. And the ones that're fantasy—they're the ones you really hang on to."

Turning to face him, Heather said earnestly, "You know how you look, even now at the age you are. You're beautiful. Thirty million people ogle you an hour a week. It's not your singing they're interested in . . . it's your incurable physical beauty."

"The same can be said for you," he said caustically. He felt tired and he yearned for the privacy and seclusion that lay there on the outskirts of Zürich, silently waiting for the two of them to come back once more. And it was as if the house wanted them to stay, not for a night or a week of nights, but forever.

"I don't show my age," Heather said.

He glanced at her, then studied her. Volumes of red hair, pale skin with a few freckles, a strong roman nose. Deep-set huge violet eyes. She was right; she didn't show her age. Of course she never tapped into the phone-grid transex net-work, as he did. But in point of fact he did so very little. So he was not hooked, and there had not been, in his case, brain damage or premature aging.

"You're a goddamn beautiful-looking person," he said grudgingly.

"And you?" Heather said.

He could not be shaken by this. He knew that he still had his charisma, the force they had inscribed on the chromo-somes forty-two years ago. True, his hair had become mostly gray and he did tint it. And a few wrinkles had appeared here and there. But—

"As long as I have my voice," he said, "I'll be okay. I'll have what I want. You're wrong about me—it's your six aloofness, your cherished so-called individuality. Okay, if you don't want to fly over to the house in Zürich, where *do* you want to go? Your place? My place?"

"I want to be married to you," Heather said. "So then it

won't be my place versus your place but it'll be our place. And I'll give up singing and have three children, all of them looking like you."

"Even the girls?"

Heather said, "They'll all be boys."

Leaning over he kissed her on the nose. She smiled, took his hand, patted it warmly. "We can go anywhere tonight," he said to her in a low, firm, controlled, and highly projected voice, almost a father voice; it generally worked well with Heather, whereas nothing else did. Unless, he thought, I walk off.

She feared that. Sometimes in their quarrels, especially at the house in Zürich, where no one could hear them or interfere, he had seen the fear on her face. The idea of being alone appalled her; he knew it; she knew it; the fear was part of the reality of their joint life. Not their public life; for them, as genuinely professional entertainers, there they had complete, rational control: however angry and estranged they became they would function together in the big worshiping world of viewers, letter writers, noisy fans. Even outright hatred could not change that.

But there could be no hate between them anyhow. They had too much in common. They got so damn much from each other. Even mere physical contact, such as this, sitting together in the Rolls skyfly, made them happy. For as long, anyhow, as it lasted.

Reaching into the inner pocket of his custom-tailored genuine silk suit—one of perhaps ten in the whole world—he brought out a wad of government-certified bills. A great number of them, compressed into a fat little bundle.

"You shouldn't carry so much cash on you," Heather said naggingly, in the tone he disliked so much: the opinionated-mother tone.

Jason said, "With this"—he displayed the package of bills—"we can buy our way into any—"

"If some unregistered student who has sneaked across from a campus burrow just last night doesn't chop your hand off at the wrist and run away with it, both your hand and your flashy money. You always have been flashy. Flashy and loud. Look at your tie. Look at it!" She had raised her voice, now; she seemed genuinely angry.

"Life is short," Jason said. "And prosperity even shorter." But he placed the package of bills back in his inside coat pocket, smoothed away at the lump it created in his otherwise perfect suit. "I wanted to buy you something with it," he said. Actually the idea had just come to him now; what he had planned to do with the money was something a little different: he intended to take it to Las Vegas, to the blackjack tables. As a six he could—and did—always win at blackjack; he had the edge over everyone, even the dealer. Even, he thought sleekly, the pit boss.

"You're lying," Heather said. "You didn't intend to get me anything; you never do, you're so selfish and always thinking about yourself. That's screwing money; you're going to buy some big-chested blonde and go to bed together with her. Probably at our place in Zürich, which, you realize, I haven't seen for four months now. I might as well be pregnant."

It struck him as odd that she would say that, out of all the possible retorts that might flow up into her conscious, talking mind. But there was a good deal about Heather that he did not understand; with him, as with her fans, she kept many things about her private.

But, over the years, he had learned a lot about her. He knew, for example, that in 1982 she had had an abortion, a well-kept secret, too. He knew that at one time she had been illegally married to a student commune leader, and that for one year she had lived in the rabbit warrens of Columbia University, along with all the smelly, bearded students kept subsurface lifelong by the pols and the nats. The police and the national guard, who ringed every campus, keeping the students from creeping across to society like so many black rats swarming out of a leaky ship.

And he knew that one year ago she had been busted for possession of drugs. Only her wealthy and powerful family had been able to buy her out of *that* one: her money and her charisma and fame hadn't worked when confrontation time with the police came.

Heather had been scarred a little by all that had overtaken her, but, he knew, she was all right now. Like all sixes she had enormous recuperative ability. It had been carefully built into each of them. Along with much, much else. Even he, at forty-two years, didn't know them all. And a lot had happened to him, too. Mostly in the form of dead bodies, the remains of other entertainers he had trampled on his long climb to the top.

"These 'flashy' ties—" he began, but then the skyfly's phone rang. He took it, said hello. Probably it was Al Bliss with the ratings on tonight's show.

But it was not. A girl's voice came to him, penetrating sharply, stridently into his ear. "Jason?" the girl said loudly.

"Yeah," he said. Cupping the mouthpiece of the phone he said to Heather, "It's Marilyn Mason. Why the hell did I give her my skyfly number?"

"Who the hell is Marilyn Mason?" Heather asked.

"I'll tell you later." He uncupped the phone. "Yes, dear; this is Jason for real, in the true reincarnated flesh. What is it? You sound terrible. Are they evicting you again?" He winked at Heather and grinned wryly.

"Get rid of her," Heather said.

Again cupping the mouthpiece of the phone he said to her, "I will; I'm trying to; can't you see?" Into the phone he said, "Okay, Marilyn. Spill your guts out to me; that's what I'm for."

For two years Marilyn Mason had been his protégée, so to speak. Anyhow, she wanted to be a singer—be famous, rich, loved—like him. One day she had come wandering into the studio, during rehearsal, and he had taken notice of her. Tight little worried face, short legs, skirt far too short—he had, as was his practice, taken it all in at first glance. And, a week later, he had arranged for an audition for her with Columbia Records, their artists and repertoire chief.

A lot had gone on in that week, but it hadn't had anything to do with singing.

Marilyn said shrilly into his ear, "I have to see you. Otherwise I'll kill myself and the guilt will be on you. For the rest of your life. And I'll tell that Heather Hart woman about us sleeping together all the time."

Inwardly he sighed. Hell, he was tired already, worn out by his hour-long show during which it was smile, smile, smile. "I'm on my way to Switzerland for the rest of tonight," he said firmly, as if speaking to a hysterical child. Usually, when Marilyn was in one of her accusatory, quasi-paranoid moods it worked. But not this time, naturally.

"It'll take you five minutes to get over here in that million-dollar Rolls skyfly of yours," Marilyn dinned in his ear. "I just want to talk to you for five seconds. I have something very important to tell you."

She's probably pregnant, Jason said to himself. Somewhere along the line she intentionally—or maybe unintentionally—forgot to take her pill.

"What can you tell me in five seconds that I don't already know?" he said sharply. "Tell me now."

"I want you here with me," Marilyn said, with her customary total lack of consideration. "You must come. I haven't seen you in six months and during that time I've done a lot of thinking about us. And in particular about that last audition."

"Okay," he said, feeling bitter and resentful. This was what he got for trying to manufacture for her—a no-talent—a career. He hung up the phone noisily, turned to Heather and said, "I'm glad you never ran into her; she's really a—"

"Bullshit," Heather said. "I didn't 'run into her' because you made damn sure you saw to that."

"Anyhow," he said, as he made a right turn for the skyfly, "I got her not one but two auditions, and she snurfled them both. And to keep her self-respect she's got to blame it on me. I somehow herded her into failing. You see the picture."

"Does she have nice boobs?" Heather said.

"Actually, yes." He grinned and Heather laughed. "You know my weakness. But I did my part of the bargain; I got her an audition—*two* auditions. The last one was six months ago and I know goddamn well she's still smoldering and brooding over it. I wonder what she wants to tell me."

He punched the control module to set up an automatic course for Marilyn's apartment building with its small but adequate roof field.

"She's probably in love with you," Heather said, as he parked the skyfly on its tail, releasing then the descent stairs.

"Like forty million others," Jason said genially.

Heather, making herself comfortable in the bucket seat of the skyfly said, "Don't be gone very long or so help me I'm taking off without you."

"Leaving me stuck with Marilyn?" he said. They both laughed. "I'll be right back." He crossed the field to the elevator, pressed the button.

When he entered Marilyn's apartment he saw, at once, that she was out of her mind. Her entire face had pinched and constricted; her body so retracted that it looked as if she were trying to ingest herself. And her eyes. Very few things around or about women made him uneasy, but this did. Her eyes, completely round, with huge pupils, bored at him as she stood silently facing him, her arms folded, everything about her unyielding and iron rigid.

"Start talking," Jason said, feeling around for the handle of the advantage. Usually—in fact virtually always—he could control a situation that involved a woman; it was, in point of fact, his specialty. But this . . . he felt uncomfortable. And still she said nothing. Her face, under layers of makeup, had become completely bloodless, as if she were an animated corpse. "You want another audition?" Jason asked. "Is that it?"

Marilyn shook her head no.

"Okay; tell me what it is," he said wearily but uneasily. He kept the unease out of his voice, however; he was far too shrewd, far too experienced, to let her hear his uncertainty. In a confrontation with a woman it ran nearly ninety per cent bluff, on both sides. It all lay in *how* you did it, not what you did.

"I have something for you," Marilyn turned, walked off out of sight into the kitchen. He strolled after her.

"You still blame me for the lack of success of both—" he began.

"Here you are," Marilyn said. She lifted up a plastic bag from the drainboard, stood holding it a moment, her face still bloodless and stark, her eyes jutting and unblinking, and then she yanked the bag open, swung it, moved swiftly up to him.

It happened too fast. He backed away out of instinct, but too slowly and too late. The gelatinlike Callisto cuddle sponge with its fifty feeding tubes clung to him, anchored itself to his chest. Already he felt the feeding tubes dig into him, into his chest.

He leaped to the overhead kitchen cabinets, grabbed out a half-filled bottle of scotch, unscrewed the lid with flying fingers, and poured the scotch onto the gelatinlike creature. His thoughts had become lucid, even brilliant; he did not panic, but stood there pouring the scotch onto the thing.

For a moment nothing happened. He still managed to hold himself together and not flee into panic. And then the thing bubbled, shriveled, fell from his chest onto the floor. It had died.

Feeling weak, he seated himself at the kitchen table. Now he found himself fighting off unconsciousness; some of the feeding tubes remained inside him, and they were still alive. "Not bad," he managed to say. "You almost got me, you fucking little tramp."

"Not almost," Marilyn Mason said flatly, emotionlessly. "Some of the feeding tubes are still in you and you know it; I can see it on your face. And a bottle of scotch isn't going to get them out. *Nothing* is going to get them out."

At that point he fainted. Dimly, he saw the green-and-gray floor rise to take him and then there was emptiness. A void without even himself in it.

Pain. He opened his eyes, reflexively touched his chest. His hand-tailored silk suit had vanished; he wore a cotton hospital

robe and he was lying flat on a gurney. "God," he said thickly
as the two staff men wheeled the gurney rapidly up the hospital corridor.

Heather Hart hovered over him, anxious and in shock,
but, like him, she retained full possession of her senses. "I
knew something was wrong," she said rapidly as the staff
men wheeled him into a room. "I didn't wait for you in the
skyfly; I came down after you."

"You probably thought we were in bed together," he said
weakly.

"The doctor said," Heather said, "that in another fifteen
seconds you would have succumbed to the somatic violation,
as he calls it. The entrance of that *thing* into you."

"I got the thing," he said. "But I didn't get all the feeding
tubes. It was too late."

"I know," Heather said. "The doctor told me. They're
planning surgery for as soon as possible; they may be able
to do something if the tubes haven't penetrated too far."

"I was good in the crisis," Jason grated; he shut his eyes
and endured the pain. "But not quite good enough. Just not
quite." Opening his eyes, he saw that Heather was crying.
"Is it that bad?" he asked her; reaching up he took hold of
her hand. He felt the pressure of her love as she squeezed
his fingers, and then there was nothing. Except the pain. But
nothing else, no Heather, no hospital, no staff men, no light.
And no sound. It was an eternal moment and it absorbed
him completely.

2

Light filtered back, filling his closed eyes with a membrane of illuminated redness. He opened his eyes, lifted his head to look around him. To search out Heather or the doctor.

He lay alone in the room. No one else. A bureau with a cracked vanity mirror, ugly old light fixtures jutting from the grease-saturated walls. And from somewhere nearby the blare of a TV set.

He was not in a hospital.

And Heather was not with him; he experienced her absence, the total emptiness of everything, because of her.

God, he thought. *What's happened?*

The pain in his chest had vanished, along with so much else. Shakily, he pushed back the soiled wool blanket, sat up, rubbed his forehead reflexively, gathered together his vitality.

This is a hotel room, he realized. A lousy, bug-infested cheap wino hotel. No curtains, no bathroom. Like he had lived in years ago, at the start of his career. Back when he had been unknown and had no money. The dark days he always shut out of his memory as best he could.

Money. He groped at his clothes, discovered that he no longer wore the hospital gown but had back, in wrinkled condition, his hand-tailored silk suit. And, in the inner coat pocket, the wad of high-denomination bills, the money he had intended to take to Vegas.

At least he had that.

Swiftly, he looked around for a phone. No, of course not. But there'd be one in the lobby. But whom to call? Heather? Al Bliss, his agent? Mory Mann, the producer of his TV show? His attorney, Bill Wolfer? Or all of them, as soon as possible, perhaps.

Unsteadily, he managed to get to his feet; he stood swaying, cursing for reasons he did not understand. An animal instinct held him; he readied himself, his strong six body, to fight. But he could not discern the antagonist, and that frightened him. For the first time in as long as he could remember he felt panic.

Has a lot of time passed? he asked himself. He could not tell; he had no sense of it either way. Daytime. Quibbles zooming and bleating in the skies outside the dirty glass of his window. He looked at his watch; it read ten-thirty. So what? It could be a thousand years off, for all he knew. His watch couldn't help him.

But the phone would. He made his way out into the dust-saturated corridor, found the stairs, descended step by step, holding on to the rail until at last he stood in the depressing, empty lobby with its ratty old overstuffed chairs.

Fortunately he had change. He dropped a one-dollar gold piece into the slot, dialed Al Bliss's number.

"Bliss Talent Agency," Al's voice came presently.

"Listen," Jason said. "I don't know where I am. In the name of Christ come and get me; get me out of here; get me someplace else. You understand, Al? Do you?"

Silence from the phone. And then in a distant, detached voice Al Bliss said, "Who am I talking to?"

He snarled his answer.

"I don't know you, Mr. Jason Taverner," Al Bliss said, again in his most neutral, uninvolved voice. "Are you sure you have the right number? Who did you want to talk to?"

"To you, Al. Al Bliss, my agent. What happened in the hospital? How'd I get out of there into here? Don't you know?" His panic ebbed as he forced control on himself; he made his words come out reasonably. "Can you get hold of Heather for me?"

"Miss Hart?" Al said, and chuckled. And did not answer.

"You," Jason said savagely, "are through as my agent. Period. No matter what the situation is. You are out."

In his ear Al Bliss chuckled again and then, with a click, the line became dead. Al Bliss had hung up.

I'll kill the son of a bitch, Jason said to himself. I'll tear that fat balding little bastard into inch-square pieces.

What was he trying to do to me? I don't understand. What all of a sudden does he have against me? What the hell did I do to him, for chrissakes? He's been my friend and agent nineteen years. And nothing like this has ever happened before.

I'll try Bill Wolfer, he decided. He's always in his office or on call; I'll be able to get hold of him and find out what this is all about. He dropped a second gold dollar into the phone's slot and, from memory, once more dialed.

"Wolfer and Blaine, Attorneys-at-law," a female receptionist's voice sounded in his ear.

"Let me talk to Bill," Jason said. "This is Jason Taverner. You know who I am."

The receptionist said, "Mr. Wolfer is in court today. Would you care to speak to Mr. Blaine instead, or shall I have Mr. Wolfer call you back when he returns to the office later on this afternoon?"

"Do you know who I am?" Jason said. "Do you know who Jason Taverner is? Do you watch TV?" His voice almost got away from him at that point; he heard it break and rise. With great effort he regained control over it, but he could not stop his hands from shaking; his whole body, in fact, shook.

"I'm sorry, Mr. Taverner," the receptionist said. "I really can't talk for Mr. Wolfer or—"

"Do you watch TV?" he said.

"Yes."

"And you haven't heard of me? The *Jason Taverner Show*, at nine on Tuesday nights?"

"I'm sorry, Mr. Taverner. You really must talk directly to Mr. Wolfer. Give me the number of the phone you're calling from and I'll see to it that he calls you back sometime today."

He hung up.

I'm insane, he thought. Or she's insane. She and Al Bliss, that son of a bitch. God. He moved shakily away from the phone, seated himself in one of the faded overstuffed chairs. It felt good to sit; he shut his eyes and breathed slowly and deeply. And pondered.

I have five thousand dollars in government high-denomination bills, he told himself. So I'm not completely helpless. And that thing is gone from my chest, including its feeding tubes. They must have been able to get at them surgically in the hospital. So at least I'm alive; I can rejoice over that. Has there been a time lapse? he asked himself. Where's a newspaper?

He found an L.A. *Times* on a nearby couch, read the date. October 12, 1988. No time lapse. This was the day after his show and the day Marilyn had sent him, dying, to the hospital.

An idea came to him. He searched through the sections of newspaper until he found the entertainment column. Currently he was appearing nightly at the Persian Room of the Hollywood Hilton—had been in fact for three weeks, but of course less Tuesdays because of his show.

The ad for him which the hotel people had been running during the past three weeks did not seem to be on the page anywhere. He thought groggily, maybe it's been moved to another page. He thereupon combed that section of the paper thoroughly. Ad after ad for entertainers but no mention of him. And his face had been on the entertainment page of some newspaper or another for ten years. Without an ellipsis.

I'll make one more try, he decided. I'll try Mory Mann.

Fishing out his wallet, he searched for the slip on which he had written Mory's number.

His wallet was very thin.

All his identification cards were gone. Cards that made it possible for him to stay alive. Cards that got him through pol

and nat barricades without being shot or thrown into a forced-labor camp.

I can't live two hours without my ID, he said to himself. I don't even dare walk out of the lobby of this rundown hotel and onto the public sidewalk. They'll assume I'm a student or teacher escaped from one of the campuses. I'll spend the rest of my life as a slave doing heavy manual labor. I am what they call an *unperson*.

So my first job, he thought, is to stay alive. The hell with Jason Taverner as a public entertainer; I can worry about that later.

He could feel within his brain the powerful six-determined constituents moving already into focus. I am not like other men, he told himself. I will get out of this, whatever it is. Somehow.

For example, he realized, with all this money I have on me I can get myself down to Watts and buy phony ID cards. A whole walletful of them. There must be a hundred little operators scratching away at that, from what I've heard. But I never thought I'd be using one of them. Not Jason Taverner. Not a public entertainer with an audience of thirty million.

Among all those thirty million people, he asked himself, isn't there one who remembers me? If "remember" is the right word. I'm talking as if a lot of time has passed, that I'm an old man now, a has-been, feeding off former glories. And that's not what's going on.

Returning to the phone, he looked up the number of the birth-registration control center in Iowa; with several gold coins he managed to reach them at last, after much delay.

"My name is Jason Taverner," he told the clerk. "I was born in Chicago at Memorial Hospital on December 16, 1946. Would you please confirm and release a copy of my certificate of birth? I need it for a job I'm applying for."

"Yes, sir." The clerk put the line on hold; Jason waited.

The clerk clicked back on. "Mr. Jason Taverner, born in Cook County on December 16, 1946."

"Yes," Jason said.

"We have no birth registration form for such a person at

that time and place. Are you absolutely sure of the facts, sir?"

"You mean do I know my name and when and where I was born?" His voice again managed to escape his control, but this time he let it; panic flooded him. "Thanks," he said and hung up, shaking violently, now. Shaking in his body and in his mind.

I don't exist, he said to himself. There is no Jason Taverner. There never was and there never will be. The hell with my career; I just want to live. If someone or something wants to eradicate my career, okay; do it. But aren't I going to be allowed to exist at all? Wasn't I even born?

Something stirred in his chest. With terror he thought, They didn't get the feed tubes out entirely; some of them are still growing and feeding inside of me. That goddamn tramp of a no-talent girl. I hope she winds up walking the streets for two bits a try.

After what I did for her: getting her those two auditions for A and R people. But hell—I did get to lay her a lot. I suppose it comes out even.

Returning to his hotel room, he took a good long look at himself in the flyspecked vanity mirror. His appearance hadn't changed, except that he needed a shave. No older. No more lines, no gray hair visible. The good shoulders and biceps. The fat-free waist that let him wear the current form-fitting men's clothing.

And that's important to your image, he said to himself. What kind of suits you can wear, especially those tucked-in-waist numbers. I must have fifty of them, he thought. Or did have. Where are they now? he asked himself. The bird is gone, and in what meadow does it now sing? Or however that goes. Something from the past, out of his days at school. Forgotten until this moment. Strange, he thought, what drifts up into your mind when you're in an unfamiliar and ominous situation. Sometimes the most trivial stuff imaginable.

If wishes were horses then beggars might fly. Stuff like that. It's enough to drive you crazy.

He wondered how many pol and nat check stations there were between this miserable hotel and the closest ID forger in Watts? Ten? Thirteen? Two? For me, he thought, all it takes is one. One random check by a mobile vehicle and crew of three. With their damn radio gear connecting them to pol-nat data central in Kansas City. Where they keep the dossiers.

He rolled back his sleeve and examined his forearm. Yes, there it was: his tattooed ident number. His somatic license plate, to be carried by him throughout his life, buried at last with him in his longed-for grave.

Well, the pols and nats at the mobile check station would read off the ident number to Kansas City and then—what then? Was his dossier still there or was it gone, too, like his birth certificate? And if it wasn't there, what would the pol-nat bureaucrats think it meant?

A clerical error. Somebody misfiled the microfilm packet that made up the dossier. It'll turn up. Someday, when it doesn't matter, when I've spent ten years of my life in a quarry on Luna using a manual pickax. If the dossier isn't there, he mused, they'll assume I'm an escaped student, because it's only students who don't have pol-nat dossiers, and even some of them, the important ones, the leaders—they're in there, too.

I am at the bottom of life, he realized. And I can't even climb my way up to mere physical existence. Me, a man who yesterday had an audience of thirty million. Someday, somehow, I will grope my way back to them. But not now. There are other things that come first. The bare bones of existence that every man is born with: I don't even have that. But I will get it; a six is not an ordinary. No ordinary could have physically or psychologically survived what's happened to me—especially the uncertainty—as I have.

A six, no matter what the external circumstances, will always prevail. Because that's the way they genetically defined us.

He left his hotel room once more, walked downstairs and up to the desk. A middle-aged man with a thin mustache was reading a copy of *Box* magazine; he did not look up but said, "Yes, sir."

Jason brought out his packet of government bills, laid a five-hundred-dollar note on the counter before the clerk. The clerk glanced at it, glanced again, this time with wide-opened eyes. Then he cautiously looked up into Jason's face, questioningly.

"My ident cards were stolen," Jason said. "That five-hundred-dollar bill is yours if you can get me to someone who can replace them. If you're going to do it, do it right now; I'm not going to wait." Wait to be picked up by a pol or a nat, he thought. Caught here in this rundown dingy hotel.

"Or caught on the sidewalk in front of the entrance," the clerk said. "I'm a telepath of sorts. I know this hotel isn't much, but we have no bugs. Once we had Martian sand fleas, but no more." He picked up the five-hundred-dollar bill. "I'll get you to someone who can help you," he said. Studying Jason's face intently, he paused, then said, "You think you're world-famous. Well, we get all kinds."

"Let's go," Jason said harshly. "Now."

"Right now," the clerk said, and reached for his shiny plastic coat.

3

As the clerk drove his old-time quibble slowly and noisily down the street he said casually to Jason, seated beside him, "I'm picking up a lot of odd material in your mind."

"Get out of my mind," Jason said brusquely, with aversion. He had always disliked the prying, curiosity-driven telepaths, and this time was no exception. "Get out of my mind," he said, "and get me to the person who's going to help me. And don't run into any pol-nat barricades. If you expect to live through this."

The clerk said mildly, "You don't have to tell me that; I know what would happen to you if we got stopped. I've done this before, many times. For students. But you're not a student. You're a famous man and you're rich. But at the same time you aren't. At the same time you're a nobody. You don't even exist, legally speaking." He laughed a thin, effete laugh, his eyes fixed on the traffic ahead of him. He drove like an old woman, Jason noted. Both hands fixedly hanging on to the steering wheel.

Now they had entered the slums of Watts proper. Tiny dark stores on each side of the cluttered streets, overflowing ashcans, the pavement littered with pieces of broken bottles, drab painted signs that advertised Coca-Cola in big letters and the name of the store in small. At an intersection an elderly black man haltingly crossed, feeling his way along as if blind with age. Seeing him, Jason felt an odd emotion. There were so few blacks alive, now, because of Tidman's notorious sterilization bill passed by Congress back in the terrible days of the Insurrection. The clerk carefully slowed his rattly quibble to a stop so as not to harass the elderly black man in his rumpled, seam-torn brown suit. Obviously he felt it, too.

"Do you realize," the clerk said to Jason, "that if I hit him with my car it would mean the death penalty for me?"

"It should," Jason said.

"They're like the last flock of whooping cranes," the clerk said, starting forward now that the old black had reached the far side. "Protected by a thousand laws. You can't jeer at them; you can't get into a fistfight with one without risking a felony rap—ten years in prison. Yet we're making them die out—that's what Tidman wanted and I guess what the majority of Silencers wanted, but"—he gestured, for the first time taking a hand off the wheel—"I miss the kids. I remember when I was ten and I had a black boy to play with . . . not far from here as a matter of fact. He's undoubtedly sterilized by now."

"But then he's had one child," Jason pointed out. "His wife had to surrender their birth coupon when their first and only child came . . . but they've got that child. The law lets them have it. And there're a million statutes protecting their safety."

"Two adults, one child," the clerk said. "So the black population is halved every generation. Ingenious. You have to hand it to Tidman; he solved the race problem, all right."

"Something had to be done," Jason said; he sat rigidly in his seat, studying the street ahead, searching for a sign of a pol-nat checkpoint or barricade. He saw neither, but how long were they going to have to continue driving?

"We're almost there," the clerk said calmly. He turned his head momentarily to face Jason. "I don't like your racist views," he said. "Even if you are paying me five hundred dollars."

"There're enough blacks alive to suit me," Jason said.

"And when the last one dies?"

Jason said, "You can read my mind; I don't have to tell you."

"Christ," the clerk said, and returned his attention to the street traffic ahead.

They made a sharp right turn, down a narrow alley, at both sides of which closed, locked wooden doors could be seen. No signs here. Just shut-up silence. And piles of ancient debris.

"What's behind the doors?" Jason asked.

"People like you. People who can't come out into the open. But they're different from you in one way: they don't have five hundred dollars . . . and a lot more besides, if I read you correctly."

"It's going to cost me plenty," Jason said acidly, "to get my ID cards. Probably all I've got."

"She won't overcharge you," the clerk said as he brought his quibble to a halt half on the sidewalk of the alley. Jason peered out, saw an abandoned restaurant, boarded up, with broken windows. Entirely dark inside. It repelled him, but apparently this was the place. He'd have to go along with it, his need being what it was: he could not be choosy.

And—they had avoided every checkpoint and barricade along the way; the clerk had picked a good route. So he had damn little to complain about, all things considered.

Together, he and the clerk approached the open-hanging broken front door of the restaurant. Neither spoke; they concentrated on avoiding the rusted nails protruding from the sheets of plywood hammered into place, presumably to protect the windows.

"Hang on to my hand," the clerk said, extending it in the shadowy dimness that surrounded them. "I know the way and it's dark. The electricity was turned off on this block three years ago. To try to get the people to vacate the buildings here so that they could be burned down." He added, "But most of them stayed on."

The moist, cold hand of the hotel clerk led him past what appeared to be chairs and tables, heaped up into irregular tumbles of legs and surfaces, interwoven with cobwebs and grainy patterns of dirt. They bumped at last against a black, unmoving wall; there the clerk stopped, retrieved his hand, fiddled with something in the gloom.

"I can't open it," he said as he fiddled. "It can only be opened from the other side, *her* side. What I'm doing is signaling that we're here."

A section of the wall groaningly slid aside. Jason, peering, saw into nothing more than additional darkness. And abandonment.

"Step on through," the clerk said, and maneuvered him forward. The wall, after a pause, slid shut again behind them.

Lights winked on. Momentarily blinded, Jason shielded his eyes and then took a good look at her workshop.

It was small. But he saw a number of what appeared to be complex and highly specialized machines. On the far side a workbench. Tools by the hundreds, all neatly mounted in place on the walls of the room. Below the workbench large cartons, probably containing a variety of papers. And a small generator-driven printing press.

And the girl. She sat on a high stool, hand-arranging a line of type. He made out pale hair, very long but thin, dribbling down the back of her neck onto her cotton work shirt. She wore jeans, and her feet, quite small, were bare. She appeared to him to be, at a guess, fifteen or sixteen. No breasts to speak of, but good long legs; he liked that. She wore no makeup whatsoever, giving her features a white, slightly pastel tint.

"Hi," she said.

The clerk said, "I'm going. I'll try not to spend the five hundred dollars in one place." Touching a button, he caused the section of wall to slide aside; as it did so the lights in the workroom clicked out, leaving them once again in absolute darkness.

From her stool the girl said, "I'm Kathy."

"I'm Jason," he said. The wall had slid shut, now, and the lights had come on again. She's really very pretty, he thought. Except that she had a passive, almost listless quality about her. As if nothing to her, he thought, is worth a damn. Apathy? No, he decided. She was shy; that was the explanation.

"You gave him five hundred dollars to bring you here?" Kathy said wonderingly; she surveyed him critically, as if seeking to make some kind of value judgment about him, based on his appearance.

"My suit isn't usually this rumpled," Jason said.

"It's a nice suit. Silk?"

"Yes." He nodded.

"Are you a student?" Kathy asked, still scrutinizing him. "No, you're not; you don't have that pulpy pasty color they have, from living subsurface. Well, that leaves only one other possibility."

"That I'm a criminal," Jason said. "Trying to change my identity before pols and nats get me."

"Are you?" she said, with no sign of uneasiness. It was a simple, flat question.

"No." He did not amplify, not at that moment. Perhaps later.

Kathy said, "Do you think a lot of those nats are robots and not real people? They always have those gas masks on so you can't really tell."

"I'm content just to dislike them," Jason said. "Without looking into it any further."

"What ID do you need? Driver's license? Police-file ident card? Proof of employment at a legal job?"

He said, "Everything. Including membership tab in the Musicians Union Local Twelve."

"Oh, you're a musician." She regarded him with more interest, now.

"I'm a vocalist," he said. "I host an hour-long TV variety show Tuesday night at nine. Maybe you've seen it. The *Jason Taverner Show.*"

"I don't own a TV set any more," the girl said. "So I guess I wouldn't recognize you. Is it fun to do?"

"Sometimes. You meet a lot of show-biz people and that's fine if that's what you like. I've found them mostly to be people like anybody else. They have their fears. They're not perfect. Some of them are very funny, both on and off camera."

"My husband always used to tell me I have no sense of humor," the girl said. "He thought everything was funny. He even thought it was funny when he was drafted into the nats."

"Did he still laugh by the time he got out?" Jason asked.

"He never did. He was killed in a surprise attack by students. But it wasn't their fault; he was shot by a fellow nat."

Jason said, "How much is it going to cost me to get my full set of ID? You better tell me now before you start on them."

"I charge people what they can afford," Kathy said, once more setting up her line of type. "I'm going to charge you a lot because I can tell you're rich, by the way you gave Eddy five hundred dollars to get you here, and by your suit. Okay?" Briefly she glanced in his direction. "Or am I wrong? Tell me."

"I have five thousand dollars on me," Jason said. "Or, rather, less five hundred. I'm a world-famous entertainer; I work a month every year at the Sands in addition to my show. In fact, I appear at a number of first-class clubs, when I can squeeze them into my tight schedule."

"Gee," Kathy said. "I wish I had heard of you; then I could be impressed."

He laughed.

"Did I say something stupid?" Kathy asked timidly.

"No," Jason said. "Kathy, how old are you?"

"I'm nineteen. My birthday is in December, so I'm almost twenty. How old did you think I am by looking at me?"

"About sixteen," he said.

Her mouth turned down in a childlike pout. "That's what everybody says," she said in a low voice. "It's because I don't have any bosom. If I had a bosom I'd look twenty-one. How old are you?" She stopped fiddling with her type and eyed him intently. "I'd guess about fifty."

Fury flowed through him. And misery.

"You look like your feelings are hurt," Kathy said.

"I'm forty-two," Jason said tightly.

"Well, what's the difference? I mean, they're both—"

"Let's get down to business," Jason broke in. "Give me a pen and paper and I'll write down what I want and what I want each card to say about me. I want this done exactly right. You better be good."

"I made you mad," Kathy said. "By saying you look fifty. I guess on closer examination you really don't. You look about thirty." She handed him pen and paper, smiling shyly. And apologetically.

Jason said, "Forget it." He patted her on the back.

"I'd rather people didn't touch me," Kathy said; she slid away.

Like a fawn in the woods, he thought. Strange; she's afraid to be touched even a little and yet she's not afraid to forge documents, a felony that could get her twenty years in prison. Maybe nobody bothered to tell her it's against the law. Maybe she doesn't know.

Something bright and colorful on the far wall caught his attention; he walked over to inspect it. A medieval illuminated manuscript, he realized. Or rather, a page from it. He had read about them but up until now he had never set eyes on one.

"Is this valuable?" he asked.

"If it was the real thing it might be worth a hundred dollars," Kathy said. "But it's not; I made it years ago, when I was in junior high school at North American Aviation. I copied it, the original, ten times before I had it right. I love good calligraphy; even when I was a kid I did. Maybe it's because my father designed book covers; you know, the dust jackets."

He said, "Would this fool a museum?"

For a moment Kathy gazed intently at him. And then she nodded yes.

"Wouldn't they know by the paper?"

"It's parchment and it's from that period. That's the same way you fake old stamps; you get an old stamp that's worthless, eradicate the imprint, then—" She paused. "You're anxious for me to get to work on your ID," she said.

"Yes," Jason said. He handed her the piece of paper on which he had written the information. Most of it called for pol-nat standard postcurfew tags, with thumbprints and photographs and holographic signatures, and everything with short expiration dates. He'd have to get a whole new set forged within three months.

"Two thousand dollars," Kathy said, studying the list.

He felt like saying, For that do I get to go to bed with you, too? But aloud he said, "How long will it take? Hours? Days? And if it's days, where am I—"

"Hours," Kathy said.

He experienced a vast wave of relief.

"Sit down and keep me company," Kathy said, pointing to a three-legged stool pushed off to one side. "You can tell me about your career as a successful TV personality. It must be fascinating, all the bodies you have to walk over to get to the top. Or did you get to the top?"

"Yes," he said shortly. "But there's no bodies. That's a myth. You make it on talent and talent alone, not what you do or say to other people either above or below you. And it's work; you don't breeze in and do a soft-shoe shuffle and then sign your contract with NBC or CBS. They're tough, experienced businessmen. Especially the A and R people. Artists and Repertoire. They decide who to sign. I'm talking about records now. That's where you have to start to be on a national level; of course you can work club dates all over everywhere until—"

"Here's your quibble driver's license," Kathy said. She carefully passed him a small black card. "Now I'll get started on your military service-status chit. That's a little harder because of the full-face and profile photos, but I can handle that over there." She pointed at a white screen, in front of which stood a tripod with camera, a flash gun mounted at its side.

"You have all the equipment," Jason said as he fixed himself rigidly against the white screen; so many photos had been taken of him during his long career that he always knew exactly where to stand and what expression to reveal.

But apparently he had done something wrong this time. Kathy, a severe expression on her face, surveying him.

"You're all lit up," she said, half to herself. "You're glowing in some sort of phony way."

"Publicity stills," Jason said. "Eight-by-ten glossy—"

"These aren't. These are to keep you out of a forced-labor camp for the rest of your life. Don't smile."

He didn't.

"Good," Kathy said. She ripped the photos from the camera, carried them cautiously to her workbench, waving them to dry them. "These damn 3-D animateds they want on the military service papers—that camera cost me a thousand dollars and I need it only for this and nothing else . . . but I have to have it." She eyed him. "It's going to cost you."

"Yes," he said, stonily. He felt aware of that already.

For a time Kathy puttered, and then, turning abruptly toward him, she said, "Who are you *really*? You're used to posing; I saw you, I saw you freeze with that glad smile in place and those lit-up eyes."

"I told you. I'm Jason Taverner. The TV personality guest host. I'm on every Tuesday night."

"No," Kathy said; she shook her head. "But it's none of my business—sorry—I shouldn't have asked." But she continued to eye him, as if with exasperation. "You're doing it all wrong. You really are a celebrity—it was reflexive, the way you posed for your picture. But you're not a celebrity. There's no one named Jason Taverner who matters, who is anything. So what are you, then? A man who has his picture taken all the time that no one's ever seen or heard of."

Jason said, "I'm going about it the way any celebrity who no one has ever heard of would go about it."

For a moment she stared at him and then she laughed. "I see. Well, that's cool; that's really cool. I'll have to remember that." She turned her attention back to the documents she was forging. "In this business," she said, absorbed in what she was doing, "I don't want to get to know people I'm making cards for. But"—she glanced up—"I'd sort of like to know you. You're strange. I've seen a lot of types—

hundreds, maybe—but none like you. Do you know what I think?"

"You think I'm insane," Jason said.

"Yes." Kathy nodded. "Clinically, legally, whatever. You're psychotic; you have a split personality. Mr. No One and Mr. Everyone. How have you survived up until now?"

He said nothing. It could not be explained.

"Okay," Kathy said. One by one, expertly and efficiently, she forged the necessary documents.

Eddy, the hotel clerk, lurked in the background, smoking a fake Havana cigar; he had nothing to say or do, but for some obscure reason he hung around. I wish he'd fuck off, Jason thought to himself. I'd like to talk to her more . . .

"Come with me," Kathy said, suddenly; she slid from her work stool and beckoned him toward a wooden door at the right of her bench. "I want your signature five times, each a little different from the others so they can't be superimposed. That's where so many documenters"—she smiled as she opened the door—"that's what we call ourselves—that's where so many of us fuck it up. They take one signature and transfer it to all the documents. See?"

"Yes," he said, entering the musty little closetlike room after her.

Kathy shut the door, paused a moment, then said, "Eddy is a police fink."

Staring at her he said, "Why?"

" 'Why?' Why what? Why is he a police fink? For money. For the same reason I am."

Jason said, "God damn you." He grabbed her by the right wrist, tugged her toward him; she grimaced as his fingers tightened. "And he's already—"

"Eddy hasn't done anything yet," she grated, trying to free her wrist. "That hurts. Look; calm down and I'll show you. Okay?"

Reluctantly, his heart hammering in fear, he let her go. Kathy turned on a bright, small light, laid three forged documents in the circle of its glare. "A purple dot on the margin of each," she said, indicating the almost invisible circle of color. "A microtransmitter, so you'll emit a bleep every five seconds as you move around. They're after conspiracies; they want the people you're with."

Jason said harshly, "I'm not with anyone."

"But they don't know that." She massaged her wrist, frowning in a girlish, sullen way. "You TV celebrities no one's ever heard of sure have quick reactions," she murmured.

"Why did you tell me?" Jason asked. "After doing all the forging, all the—"

"I want you to get away," she said, simply.

"Why?" He still did not understand.

"Because hell, you've got some sort of magnetic quality about you; I noticed it as soon as you came into the room. You're"—she groped for the word—"sexy. Even at your age."

"My presence," he said.

"Yes." Kathy nodded. "I've seen it before in public people, from a distance, but never up close like this. I can see why you imagine you're a TV personality; you really seem like you are."

He said, "How do I get away? Are you going to tell me that? Or does that cost a little more?"

"God, you're so cynical."

He laughed, and again took hold of her by the wrist.

"I guess I don't blame you," Kathy said, shaking her head and making a masklike face. "Well, first of all, you can buy Eddy off. Another five hundred should do it. Me you don't have to buy off—*if*, and only if, and I mean it, if you stay with me awhile. You have . . . allure, like a good perfume. I respond to you and I just never do that with men."

"With women, then?" he said tartly.

It passed her without registering. "Will you?" she said.

"Hell," he said, "I'll just leave." Reaching, he opened the door behind her, shoved past her and out into her workroom. She followed, rapidly.

Among the dim, empty shadows of the abandoned restaurant she caught up with him; she confronted him in the gloom. Panting, she said, "You've already got a transmitter planted on you."

"I doubt it," he answered.

"It's true. Eddy planted it on you."

"Bullshit," he said, and moved away from her toward the light of the restaurant's sagging, broken front door.

Pursuing him like a deft-footed herbivore, Kathy gasped, "But suppose it's true. It could be." At the half-available doorway she interposed herself between him and freedom; standing there, her hands lifted as if to ward off a physical blow, she said swiftly, "Stay with me one night. Go to bed with me. Okay? That's enough. I promise. Will you do it, for just one night?"

He thought, Something of my abilities, my alleged and well-known properties, have come with me, to this strange place I now live in. This place where I do not exist except on forged cards manufactured by a pol fink. Eerie, he thought, and he shuddered. Cards with microtransmitters built into them, to betray me and everyone with me to the pols. I haven't done very well here. Except that, as she says, I've got allure. Jesus, he thought. And that's all that stands between me and a forced-labor camp.

"Okay," he said, then. It seemed the wiser choice—by far.

"Go pay Eddy," she said. "Get that over with and him out of here."

"I wondered why he's still hanging around," Jason said. "Did he scent more money?"

"I guess so," Kathy said.

"You do this all the time," Jason said as he got out his money. SOP: standard operating procedure. And he had tumbled for it.

Kathy said blithely, "Eddy is psionic."

4

Two city blocks away, upstairs in an unpainted but once white wooden building, Kathy had a single room with a hot-compart in which to fix one-person meals.

He looked around him. A girl's room: the cotlike bed had a handmade spread covering it, tiny green balls of textile fibers in row after row. Like a graveyard for soldiers, he thought morbidly as he moved about, feeling compressed by the smallness of the room.

On a wicker table a copy of Proust's *Remembrance of Things Past*.

"How far'd you get into it?" he asked her.

"To *Within a Budding Grove*." Kathy double-locked the door after them and set into operation some kind of electronic gadget; he did not recognize it.

"That's not very far," Jason said.

Taking off her plastic coat, Kathy asked, "How far did you get into it?" She hung her coat in a tiny closet, taking his, too.

"I never read it," Jason said. "But on my program we did a dramatic rendering of a scene . . . I don't know which. We got a lot of good mail about it, but we never tried it again. Those out things, you have to be careful and not dole out too much. If you do it kills it dead for everybody, all networks, for the rest of the year." He prowled, crampedly, about the room, examining a book here, a cassette tape, a micromag. She even had a talking toy. Like a kid, he thought; she's not really an adult.

With curiosity, he turned on the talking toy.

"Hi!" it declared. "I'm Cheerful Charley and I'm definitely tuned in on your wavelength."

"Nobody named Cheerful Charley is tuned in on my wavelength," Jason said. He started to shut it off, but it protested. "Sorry," Jason told it, "but I'm tuning you out, you creepy little bugger."

"But I love you!" Cheerful Charley complained tinnily.

He paused, thumb on off button. "Prove it," he said. On his show he had done commercials for junk like this. He hated it and them. Equally. "Give me some money," he told it.

"I know how you can get back your name, fame, and game," Cheerful Charley informed him. "Will that do for openers?"

"Sure," he said.

Cheerful Charley bleated, "Go look up your girl friend."

"Who do you mean?" he said guardedly.

"Heather Hart," Cheerful Charley bleeped.

"Hard by," Jason said, pressing his tongue against his upper incisors. He nodded. "Any more advice?"

"I've heard of Heather Hart," Kathy said as she brought a bottle of orange juice out of the cold-cupboard of the room's wall. The bottle had already become three-fourths empty; she shook it up, poured foamy instant ersatz orange juice into two jelly glasses. "She's beautiful. She has all that long red hair. Is she really your girl friend? Is Charley right?"

"Everybody knows," he said, "that Cheerful Charley is always right."

"Yes, I guess that's true." Kathy poured bad gin (Mountbatten's Privy Seal Finest) into the orange juice. "Screwdrivers," she said, proudly.

"No, thanks," he said. "Not at this hour of the day." Not even B & L scotch bottled in Scotland, he thought. This damn little room . . . isn't she making anything out of polfinking and card-forging, whichever it is she does? Is she really a police informer, as she says? he wondered. Strange. Maybe she's both. Maybe neither.

"Ask me!" Cheerful Charley piped. "I can see you have something on your mind, mister. You good-looking bastard, you."

He let that pass. "This girl," he began, but instantly Kathy grabbed Cheerful Charley away from him, stood holding it, her nostrils flaring, her eyes filled with indignation.

"The hell you're going to ask my Cheerful Charley about me," she said, one eyebrow raised. Like a wild bird, he thought, going through elaborate motions to protect her nest. He laughed. "What's funny?" Kathy demanded.

"These talking toys," he said, "are more nuisance than utilitarian. They ought to be abolished." He walked away from her, then to a clutter of mail on a TV-stand table. Aimlessly, he sorted among the envelopes, noticing vaguely that none of the bills had been opened.

"Those are mine," Kathy said defensively, watching him.

"You get a lot of bills," he said, "for a girl living in a one-room schmalch. You buy your clothes—or what else?—at Metter's? Interesting."

"I—take an odd size."

He said, "And Sax and Crombie shoes."

"In my work—" she began, but he cut her off with a convulsive swipe of his hand.

"Don't give me that," he grated.

"Look in my closet. You won't see much there. Nothing out of the ordinary, except that what I do have is good. I'd rather have a little amount of something good . . ." Her words trailed off. "You know," she said vaguely, "than a lot of junk."

Jason said, "You have another apartment."

It registered; her eyes flickered as she looked into herself for an answer. That, for him, constituted plenty.

"Let's go there," he said. He had seen enough of this cramped little room.

"I can't take you there," Kathy said, "because I share it

with two other girls and the way we've divided up the use, this time is—"

"Evidently you weren't trying to impress me." It amused him. But also it irritated him; he felt downgraded, nebulously.

"I would have taken you there if today were my day," Kathy said. "That's why I have to keep this little place going; I've got to have *someplace* to go when it's not my day. My day, my next one, is Friday. From noon on." Her tone had become earnest. As if she wished very much to convince him. Probably, he mused, it was true. But the whole thing irked him. Her and her whole life. He felt, now, as if he had been snared by something dragging him down into depths he had never known about before, even in the early, bad days. And he did not like it.

He yearned all at once to be out of here. The animal at bay was himself.

"Don't look at me like that," Kathy said, sipping her screwdriver.

To himself, but aloud, he said, "You have bumped the door of life open with your big, dense head. And now it can't be closed."

"What's that from?" Kathy asked.

"From my life."

"But it's like poetry."

"If you watched my show," he said, "you'd know I come up with sparklers like that every so often."

Appraising him calmly, Kathy said, "I'm going to look in the TV log and see if you're listed." She set down her screwdriver, fished among discarded newspapers piled at the base of the wicker table.

"I wasn't even born," he said. "I checked on that."

"And your show isn't listed," Kathy said, folding the news-print page back and studying the log.

"That's right," he said. "So now you have all the answers about me." He tapped his vest pocket of forged ID cards. "Including these. With their microtransmitters, if that much is true."

"Give them back to me," Kathy said, "and I'll erad the microtransmitters. It'll only take a second." She held out her hand.

He returned them to her.

"Don't you care if I take them off?" Kathy inquired.

Candidly, he answered, "No, I really don't. I've lost the ability to tell what's good or bad, true or not true, anymore. If you want to take the dots off, do it. If it pleases you."

A moment later she returned the cards, smiling her sixteen-year-old hazy smile.

Observing her youth, her automatic radiance, he said, " 'I feel as old as yonder elm.' "

"From *Finnegans Wake*," Kathy said happily. "When the old washerwomen at dusk are merging into trees and rocks."

"You've read *Finnegans Wake*?" he asked, surprised.

"I saw the film. Four times. I like Hazeltine; I think he's the best director alive."

"I had him on my show," Jason said. "Do you want to know what he's like in real life?"

"No," Kathy said.

"Maybe you ought to know."

"No," she repeated, shaking her head; her voice had risen. "And don't try to tell me—okay? I'll believe what I want to believe, and you believe what you believe. All right?"

"Sure," he said. He felt sympathetic. The truth, he had often reflected, was overrated as a virtue. In most cases a sympathetic lie did better and more mercifully. Especially between men and women; in fact, whenever a woman was involved.

This, of course, was not, properly speaking, a woman, but a girl. And therefore, he decided the kind lie was even more of a necessity.

"He's a scholar and an artist," he said.

"Really?" She regarded him hopefully.

"Yes."

At that she sighed in relief.

"Then you believe," he said, pouncing, "that I have met Michael Hazeltine, the finest living film director, as you said yourself. So you do believe that I am a six—" He broke off; that had not been what he intended to say.

" 'A six,' " Kathy echoed, her brow furrowing, as if she were trying to remember. "I read about them in *Time*. Aren't they all dead now? Didn't the government have them all rounded up and shot, after that one, their leader—what was his name?—Teagarden; yes, that's his name. Willard Teagarden. He tried to—how do you say it?—pull off a coup against the federal nats? He tried to get them disbanded as an illegal parimutuel—"

"Paramilitary," Jason said.

"You don't give a damn about what I'm saying."

Sincerely, he said, "I sure do." He waited. The girl did not continue. "Christ," he spat out. "Finish what you were saying!"

"I think," Kathy said at last, "that the *sevens* made the coup not come off."

He thought. Sevens. Never in his life had he heard of sevens. Nothing could have shocked him more. Good, he thought, that I let out that lapsus linguae. I have genuinely learned something, now. At last. In this maze of confusion and the half real.

A small section of wall creaked meagerly open and a cat, black and white and very young, entered the room. At once Kathy gathered him up, her face shining.

"Dinman's philosophy," Jason said. "The mandatory cat." He was familiar with the viewpoint; he had in fact introduced Dinman to the TV audience on one of his fall specials.

"No, I just love him," Kathy said, eyes bright as she carried the cat over to him for his inspection.

"But you do believe," he said, as he patted the cat's little head, "that owning an animal increases a person's empathic—"

"Screw that," Kathy said, clutching the cat to her throat as if she were a five-year-old with its first animal. Its school project: the communal guinea pig. "This is Domenico," she said.

"Named after Domenico Scarlatti?" he asked.

"No, after Domenico's Market, down the street; we passed it on our way here. When I'm at the Minor Apartment—this room—I shop there. Is Domenico Scarlatti a musician? I think I've heard of him."

Jason said, "Abraham Lincoln's high school English teacher."

"Oh." She nodded absently, now rocking the cat back and forth.

"I'm kidding you," he said, "and it's mean. I'm sorry."

Kathy gazed up at him earnestly as she clutched her small cat. "I never know the difference," she murmured.

"That's why it's mean," Jason said.

"Why?" she asked. "If I don't even know. I mean, that means I'm just dumb. Doesn't it?"

"You're not dumb," Jason said. "Just inexperienced." He calculated, roughly, their age difference. "I've lived over twice as long as you," he pointed out. "And I've been in the position, in the last ten years, to rub elbows with some of the most famous people on earth. And—"

"And," Kathy said, "you're a six."

She had not forgotten his slip. Of course not. He could tell her a million things, and all would be forgotten ten minutes later, except the one real slip. Well, such was the way of the world. He had become used to it in his time; that was part of being his age and not hers.

"What does Domenico mean to you?" Jason said, changing the subject. Crudely, he realized, but he went ahead. "What do you get from him that you don't get from human beings?"

She frowned, looked thoughtful. "He's always busy. He always has some project going. Like following a bug. He's very good with flies; he's learned how to eat them without their flying away." She smiled engagingly. "And I don't have to ask myself about him, Should I turn him in to Mr. McNulty? Mr. McNulty is my pol contact. I give him the analog receivers for the microtransmitters, the dots I showed you—"

"And he pays you."

She nodded.

"And yet you live like this."

"I—" she struggled to answer—"I don't get many customers."

"Nonsense. You're good; I watched you work. You're experienced."

"A talent."

"But a trained talent."

"Okay; it all goes into the apartment uptown. My Major Apartment." She gritted her teeth, not enjoying being badgered.

"No." He didn't believe it.

Kathy said, after a pause, "My husband's alive. He's in a forced-labor camp in Alaska. I'm trying to buy his way out by giving information to Mr. McNulty. In another year"— she shrugged, her expression moody now, introverted—"he *says* Jack can come out. And come back here."

So you send other people into the camps, he thought, to get your husband out. It sounds like a typical police deal. It's probably the truth.

"It's a terrific deal for the police," he said. "They lose one man and get—how many would you say you've bugged for them? Scores? Hundreds?"

Pondering, she said at last, "Maybe a hundred and fifty."

"It's evil," he said.

"Is it?" She glanced at him nervously, clutching Domenico to her flat chest. Then, by degrees, she became angry; it showed on her face and in the way she crushed the cat against her rib cage. "The hell it is," she said fiercely, shaking her head no. "I love Jack and he loves me. He writes to me all the time."

Cruelly, he said, "Forged. By some pol employee."

Tears spilled from her eyes in an amazing quantity; they dimmed her gaze. "You think so? Sometimes I think they are, too. Do you want to look at them? Could you tell?"

"They're probably not forged. It's cheaper and simpler to keep him alive and let him write his own letters." He hoped that would make her feel better, and evidently it did; the tears stopped coming.

"I hadn't thought of that," she said, nodding, but still not smiling; she gazed off into the distance, reflexively still rocking the small black and white cat.

"If your husband's alive," he said, cautiously this time, "do you believe it to be all right for you to go to bed with other men, such as me?"

"Oh, sure. Jack never objected to that. Even before they got him. And I'm sure he doesn't object now. As a matter of fact, he wrote me about that. Let's see; it was maybe six months ago. I think I could find the letter; I have them all on microfilm. Over in the shop."

"Why?"

Kathy said, "I sometimes lens-screen them for customers. So that later on they'll understand why I do what I did."

At this point he frankly did not know what emotion he felt toward her, nor what he ought to feel. She had become, by degrees, over the years, involved in a situation from which she could not now extricate herself. And he saw no way out for her now; it had gone on too long. The formula had become fixed. The seeds of evil had been allowed to grow.

"There's no turning back for you," he said, knowing it, knowing that she knew it. "Listen," he said to her in a gentle voice. He put his hand on her shoulder, but as before she at once shrank away. "Tell them you want him out right now, and you're not turning in any more people."

"Would they release him, then, if I said that?"

"Try it." Certainly it wouldn't do any harm. But—he could imagine Mr. McNulty and how he looked to the girl. She could never confront him; the McNultys of the world did not get confronted by anyone. Except when something went strangely wrong.

"Do you know what you are?" Kathy said. "You're a very good person. Do you understand that?"

He shrugged. Like most truths it was a matter of opinion. Perhaps he was. In this situation, anyhow. Not so in others. But Kathy didn't know about that.

"Sit down," he said, "pet your cat, drink your screwdriver. Don't think about anything; just be. Can you do that? Empty your mind for a little while? Try it." He brought her a chair; she dutifully seated herself on it.

"I do it all the time," she said emptily, dully.

Jason said, "But not negatively. Do it positively."

"How? What do you mean?"

"Do it for a real purpose, not just to avoid facing unfortunate verities. Do it because you love your husband and you want him back. You want everything to be as it was before."

"Yes," she agreed. "But now I've met you."

"Meaning what?" He proceeded cautiously; her response puzzled him.

Kathy said, "You're more magnetic than Jack. He's magnetic, but you're so much, much more. Maybe after meeting you I couldn't really love him again. Or do you think a person can love two people equally, but in different ways? My therapy group says no, that I have to choose. They say that's one of the basic aspects of life. See, this has come up before; I've met several men more magnetic than Jack . . . but none of them as magnetic as you. Now I really don't know what to do. It's very difficult to decide such things because there's no one you can talk to: no one understands. You have to go through it alone, and sometimes you choose wrong. Like, what if I choose you over Jack and then he comes back and I don't give a shit about him; what then? How is he going to feel? That's important, but it's also important how I feel. If I like you or someone like you better than him, then I have to act it out, as our therapy group puts it. Did you know I was in a psychiatric hospital for eight weeks? Morningside Mental Hygiene Relations in Atherton. My folks paid for it. It cost a fortune because for some reason we weren't eligible for community or federal aid. Anyhow, I learned a lot about myself and I made a whole lot of friends, there. Most of the people I truly know I met at Morningside. Of course, when I originally met them back then I had the delusion that they were famous people like Mickey Quinn and Arlene Howe. You know—celebrities. Like you."

He said, "I know both Quinn and Howe, and you haven't missed anything."

Scrutinizing him, she said, "Maybe you're not a celebrity; maybe I've reverted back to my delusional period. They said I probably would, sometime. Sooner or later. Maybe it's later now."

"That," he pointed out, "would make me a hallucination of yours. Try harder; I don't feel completely real."

She laughed. But her mood remained somber. "Wouldn't that be strange if I made you up, like you just said? That if I fully recovered you'd disappear?"

"I wouldn't disappear. But I'd cease to be a celebrity."

"You already have." She raised her head, confronted him steadily. "Maybe that's it. Why you're a celebrity that no one's ever heard of. I made you up, you're a product of my delusional mind, and now I'm becoming sane again."

"A solipsistic view of the universe—"

"Don't do that. You know I haven't any idea what words like that mean. What kind of person do you think I am? I'm not famous and powerful like you; I'm just a person doing a terrible, awful job that puts people in prison, because I love Jack more than all the rest of humanity. Listen." Her tone became firm and crisp. "The only thing that got me back to sanity was that I loved Jack more than Mickey Quinn. See, I thought this boy named David was really Mickey Quinn, and it was a big secret that Mickey Quinn had lost his mind and he had gone to this mental hospital to get himself back in shape, and no one was supposed to know about it because it would ruin his image. So he pretended his name was David. But I knew. Or rather, I thought I knew. And Dr. Scott said I had to chose between Jack and David, or Jack and Mickey Quinn, which I thought it was. And I chose Jack. So I came out of it. Maybe"—she wavered, her chin trembling—"maybe now you can see why I have to believe Jack is more important than anything or anybody, or a lot of anybodys, else. See?"

He saw. He nodded.

"Even men like you," Kathy said, "who're more magnetic than him, even you can't take me away from Jack."

"I don't want to." It seemed a good idea to make that point.

"Yes—you do. On some level you do. It's a competition."

Jason said, "To me you're just one small girl in one small room in one small building. For me the whole world is mine, and everybody in it."

"Not if you're in a forced-labor camp."

He had to nod in agreement to that, too. Kathy had an annoying habit of spiking the guns of rhetoric.

"You understand a little now," she said, "don't you? About me and Jack, and why I can go to bed with you without wronging Jack? I went to bed with David when we were at Morningside, but Jack understood; he knew I had to do it. Would you have understood?"

"If you were psychotic—"

"No, not because of that. Because it was my destiny to go to bed with Mickey Quinn. It had to be done; I was fulfilling my cosmic role. Do you see?"

"Okay," he said, gently.

"I think I'm drunk." Kathy examined her screwdriver. "You're right; it's too early to drink one of these." She set the half-empty glass down. "Jack saw. Or anyhow he said he saw. Would he lie? So as not to lose me? Because if I had had to chose between him and Mickey Quinn"—she paused—"but I chose Jack. I always would. But still I had to go to bed with David. With Mickey Quinn, I mean."

I have gotten myself mixed up with a complicated, peculiar, malfunctioning creature, Jason Taverner said to himself. As bad as—worse than—Heather Hart. As bad as I've yet encountered in forty-two years. But how do I get away from her without Mr. McNulty hearing all about it? Christ, he thought dismally. Maybe I don't. Maybe she plays with me until she's bored, and then she calls in the pols. And that's it for me.

"Wouldn't you think," he said aloud, "that in four decades plus, I could have learned the answer to this?"

"To me?" she said. Acutely.

He nodded.

"You think after you go to bed with me I'll turn you in."

At this point he had not boiled it down to precisely that.

But the general idea was there. So, carefully, he said, "I think you've learned in your artless, innocent, nineteen-year-old way, to use people. Which I think is very bad. And once you begin you can't stop. You don't even know you're doing it."

"I would never turn you in. I love you."

"You've known me perhaps five hours. Not even that."

"But I can always tell." Her tone, her expression, both were firm. And deeply solemn.

"You're not even sure who I am!"

Kathy said, "I'm never sure who *anybody* is."

That, evidently, had to be granted. He tried, therefore, another tack. "Look. You're an odd combination of the innocent romantic, and a"—he paused; the word "treacherous" had come to mind, but he discarded it swiftly—"and a calculating, subtle manipulator." You are, he thought, a prostitute of the mind. And it's your mind that is prostituting itself, before and beyond anyone else's. Although you yourself would never recognize it. And, if you did, you'd say you were forced into it. Yes; forced into it, but by whom? By Jack? By David? By yourself, he thought. By wanting two men at the same time—and getting to have both.

Poor Jack, he thought. You poor goddamn bastard. Shoveling shit at the forced-labor camp in Alaska, waiting for this elaborately convoluted waif to save you. Don't hold your breath.

That evening, without conviction, he had dinner with Kathy at an Italian-type restaurant a block from her room. She seemed to know the owner and the waiters, in some dim fashion; anyhow, they greeted her and she responded absentmindedly, as if only half hearing them. Or, he thought, only half aware of where she was.

Little girl, he thought, where is the rest of your mind?

"The lasagna is very good," Kathy said, without looking at the menu; she seemed a great distance away now. Receding further and further. With each passing moment. He sensed an approaching crisis. But he did not know her well enough;

he had no idea what form it would take. And he did not like that.

"When you blep away," he said abruptly, trying to catch her off guard, "how do you do it?"

"Oh," she said tonelessly. "I throw myself down on the floor and scream. Or else I kick. Anyone who tries to stop me. Who interferes with my freedom."

"Do you feel like doing that now?"

She glanced up. "Yes." Her face, he saw, had become a mask, both twisted and agonized. But her eyes remained totally dry. This time no tears would be involved. "I haven't been taking my medication. I'm supposed to take twenty milligrams of Actozine per diem."

"Why don't you take it?" They never did; he had run across that anomaly several times.

"It dulls my mind," she answered, touching her nose with her forefinger, as if involved in a complex ritual that had to be done absolutely correctly.

"But if it—"

Kathy said sharply, "They can't fuck with my mind. I'm not letting any MFs get to me. Do you know what a MF is?"

"You just said." He spoke quietly and slowly, keeping his attention firmly fixed on her . . . as if trying to hold her there, to keep her mind together.

The food came. It was terrible.

"Isn't this wonderfully authentically Italian?" Kathy said, deftly winding spaghetti on her fork.

"Yes," he agreed, aimlessly.

"You think I'm going to blep away. And you don't want to be involved with it."

Jason said, "That's right."

"Then leave."

"I"—he hesitated—"I like you. I want to make sure you're all right." A benign lie, of the kind he approved. It seemed better than saying, Because if I walk out of here you will be on the phone to Mr. McNulty in twenty seconds. Which, in fact, was the way he saw it.

"I'll be all right. They'll take me home." She vaguely indicated the restaurant around them, the customers, waiters, cashier. Cook steaming away in the overheated, underventilated kitchen. Drunk at the bar, fiddling with his glass of Olympia beer.

He said, calculating carefully, fairly, reasonably sure that he was doing the right thing, "You're not taking responsibility."

"For who? I'm not taking responsibility for your life, if that's what you mean. That's your job. Don't burden me with it."

"Responsibility," he said, "for the consequences to others of your acts. You're morally, ethically drifting. Hitting out here and there, then submerging again. As if nothing happened. Leaving it to everyone else to pick up the sweltering moons."

Raising her head she confronted him and said, "Have I hurt you? I saved you from the pols; that's what I did for you. Was that the wrong thing to do? Was it?" Her voice increased in volume; she stared at him pitilessly, unblinkingly, still holding her forkful of spaghetti.

He sighed. It was hopeless. "No," he said, "it wasn't the wrong thing to do. Thanks. I appreciate it." And, as he said it, he felt unwavering hatred toward her. For enmeshing him this way. One puny nineteen-year-old ordinary, netting a full-grown six like this—it was so improbable that it seemed absurd; he felt on one level like laughing. But on the other levels he did not.

"Are you responding to my warmth?" she inquired.

"Yes."

"You do feel my love reaching out to you, don't you? Listen. You can almost hear it." She listened intently. "My love is growing, and it's a tender vine."

Jason signaled the waiter. "What have you got here?" he asked the waiter brusquely. "Just beer and wine?"

"And pot, sir. The best-grade Acapulco Gold. And hash, grade A."

"But no hard liquor."

"No, sir."

Gesturing, he dismissed the waiter.

"You treated him like a servant," Kathy said.

"Yeah," he said, and groaned aloud. He shut his eyes and massaged the bridge of his nose. Might as well go the whole way now; he had managed, after all, to inflame her ire. "He's a lousy waiter," he said, "and this is a lousy restaurant. Let's get out of here."

Kathy said bitterly, "So that's what it means to be a celebrity. I understand." She quietly put down her fork.

"What do you think you understand?" he said, letting it all hang out; his conciliatory role was gone for good now. Never to be gotten back. He rose to his feet, reached for his coat. "I'm leaving," he told her. And put on his coat.

"Oh, God," Kathy said, shutting her eyes; her mouth, bent out of shape, hung open. "Oh, God. No. What have you done? Do you know what you've done? Do you understand fully? Do you grasp it at all?" And then, eyes shut, fists clenched, she ducked her head and began to scream. He had never heard screams like it before, and he stood paralyzed as the sound—and the sight of her constricted, broken face— dinned at him, numbing him. These are psychotic screams, he said to himself. From the racial unconscious. Not from a person but from a deeper level; from a collective entity.

Knowing that did not help.

The owner and two waiters hustled over, still clutching menus; Jason saw and marked details, oddly; it seemed as if everything, at her screams, had frozen over. Become fixed. Customers raising forks, lowering spoons, chewing . . . everything stopped and there remained only the terrible, ugly noise.

And she was saying words. Crude words, as if read off some back fence. Short, destructive words that tore at everyone in the restaurant, including himself. Especially himself.

The owner, his mustache twitching, nodded to the two waiters, and they lifted Kathy bodily from her chair; they raised her by her shoulders, held her, then, at the owner's curt nod, dragged her from the booth, across the restaurant and out onto the street.

He paid the bill, hurried after them.

At the entrance, however, the owner stopped him. Holding out his hand. "Three hundred dollars," the owner said.

"For what?" he demanded. "For dragging her outside?"

The owner said, "For not calling the pols."

Grimly, he paid.

The waiters had set her down on the pavement, at the curb's edge. She sat silent now, fingers pressed to her eyes, rocking back and forth, her mouth making soundless images. The waiters surveyed her, apparently essaying whether or not she would make any more trouble, and then, their joint decision made, they hurried back into the restaurant. Leaving him and Kathy there on the sidewalk, under the red-and-white neon sign, together.

Kneeling by her, he put his hand on her shoulder. This time she did not try to pull away. "I'm sorry," he said. And he meant it. "For pushing you." I called your bluff, he said to himself, and it was not a bluff. Okay; you won. I give up. From now on it's whatever you want. Name it. He thought, Just make it brief, for God's sake. Let me out of this as quickly as you possibly can.

He had an intuition that it would not be soon.

5

Together, hand in hand, they strolled along the evening side-walk, past the competing, flashing, winking, flooding pools of color created by the rotating, pulsating, jiggling, lit-up signs. This kind of neighborhood did not please him; he had seen it a million times, duplicated throughout the face of earth. It had been from such as this that he had fled, early in his life, to use his sixness as a method of getting out. And now he had come back.

He did not object to the people: he saw them as trapped here, the ordinaries, who through no fault of their own had to remain. They had not invented it; they did not like it; they endured it, as he had not had to. In fact, he felt guilty, seeing their grim faces, their turned-down mouths. Jagged, unhappy mouths.

"Yes," Kathy said at last, "I think I really am falling in love with you. But it's your fault; it's your powerful magnetic field that you radiate. Did you know I can see it?"

"Gee," he said mechanically.

"It's dark velvet purple," Kathy said, grasping his hand tightly with her surprisingly strong fingers. "Very intense. Can you see mine? My magnetic aura?"

"No," he said.

"I'm surprised. I would have thought you could." She seemed calm, now; the explosive screaming episode had left, trailing after it, relative stability. An almost pseudo-epileptoid personality structure, he conjectured. That works up day after day to—

"My aura," she broke into his thoughts, "is bright red. The color of passion."

"I'm glad for you," Jason said.

Halting, she turned to peer into his face. To decipher his expression. He hoped it was appropriately opaque. "Are you mad because I lost my temper?" she inquired.

"No," he said.

"You *sound* mad. I think you are mad. Well, I guess only Jack understands. And Mickey."

"Mickey Quinn," he said reflexively.

"Isn't he a remarkable person?" Kathy said.

"Very." He could have told her a lot, but it was pointless. She did not really want to know; she believed she understood already.

What else do you believe, little girl? he wondered. For example, what do you believe you know about me? As little as you know about Mickey Quinn and Arlene Howe and all the rest of them who, for you, do not in reality exist? Think what I could tell you if, for a moment, you were able to listen. But you can't listen. It would frighten you, what you might hear. And anyhow, you know everything already.

"How does it feel," he asked, "to have slept with so many famous people?"

At that she stopped short. "Do you think I slept with them because they were famous? Do you think I'm a CF, a celebrity fucker? Is that your real opinion of me?"

Like flypaper, he thought. She enmeshed him by every word he said. He could not win.

"I think," he said, "you've led an interesting life. You're an interesting person."

"And important," Kathy added.

"Yes," he said. "Important, too. In some ways the most important person I've ever encountered. It's a thrilling experience."

"Do you mean that?"

"Yes," he said emphatically. And in a peculiar, assbackward way, it was true. No one, not even Heather, had ever tied him up so completely as this. He could not endure what he found himself going through, and he could not get away. It seemed to him as if he sat behind the tiller of his custom-made unique quibble, facing a red light, green light, amber light all at once; no rational response was possible. Her irrationality made it so. The terrible power, he thought, of illogic. Of the archetypes. Operating out of the drear depths of the collective unconscious which joined him and her—and everyone else—together. In a knot which never could be undone, as long as they lived.

No wonder, he thought, some people, many people, long for death.

"You want to go watch a captain kirk?" Kathy asked.

"Whatever," he said, briefly.

"There's a good one on at Cinema Twelve. It's set on a planet in the Betelgeuse System, a lot like Tarberg's Planet—you know, in the Proxima System. Only in the captain kirk it's inhabited by minions of an invisible—"

"I saw it," he said. As a matter of fact, a year ago they had had Jeff Pomeroy, who played the captain kirk in the picture, on his show; they had even run a short scene: the usual flick-plugging, you-visit-us deal with Pomeroy's studio. He had not liked it then and he doubted if he would like it now. And he detested Jeff Pomeroy, both on and off the screen. And that, as far as he was concerned, was that.

"It really wasn't any good?" Kathy asked trustingly.

"Jeff Pomeroy," he said, "as far as I'm concerned, is the itchy asshole of the world. He and those like him. His imitators."

Kathy said, "He was at Morningside for a while. I didn't get to know him, but he was there."

"I can believe it," he said, half believing it.

"Do you know what he said to me once?"

"Knowing him," Jason began, "I'd say—"

"He said I was the tamest person he ever knew. Isn't that interesting? And he saw me go into one of my mystic states—

you know; when I lie down and scream—and still he said that. I think he's a very perceptive person; I really do. Don't you?"

"Yes," he said.

"Shall we go back to my room, then?" Kathy asked. "And screw like minks?"

He grunted in disbelief. Had she really said that? Turning, he tried to make out her face, but they had come to a patch between signs; all was dark for the moment. Jesus, he said to himself. *I've got to get myself out of this.* I've got to find my way back to my own world!

"Does my honesty bother you?" she asked.

"No," he said grimly. "Honesty never bothers me. To be a celebrity you have to be able to take it." Even that, he thought. "All kinds of honesty," he said. "Your kind most of all."

"What kind is mine?" Kathy asked.

"Honest honesty," he said.

"Then you do understand me," she said.

"Yes," he said, nodding. "I really do."

"And you don't look down on me? As a little worthless person who ought to be dead?"

"No," he said, "you're a very important person. And very honest, too. One of the most honest and straightforward individuals I've ever met. I mean that; I swear to God I do."

She patted him friendlily on the arm. "Don't get all worked up over it. Let it come naturally."

"It comes naturally," he assured her. "It really does."

"Good," Kathy said. Happily. He had, evidently, eased her worries; she felt sure of him. And on that his life depended . . . or did it really? Wasn't he capitulating to her pathological reasoning? At the moment he did not really know.

"Listen," he said haltingly. "I'm going to tell you something and I want you to listen carefully. You belong in a prison for the criminally insane."

Eerily, frighteningly, she did not react; she said nothing.

"And," he said, "I'm getting as far away from you as I

can." He yanked his hand loose from hers, turned, made his way off in the opposite direction. Ignoring her. Losing himself among the ordinaries who milled in both directions along the cheap, neon-lit sidewalks of this unpleasant part of town.

I've lost her, he thought, and in doing so I have probably lost my goddamn life.

Now what? He halted, looked around him. Am I carrying a microtransmitter, as she says? he asked himself. Am I giving myself away with every step I take?

Cheerful Charley, he thought, told me to look up Heather Hart. And as everybody in TV-land knows, Cheerful Charley is never wrong.

But will I live long enough, he asked himself, to reach Heather Hart? And if I do reach her and I'm bugged, won't I simply be carrying my death onto her? Like a mindless plague? And, he thought, if Al Bliss didn't know me and Bill Wolfer didn't know me, why should Heather know me? But Heather, he thought, is a six, like myself. The only other six I know. Maybe that will be the difference. If there is any difference.

He found a public phone booth, entered, shut the door against the noise of traffic, and dropped a gold quinque into the slot.

Heather Hart had several unlisted numbers. Some for business, some for personal friends, one for—to put it bluntly— lovers. He, of course, knew that number, having been to Heather what he had, and still was, he hoped.

The viewscreen lit up. He made out the changing shapes as indicating that she was taking the call on her carphone.

"Hi," Jason said.

Shading her eyes to make him out, Heather said, "Who the hell are you?" Her green eyes flashed. Her red hair dazzled.

"Jason."

"I don't know anybody named Jason. How'd you get this number?" Her tone was troubled but also harsh. "Get the hell off my goddamn phone!" she scowled at him from the viewscreen and said, "Who gave you this number? I want his name."

Jason said, "You told me the number six months ago. When you first had it installed. Your private of the private lines; right? Isn't that what you called it?"

"Who told you that?"

"You did. We were in Madrid. You were on location and I had me a six-day vacation half a mile from your hotel. You used to drive over in your Rolls quibble about three each afternoon. Right?"

Heather said in a chattering, staccato tone, "Are you from a magazine?"

"No," Jason said. "I'm your number one paramour."

"My *what*?"

"Lover."

"Are you a fan? You're a fan, a goddamn twerp fan. I'll kill you if you don't get off my phone." The sound and image died; Heather had hung up.

He inserted another quinque into the slot, redialed.

"The twerp fan again," Heather said, answering. She seemed more poised, now. Or was it resigned?

"You have one imitation tooth," Jason said. "When you're with one of your lovers you glue it into place in your mouth with a special epoxy cement that you buy at Harney's. But with me you sometimes take it out, put it in a glass with Dr. Sloom's denture foam. That's the denture cleanser you prefer. Because, you always say, it reminds you of the days when Bromo Seltzer was legal and not just black market made in somebody's basement lab, using all three bromides that Bromo Seltzer discontinued years ago when—"

"How," Heather interrupted, "did you get hold of this information?" Her face was stiff—her words brisk and direct. Her tone . . . he had heard it before. Heather used it with people she detested.

"Don't use that 'I don't give a fuck' tone with me," he said angrily. "Your false tooth is a molar. You call it Andy. Right?"

"A twerp fan knows all this about me. God. My worst nightmare confirmed. What's the name of your club and how many fans are there in it and where are you from and how,

God damn it, did you get hold of personal details from my private life that you have no right to know in the first place? I mean, what you're doing is illegal; it's an invasion of privacy. I'll have the pols after you if you call me once more." She reached to hang up the receiver.

"I'm a six," Jason said.

"A what? A six what? You have six legs; is that it? Or more likely six heads."

Jason said, "You're a six, too. That's what's kept us together all this time."

"I'm going to die," Heather said, ashen, now; even in the dim light of her quibble he could make out the change of color in her features. "What'll it cost me to have you leave me alone? I always knew that some twerp fan would eventually—"

"Stop calling me a twerp fan," Jason said bitingly; it infuriated him absolutely. It struck him as the ultimate in something or other; maybe a bird down, as the expression went now.

Heather said, "What do you want?"

"To meet you at Altrocci's."

"Yes, you'd know about that, too. The one place I can go without being ejaculated on by nerds who want me to sign menus that don't even belong to them." She sighed wretchedly. "Well, now that's over. I won't meet you at Altrocci's or anywhere. Keep out of my life or I'll have my prive-pols deball you and—"

"You have *one* private pol," Jason interrupted. "He's sixty-two years old and his name is Fred. Originally he was a sharpshooter with the Orange County Minutemen; used to pick off student jeters at Cal State Fullerton. He was good then, but he's nothing to worry about now."

"Is that so," Heather said.

"Okay, let me tell you something else that how do you think I would know. Remember Constance Ellar?"

"Yes," Heather said. "That nonentity starlet that looked like a Barbie Doll except that her head was too small and her body looked as if someone had inflated her with a CO_2 cartridge, overinflated her." Her lip curled. "She was utterly damn dumb."

"Right," he agreed. "Utterly damn dumb. That's the exact word. Remember what we did to her on my show? Her first planetwide exposure, because I had to take her in a tie-in deal. Do you remember that, what we did, you and I?"

Silence.

Jason said, "As a sop to us for having her on the show, her agent agreed to let her do a commercial for one of our quarter-time sponsors. We got curious as to what the product was, so before Miss Ellar showed up we opened the paper bag and discovered it was a cream for removing leg hair. God, Heather, you must—"

"I'm listening," Heather said.

Jason said, "We took the spray can of leg-hair cream out and put a spray can of FDS back in with the same ad copy, which simply read, 'Demonstrate use of product with expression of contentment and satisfaction,' and then we got the hell out of there and waited."

"Did we."

"Miss Ellar finally showed up, went into her dressing room, opened the paper bag, and then—and this is the part that still makes me break up—she came up to me, perfectly seriously, and said, 'Mr. Taverner, I'm sorry to bother you about this, but to demonstrate the Feminine Hygiene Deodorant Spray I'll have to take off my skirt and underpants. Right there before the TV camera.' 'So?' I said. 'So what's the problem?' And Miss Ellar said, 'I'll need a little table on which I can put my clothes. I can't just drop them on the floor; that wouldn't look right. I mean, I'll be spraying that stuff into my vagina in front of sixty million people, and when you're doing that you can't just leave your clothes lying all around you on the floor; that isn't elegant.' She really would have done it, too, right on the air, if Al Bliss hadn't—"

"It's a tasteless story."

"All the same, you thought it was pretty funny. That utterly dumb girl with her first big break ready to do that. 'Demonstrate use of product with expression of contentment and—' "

Heather hung up.

How do I make her understand? he asked himself savagely, grinding his teeth together, nearly biting off a silver filling. He hated that sensation: grinding off a piece of filling. Destroying his own body, impotently. Can't she see that my knowledge of everything about her means something important? he asked himself. Who would know these things? Obviously only someone who had been very close physically with her for some time. There could be no other explanation, and yet she had conjured up such an elaborate other reason that he couldn't penetrate through to her. And it hung directly in front of her eyes. Her six's eyes.

Once more he dropped in a coin, dialed.

"Hi again," he said, when Heather at last picked up the phone in her car. "I know that about you, too," he said. "You can't let a phone ring; that's why you have ten private numbers, each for a different purpose of your very special own."

"I have three," Heather said. "So you don't know everything."

Jason said, "I merely meant—"

"How much?"

"I've had enough of that today," he said sincerely. "You can't buy me off because that's not what I want. I want—listen to me, Heather—I want to find out why nobody knows me. You most of all. And since you're a six I thought you might be able to explain it. Do you have *any* memory of me? Look at me on the picture screen. Look!"

She peered, one eyebrow cocked. "You're young but not too young. You're good-looking. Your voice is commanding and you have no reluctance about brigging me like this. You're exactly what a twerp fan would look like, sound like, act like. Okay; are you satisfied?"

"I'm in trouble," he said. It was blatantly irrational for him to tell her this, since she had no recollection of any sort of him. But over the years he had become accustomed to laying his troubles before her—and listening to hers—and the habit had not died. The habit ignored what he saw the reality situation to be: it cruised on under its own power.

"That's a shame," Heather said.

Jason said, "Nobody remembers me. And I have no birth certificate; I was never born, never even born! So naturally I have no ID cards except a forged set I bought from a pol fink for two thousand dollars plus one thousand for my contact. I'm carrying them around, but, God: they may have microtransmitters built into them. Even knowing that I have to keep them on me; you know why—even you up at the top, even you know how this society works. Yesterday I had thirty million viewers who would have shrieked their aggrieved heads off if a pol or a nat so much as touched me. Now I'm looking into the eyes of an FLC."

"What's an FLC?"

"Forced-labor camp." He snarled the words at her, trying to pin her down and finally nail her. "The vicious little bitch who forged my papers made me take her out to some God-forsaken broken-down wop restaurant, and while we were there, just talking, she threw herself down on the floor screaming. Psychotic screaming; she's an escapee from Morn-ingside, by her own admission. That cost me another three hundred dollars and by now who knows? She's probably sicced the pols and nats *both* on me." Pushing his self-pity gingerly a little further, he said, "They're probably monitoring this phone line right now."

"Oh, Christ, no!" Heather shrieked and again hung up.

He had no more gold quinques. So, at this point, he gave up. That was a stupid thing to say, he realized, that about the phone lines. That would make anybody hang up. I strangled myself in my own word web, right down the old freeber. Straight down the middle. Beautifully flat at both ends, too. Like a great artificial anus.

He shoved the door of the phone booth aside and stepped out onto the busy nocturnal sidewalk . . . down here, he thought acidly, in Slumsville. Down where the pol finks hang out. Jolly good show, as that classic TV muffin ad went that we studied in school, he said to himself.

It would be funny, he thought, if it were happening to someone else. But it's happening to me. No, it's not funny either way. Because there is real suffering and real death passing the time of day in the wings. Ready to come on any minute.

I wish I could have taped the phone call, plus everything Kathy said to me and me to her. In 3-D color, on videotape it would be a nice bit on my show, somewhere near the end where we run out of material occasionally. Occasionally, hell: generally. Always. For the rest of my life.

He could hear his intro now. "What can happen to a man, a good man without a pol record, a man who suddenly one day loses his ID cards and finds himself facing . . ." And so forth. It would hold them, all thirty million of them. Because that was what each of them feared. "An invisible man," his intro would go, "yet a man all too conspicuous. Invisible legally; conspicuous illegally. What becomes of such a man, if he cannot replace . . ." Blah blah. On and on. The hell with it. Not everything that he did or said or had happen to him got onto the show; so it went with this. Another loser, among many. Many are called, he said to himself, but few are chosen. That's what it means to be a pro. That's how I manage things, public and private. Cut your losses and run when you have to, he told himself, quoting himself from back in the good days when his first full worldwide show got piped onto the satellite grid.

I'll find another forger, he decided, one that isn't a pol informer, and get a full new set of ID cards, ones without microtransmitters. And then, evidently, I need a gun.

I should have thought of that about the time I woke up in that hotel room, he said to himself. Once, years ago, when the Reynolds syndicate had tried to buy into his show, he had learned to use—and had carried—a gun: a Barber's Hoop with a range of two miles with no loss of peak trajectory until the final thousand feet.

Kathy's "mystical trance," her screaming fit. The audio

portion would carry a mature male voice saying against her screams as BG, "This is what it is to be psychotic. To be psychotic is to suffer, suffer beyond . . ." And so forth. Blah blah. He inhaled a great, deep lungful of cold night air, shuddered, joined the passengers on the sea of sidewalk, his hands thrust deep into his trouser pockets.

And found himself facing a queue lined up ten deep before a pol random checkpoint. One gray-clad policeman stood at the end of the line, loitering there to make sure no one doubled back in the opposite direction.

"Can't you pass it, friend?" the pol said to him as he involuntarily started to leave.

"Sure," Jason said.

"That's good," the pol said good-humoredly. "Because we've been checking here since eight this morning and we still don't have our work quota."

6

Two husky gray pols, confronting the man ahead of Jason, said in unison, "These were forged an hour ago; they're still damp. See? See the ink run under the heat? Okay." They nodded, and the man, gripped by four thungly pols, disappeared into a parked van-quibble, ominously gray and black: police colors.

"Okay," one of the husky pols said genially to Jason, "let's see when yours were printed."

Jason said, "I've been carrying these for years." He handed his wallet, with the seven ID cards, to the pols.

"Graph his signatures," the senior pol told his companion. "See if they superimpose."

Kathy had been right.

"Nope," the junior pol said, putting away his official camera. "They don't super. But it looks like this one, the military service chit, had a trans dot on it that's been scraped off. Very expertly, too, if so. You have to view it through the glass." He swung the portable magnifying lens and light over, illuminating Jason's forged cards in stark white detail. "See?"

"When you left the service," the senior pol said to Jason, "did this record have an electronic dot on it? Do you remember?" Both of them scrutinized Jason as they awaited his response.

What the hell to say? he asked himself. "I don't know,"

he said. "I don't even know what a"—he started to say, "microtransmitter dot," but quickly corrected himself—soon enough, he hoped—"what an electronic dot looks like."

"It's a dot, mister," the junior pol informed him. "Aren't you listening? Are you on drugs? Look; on his drug-status card there isn't an entry for the last year."

One of the thungly pols spoke up. "Proves they're not faked, though, because who would fake a felony onto an ID card? They'd have to be out of their minds."

"Yes," Jason said.

"Well, it's not part of our area," the senior pol said. He handed Jason's ID cards back to him. "He'll have to take it up with his drug inspector. Move on." With his nightstick the pol shoved Jason out of the way, reaching meanwhile for the ID cards of the man behind him.

"That's it?" Jason said to the thungly pols. He could not believe it. Don't let it show, he said to himself. Just *move on*!

He did so.

From the shadows beneath a broken streetlight, Kathy reached out, touched him; he froze at the touch, feeling himself turn to ice, starting with his heart. "What do you think of me now?" Kathy said. "My work, what I did for you."

"They did it," he said shortly.

"I'm not going to turn you in," Kathy said, "even though you insulted and abandoned me. But you have to stay with me tonight like you promised. You understand?"

He had to admire her. By lurking around the random checkpoint she had obtained firsthand proof that her forged documents had been well enough done to get him past the pols. So all at once the situation between them had altered: he was now in her debt. He no longer held the status of aggrieved victim.

Now she owned a moral share of him. First the stick: the threat of turning him in to the pols. Then the carrot: the adequately forged ID cards. The girl had him, really. He had to admit it, to her and to himself.

"I could have gotten you through anyhow," Kathy said. She held up her right arm, pointing to a section of her sleeve. "I've got a gray pol-ident tab, there; it shows up under their macrolens. So I don't get picked up by mistake. I would have said—"

"Let it lie there," he broke in harshly. "I don't want to hear about it." He walked away from her; the girl skimmed after him, like a skillful bird.

"Want to go back to my Minor Apartment?" Kathy asked.

"That goddamn shabby room." I have a floating house in Malibu, he thought, with eight bedrooms, six rotating baths and a four-dimensional living room with an infinity ceiling. And, because of something I don't understand and can't control, I have to spend my time like this. Visiting run-down marginal places. Crappy eateries, crappier workshops, crappiest one-room lodgings. Am I being paid back for something I did? he asked himself. Something I don't know about or remember? But nobody pays back, he reflected. I learned that a long time ago: you're not paid back for the bad you do nor the good you do. It all comes out uneven at the end. Haven't I learned that by now, if I've learned anything?

"Guess what's at the top of my shopping list for tomorrow," Kathy was saying. "Dead flies. Do you know why?"

"They're high in protein."

"Yes, but that's not why; I'm not getting them for myself. I buy a bag of them every week for Bill, my turtle."

"I didn't see any turtle."

"At my Major Apartment. You didn't really think I'd buy dead flies for myself, did you?"

"De gustibus non disputandum est," he quoted.

"Let's see. In matters of taste there's no dispute. Right?"

"Right," he said. "Meaning that if you want to eat dead flies go ahead and eat them."

"Bill does; he likes them. He's just one of those little green turtles . . . not a land tortoise or anything. Have you ever watched the way they snap at food, at a fly floating on their water? It's very small but it's awful. One second the fly's there and then the next, glunk. It's inside the turtle." She laughed. "Being digested. There's a lesson to be learned there."

"What lesson?" He anticipated it then. "That when you bite," he said, "you either get all of it or none of it, but never part."

"That's how I feel."

"Which do you have?" he asked her. "All or none?"

"I—don't know. Good question. Well, I don't have Jack. But maybe I don't want him anymore. It's been so fucking long. I guess I still need him. But I need you more."

Jason said, "I thought you were the one who could love two men equally."

"Did I say that?" She pondered as they walked. "What I meant was is that's ideal, but in real life you can only approximate it . . . do you see? Can you follow my line of thought?"

"I can follow it," he said, "and I can see where it's leading. It's leading to a temporary abandonment of Jack while I'm around and then a psychological returning to him when I'm gone. Do you do it every time?"

"I never abandon him," Kathy said sharply. They then continued on in silence until they reached her great old apartment building with its forest of no-longer-used TV masts jutting from every part of the roof. Kathy fumbled in her purse, found her key, unlocked the door to her room.

The lights had been turned on. And, seated on the moldering sofa facing them, a middle-aged man with gray hair and a gray suit. A heavy-set but immaculate man, with perfectly shaved jowls: no nicks, no red spots, no errors. He was perfectly attired and groomed; each hair on his head stood individually in place.

Kathy said falteringly, "Mr. McNulty."

Rising to his feet, the heavy-set man extended his right hand toward Jason. Automatically, Jason reached out to shake it.

"No," the heavy-set man said. "I'm not shaking hands with you; I want to see your ID cards, the ones she made for you. Let me have them."

Wordlessly—there was nothing to say—Jason passed him his wallet.

"You didn't do these," McNulty said, after a short inspection. "Unless you're getting a hell of a lot better."

Jason said, "I've had some of those cards for years."

"Have you," McNulty murmured. He returned the wallet and cards to Jason. "Who planted the microtrans on him? You?" He addressed Kathy. "Ed?"

"Ed," Kathy said.

"What do we have here?" McNulty said, scrutinizing Jason as if measuring him for a coffin. "A man in his forties, well dressed, modern clothing style. Expensive shoes . . . made of actual authentic leather. Isn't that right, Mr. Taverner?"

"They're cowhide," Jason said.

"Your papers identify you as a musician," McNulty said. "You play an instrument?"

"I sing."

McNulty said, "Sing something for us now."

"Go to hell," Jason said, and managed to control his breathing; his words came out exactly as he wanted them to. No more, no less.

To Kathy, McNulty said, "He's not exactly cowering. Does he know who I am?"

"Yes," Kathy said. "I—told him. Part of it."

"You told him about Jack," McNulty said. To Jason he said, "There is no Jack. She thinks so but it's a psychotic delusion. Her husband died three years ago in a quibble accident; he was never in a forced-labor camp."

"Jack is still alive," Kathy said.

"You see?" McNulty said to Jason. "She's made a pretty fair adjustment to the outside world except for this one fixed idea. It will never go away; she'll have it for the balance of her life." He shrugged. "It's a harmless idea and it keeps her going. So we've made no attempt to deal with it psychiatrically."

Kathy, quietly, had begun to cry. Large tears slid down her cheeks and dropped, bloblike, onto her blouse. Tear stains, in the form of dark circles, appeared here and there.

"I'll be talking to Ed Pracim in the next couple of days," McNulty said. "I'll ask him why he put the microtrans on you. He has hunches; it must have been a hunch." He reflected. "Bear in mind, the ID cards in your wallet are reproductions of actual documents on file at various central data banks throughout earth. Your reproductions are satisfactory, but I may want to check on the originals. Let's hope they're in as good order as the repros you carry."

Kathy said feebly, "But that's a rare procedure. Statistically—"

"In this case," McNulty said, "I think it's worth trying."

"Why?" Kathy said.

"Because we don't think you're turning everyone over to us. Half an hour ago this man Taverner passed successfully through a random checkpoint. We followed him using the microtrans. And his papers look fine to me. But Ed says—"

"Ed drinks," Kathy said.

"But we can count on him." McNulty smiled, a professional beam of sunshine in the shabby room. "And we can't, not quite, on you."

Bringing forth his military-service chit, Jason rubbed the small profile 4-D picture of himself. And it said tinnily, "How now, brown cow?"

"How can that be faked?" Jason said. "That's the tone of voice I had back ten years ago when I was an invol-nat."

"I doubt that," McNulty said. He examined his wristwatch. "Do we owe you anything, Miss Nelson? Or are we clear for this week?"

"Clear," she said, with an effort. Then, in a low, unsteady voice, she half-whispered, "After Jack gets out you won't be able to count on me at all."

"For you," McNulty said genially, "Jack will never get out." He winked at Jason. Jason winked back. Twice. He understood McNulty. The man preyed on the weaknesses of others; the kind of manipulation that Kathy employed had probably been learned from him. And from his quaint, genial companions.

He could understand now how she had become what she

had become. Betrayal was an everyday event; a refusal to betray, as in his case, was miraculous. He could only wonder at it and thank it dimly.

We have a betrayal state, he realized. When I was a celebrity I was exempt. Now I'm like everyone else: I now have to face what they've always faced. And—what I faced in the old days, faced and then later on repressed from my memory. Because it was too distressing to believe . . . once I had a choice, and could choose not to believe.

McNulty put his fleshy, red-speckled hand on Jason's shoulder and said, "Come along with me."

"Where to?" Jason demanded, moving away from McNulty exactly, he realized, the way Kathy had moved away from *him*. She had learned this, too, from the McNultys of the world.

"You don't have anything to charge him with!" Kathy said hoarsely, clenching her fists.

Easily, McNulty said, "We're not going to charge him with anything; I just want a fingerprint, voiceprint, footprint, EEG wave pattern from him. Okay, Mr. Tavern?"

Jason started to say, "I hate to correct a police officer—" and then broke off at the warning look on Kathy's face— "who's doing his duty," he finished, "so I'll go along." Maybe Kathy had a point; maybe it was worth something for the pol officer to get Jason Taverner's name wrong. Who knew? Time would tell.

" 'Mr. Tavern,' " McNulty said lazily, propelled him toward the door of the room. "Suggests beer and warmth and coziness, doesn't it?" He looked back at Kathy and said in a sharp voice, "Doesn't it?"

"Mr. Tavern is a warm man," Kathy said, her teeth locked together. The door shut after them, and McNulty steered him down the hallway to the stairs, breathing, meanwhile, the odor of onion and hot sauce in every direction.

At the 469th Precinct station, Jason Taverner found himself lost in a multitude of men and women who moved aimlessly, waiting to get in, waiting to get out, waiting for information, waiting to be told what to do. McNulty had pinned a colored tag on his lapel; God and the police alone knew what it meant.

Obviously it did mean something. A uniformed officer behind a desk which ran from wall to wall beckoned to him.

"Okay," the cop said. "Inspector McNulty filled out part of your J-2 form. Jason Tavern. Address: 2048 Vine Street."

Where had McNulty come up with that? Jason wondered. Vine Street. And then he realized that it was Kathy's address. McNulty had assumed they were living together; overworked, as was true of all the pols, he had written down the information that took the least effort. A law of nature: an object— or living creature—takes the shortest route between two points. He filled out the balance of the form.

"Put your hand into that slot," the officer said, indicating a fingerprinting machine. Jason did so. "Now," the officer said, "remove one shoe, either left or right. And that sock. You may sit down here." He slid a section of desk aside, revealing an entrance and a chair.

"Thanks," Jason said, seating himself.

After the recording of the footprint he spoke the sentence, "Down goes the right hut and ate a put object beside his horse." That took care of the voiceprint. After that, again seated, he allowed terminals to be placed here and there on his head; the machine cranked out three feet of scribbled-on paper, and that was that. That was the electrocardiogram. It ended the tests.

Looking cheerful, McNulty appeared at the desk. In the harsh white overhead light his five-o'clock shadow could be seen over all his jaw, his upper lip, the higher part of his neck. "How's it going with Mr. Tavern?" he asked.

The officer said, "We're ready to do a nomenclature file-pull."

"Fine," McNulty said. "I'll stick around and see what comes up."

The uniformed officer dropped the form Jason had filled

out into a slot, pressed lettered buttons, all of which were green. For some reason Jason noticed that. And the letters capitals.

From a mouthlike aperture on the very long desk a Xeroxed document slid out, dropped into a metal basket.

"Jason Tavern," the uniformed officer said, examining the document. "Of Kememmer, Wyoming. Age: thirty-nine. A diesel engine mechanic." He glanced at the photo. "Pic taken fifteen years ago."

"Any police record?" McNulty asked.

"No trouble of any kind," the uniformed officer said.

"There are no other Jason Taverns on record at Pol-Dat?" McNulty asked. The officer pressed a yellow button, shook his head. "Okay," McNulty said. "That's him." He surveyed Jason. "You don't look like a diesel engine mechanic."

"I don't do that anymore," Jason said. "I'm now in sales. For farm equipment. Do you want my card?" A bluff; he reached toward the upper right-hand pocket of his suit. McNulty shook his head no. So that was that; they had, in their usual bureaucratic fashion, pulled the wrong file on him. And, in their rush, they had let it stand.

He thought, Thank God for the weaknesses built into a vast, complicated, convoluted, planetwide apparatus. Too many people; too many machines. This error began with a pol inspec and worked its way to Pol-Dat, their pool of data at Memphis, Tennessee. Even with my fingerprint, footprint, voiceprint and EEG print they probably won't be able to straighten it out. Not now; not with my form on file.

"Shall I book him?" the uniformed officer asked McNulty.

"For what?" McNulty said. "For being a diesel mechanic?" He slapped Jason convivially on the back. "You can go home, Mr. Tavern. Back to your child-faced sweetheart. Your little virgin." Grinning, he moved off into the throng of anxious and bewildered human men and women.

"You may go, sir," the uniformed officer told Jason.

Nodding, Jason made his way out of the 469th Precinct police station, onto the nighttime street, to mix with the free and self-determined people who resided there.

But they will get me finally, he thought. They'll match up the prints. And yet—if it's been fifteen years since the photo was taken, maybe it's been fifteen years since they took an EEG and a voiceprint.

But that still left the finger- and footprints. They did not change.

He thought, Maybe they'll just toss the Xerox copy of the file into a shredding bin, and that will be that. And transmit the data they got out of me to Memphis, there to be incorporated in my—or rather "my"—permanent file. In Jason Tavern's file, specifically.

Thank God Jason Tavern, diesel mechanic, had never broken a law, had never tangled with the pols or nats. Good for him.

A police flipflap wobbled overhead, its red searchlight glimmering, and from its PA speakers it said, "Mr. Jason Tavern, return to 469th Precinct Police Station at once. This is a police order. Mr. Jason Tavern—" It raved on and on as Jason stood stunned. They had figured it out already. In a matter not of hours, days, or weeks, but minutes.

He returned to the police station, climbed the styraplex stairs, passed through the light-activated doors, through the milling throng of the unfortunate, back to the uniformed officer who had handled his case—and there stood McNulty, too. The two of them were in the process of frowningly conferring.

"Well," McNulty said, glancing up, "here's our Mr. Tavern again. What are you doing back here, Mr. Tavern?"

"The police flipflap—" he began, but McNulty cut him off.

"That was unauthorized. We merely put out an APB and some figtail hoisted it to flipflap level. But as long as you're here"—McNulty turned the document so that Jason could see the photo—"is that how you looked fifteen years ago?"

"I guess so," Jason said. The photo showed a sallow-faced individual with protruding Adam's apple, bad teeth and eyes, sternly staring into nothing. His hair, frizzy and corn-colored, hung over two near-jug ears.

"You've had plastic S," McNulty said.

Jason said, "Yes."

"Why?"

Jason said, "Who would want to look like that?"

"So no wonder you're so handsome and dignified," McNulty said. "So stately. So"—he groped for the word— "commanding. It's really hard to believe that they could do to *that*"—he put his index finger on the fifteen-year-old photo—"something to make it look like *that*." He tapped Jason friendlily on the arm. "But where'd you get the money?"

While McNulty talked, Jason had begun swiftly reading the data printed on the document. Jason Tavern had been born in Cicero, Illinois, his father had been a turret lathe operator, his grandfather had owned a chain of retail farm-equipment stores—a lucky break, considering what he had told McNulty about his current career.

"From Windslow," Jason said. "I'm sorry; I always think of him like that, and I forget that others can't." His professional training had helped him: he had read and assimilated most of the page while McNulty was talking to him. "My grandfather. He had a good deal of money, and I was his favorite. I was the only grandson, you see."

McNulty studied the document, nodded.

"I looked like a rural hick," Jason said. "I looked like what I was: a hayseed. The best job I could get involved repairing diesel engines, and I wanted more. So I took the money that Windslow left me and headed for Chicago—"

"Okay," McNulty said still nodding. "It fits together. We are aware that such radical plastic surgery can be accomplished, and at not too large a cost. But generally it's done by unpersons or labor-camp inmates who've escaped. We monitor all graft-shops, as we call them."

"But look how ugly I was," Jason said.

McNulty laughed a deep, throaty laugh. "You sure were, Mr. Tavern. Okay; sorry to trouble you. Go on." He gestured, and Jason began to part the throng of people before

him. "Oh!" McNulty called, gesturing to him. "One more—"
His voice, drowned out by the noise of the milling, did not
reach Jason. So, his heart frozen in ice, he walked out.

Once they notice you, Jason realized, *they never completely
close the file.* You can never get back your anonymity. It is
vital not to be noticed in the first place. But I have been.

"What is it?" he asked McNulty, feeling despair. They were
playing games with him, breaking him down; he could feel,
inside him, his heart, his blood, all his vital parts, stagger in
their processes. Even the superb physiology of a six tumbled
at this.

McNulty held out his hand. "Your ID cards. I want some
lab work on them. If they're okay you'll get them back the
day after tomorrow."

Jason said protestingly. "But if a random pol-check—"

"We'll give you a police pass," McNulty said. He nodded
to a great-bellied older officer to his right. "Get a 4-D photo
of him and set up a blanket pass."

"Yes, Inspector," the tub of guts said, reaching out an
overstuffed paw to turn on the camera equipment.

Ten minutes later, Jason Taverner found himself out once
more on the now almost deserted early evening sidewalk,
and this time with a bona fide pol-pass—better than anything
Kathy could have manufactured for him . . . except that the
pass was valid only for one week. But still . . .

He had one week during which he could afford not to
worry. And then, after that . . .

He had done the impossible: he had traded a walletful of
bogus ID cards for a genuine pol-pass. Examining the pass
under the streetlights, he saw that the expiration notice was
holographic . . . and there was room for the insertion of an
additional number. It read *seven.* He could get Kathy to alter
that to seventy-five or ninety-seven, or whatever was easiest.

And then it occurred to him that as soon as the pol lab
made out that his ID cards were spurious the number of his
pass, his name, his photo, would be transmitted to every
police checkpoint on the planet.

But until that happened he was safe.

PART TWO

Down, vain lights, shine you no more!
No nights are black enough for those
That in despair their lost fortunes deplore.
Light doth but shame disclose.

PART TWO

Down, vain lights, shine you no more!
No nights are black enough for those
That in despair their lost fortunes deplore.
Light doth but shame disclose.

7

Early in the gray of evening, before the cement sidewalks bloomed with nighttime activity, Police General Felix Buckman landed his opulent official quibble on the roof of the Los Angeles Police Academy building. He sat for a time, reading page-one articles on the sole evening newspaper, then, folding the paper up carefully, he placed it on the back seat of the quibble, opened the locked door, and stepped out.

No activity below him. One shift had begun to trail off; the next had not quite begun to arrive.

He liked this time: the great building, in these moments, seemed to belong to him. "And leaves the world to darkness and to me," he thought, recalling a line from Thomas Gray's *Elegy*. A long cherished favorite of his, in fact from boyhood.

With his rank key he opened the building's express descent sphincter, dropped rapidly by chute to his own level, fourteen. Where he had worked most of his adult life.

Desks without people, rows of them. Except that at the far end of the major room one officer still sat painstakingly writing a report. And, at the coffee machine, a female officer drinking from a Dixie cup.

"Good evening," Buckman said to her. He did not know her, but it did not matter: she—and everyone else in the building—knew *him*.

"Good evening, Mr. Buckman." She drew herself upright, as if at attention.

"Be tired," Buckman said.

"Pardon, sir?"

"Go home." He walked away from her, passed by the posterior row of desks, the rank of square gray metal shapes upon which the business of this branch of earth's police agency was conducted.

Most of the desks were clean: the officers had finished their work neatly before leaving. But, on desk 37, several papers. Officer Someone worked late, Buckman decided. He bent to see the nameplate.

Inspector McNulty, of course. The ninety-day wonder of the academy. Busily dreaming up plots and remnants of treason . . . Buckman smiled, seated himself on the swivel chair, picked up the papers.

TAVERNER, JASON. CODE BLUE.

A Xeroxed file from police vaults. Summoned out of the void by the overly eager—and overweight—Inspector McNulty. A small note in pencil: "Taverner does not exist."

Strange, he thought. And began to leaf through the papers.

"Good evening, Mr. Buckman." His assistant, Herbert Maime, young and sharp, nattily dressed in a civilian suit: he rated that privilege, as did Buckman.

"McNulty seems to be working on the file of someone who does not exist," Buckman said.

"In which precinct doesn't he exist?" Maime said, and both of them laughed. They did not particularly like McNulty, but the gray police required his sort. Everything would be fine unless the McNultys of the academy rose to policy-making levels. Fortunately that rarely happened. Not, anyhow, if *he* could help it.

Subject gave false name Jason Tavern. Wrong file pulled of Jason Tavern of Kememmer, Wyoming, diesel motor repairman. Subject claimed to be Tavern, with plastic S. ID cards identify him as Taverner, Jason, but no file.

Interesting, Buckman thought as he read McNulty's notes. Absolutely no file on the man. He finished the notes:

Well-dressed, suggest has money, perhaps influence to get his file pulled out of data bank. Look into relationship with Katharine Nelson, pol contact in area. Does she know who he is? Tried not to turn him in, but pol contact 1659BD planted microtrans on him. Subject now in cab. Sector N8823B, moving east in the direction of Las Vegas. Due 11/4 10:00 P.M. academy time. Next report due at 2:40 P.M. academy time.

Katharine Nelson. Buckman had met her once, at a pol-contact orientation course. She was the girl who only turned in individuals whom she did not like. In an odd elliptical way he admired her; after all, had he not intervened, she would have been shipped on 4/8/82 to a forced-labor camp in British Columbia.

To Herb Maime, Buckman said, "Get me McNulty on the phone. I think I'd better talk to him about this."

A moment later, Maime handed him the instrument. On the small gray screen McNulty's face appeared, looking rumpled. As did his living room. Small and untidy, both of them.

"Yes, Mr. Buckman," McNulty said, focusing on him and coming to a stiff attention, tired as he was. Despite fatigue and a little hype of something, McNulty knew exactly how to comport himself in relation to his superiors.

Buckman said, "Give me the story, briefly, on this Jason Taverner. I can't piece it together from your notes."

"Subject rented hotel room at 453 Eye Street. Approached pol contact 1659BD, known as Ed, asked to be taken to ID forger. Ed planted microtrans on him, took him to pol contact 1980CC, Kathy."

"Katharine Nelson," Buckman said.

"Yes, sir. Evidently she did an unusually expert job on the

ID cards; I've put them through prelim lab tests and they work out *almost* okay. She must have wanted him to get away."

"You contacted Katharine Nelson?"

"I met both of them at her room. Neither cooperated with me. I examined subject's ID cards, but—"

"They seemed genuine," Buckman interrupted.

"Yes, sir."

"You still think you can do it by eye."

"Yes, Mr. Buckman. But it got him through a random pol checkpoint; the stuff was that good."

"How nice for him."

McNulty bumbled on. "I took his ID cards and issued him a seven-day pass, subject to recall. Then I took him to the 469th Precinct station, where I have my aux office, and had his file pulled . . . the Jason Tavern file, it turned out. Subject went into a long song and dance about plastic S; it sounded plausible, so we let him go. No, wait a minute; I didn't issue him the pass until—"

"Well," Buckman interrupted, "what's he up to? Who is he?"

"We're following him, via the microtrans. We're trying to come up with data-bank material on him. But as you read in my notes, I think subject has managed to get his file out of every central data bank. It's just not there, and it has to be because we have a file on everyone, as every school kid knows; it's the law, we've got to."

"But we don't," Buckman said.

"I know, Mr. Buckman. But when a file isn't there, there has to be a reason. It didn't just *happen* not to be there: someone filched it out of there."

" 'Filched,' " Buckman said, amused.

"Stole, purloined." McNulty looked discomfited. "I've just begun to go into it, Mr. Buckman; I'll know more in twenty-four hours. Hell, we can pick him up any time we want. I don't think this is important. He's just some well-heeled guy with enough influence to get his file out—"

"All right," Buckman said. "Go to bed." He rang off,

stood for a moment, then walked in the direction of his inner offices. Pondering.

In his main office, asleep on the couch, lay his sister Alys. Wearing, Felix Buckman saw with acute displeasure, skin-tight black trousers, a man's leather shirt, hoop earrings, and a chain belt with a wrought-iron buckle. Obviously she had been drugging. And had, as so often before, gotten hold of one of his keys.

"God damn you," he said to her, closing the office door before Herb Maime could catch a glimpse of her.

In her sleep Alys stirred. Her catlike face screwed up into an irritable frown and, with her right hand, she groped to put out the overhead fluorescent light, which he had now turned on.

Grabbing her by the shoulders—and experiencing without pleasure her taut muscles—he dragged her to a sitting position. "What was it this time?" he demanded. "Termaline?"

"No." Her speech, of course, came out slurred. "Hexo-phenophrine hydrosulphate. Uncut. Subcutaneous." She opened her great pale eyes, stared at him with rebellious displeasure.

Buckman said, "Why in hell do you always come here?" Whenever she had been heavily fetishing and/or drugging she crashed here in his main office. He did not know why, and she had never said. The closest she had come, once, was a mumbled declaration about the "eye of the hurricane," suggesting that she felt safe from arrest here at the core offices of the Police Academy. Because, of course, of his position.

"Fetishist," he snapped at her, with fury. "We process a hundred of you a day, you and your leather and chain mail and dildoes. God." He stood breathing noisily, feeling himself shake.

Yawning, Alys slid from the couch, stood straight upright and stretched her long, slender arms. "I'm glad it's evening," she said airily, her eyes squeezed shut. "Now I can go home and go to bed."

"How do you plan to get out of here?" he demanded. But

he knew. Every time the same ritual unfolded. The ascent tube for "secluded" political prisoners got brought into use: it led from his extreme north office to the roof, hence to the quibble field. Alys came and went that way, his key breezily in hand. "Someday," he said to her darkly, "an officer will be using the tube for a legitimate purpose, and he'll run into you."

"And what would he do?" She massaged his short-cropped gray hair. "Tell me, please, sir. Muff-dive me into panting contrition?"

"One look at you with that sated expression on your face—"

"They know I'm your sister."

Buckman said harshly, "They know because you're always coming in here for one reason or another or no damn reason at all."

Perching knees up on the edge of a nearby desk, Alys eyed him seriously. "It really bothers you."

"Yes, it really bothers me."

"That I come here and make your job unsafe."

"You can't make my job unsafe," Buckman said. "I've got only five men over me, excluding the national director, and all of them know about you and they can't do anything. So you can do what you want." Thereupon he stormed out of the north office, down the dull corridor to the larger suite where he did most of his work. He tried to avoid looking at her.

"But you carefully closed the door," Alys said, sauntering after him, "so that that Herbert Blame or Mame or Maine or whatever it is wouldn't see me."

"You," Buckman said, "are repellent to a natural man."

"Is Maime natural? How do you know? Have you screwed him?"

"If you don't get out of here," he said quietly, facing her across two desks. "I'll have you shot. So help me God."

She shrugged her muscular shoulders. And smiled.

"Nothing scares you," he said, accusingly. "Since your brain operation. You systematically, deliberately, had all your human centers removed. You're now a"—he struggled to find the words; Alys always hamstrung him like this, even managed to abolish his ability to use words—"you," he said chokingly, "are a reflex machine that diddles itself endlessly like a rat in an experiment. You're wired into the pleasure nodule of your brain and you push the switch five thousand times an hour every day of your life when you're not sleeping. It's a mystery to me why you bother to sleep; why not diddle yourself a full twenty-four hours a day?"

He waited, but Alys said nothing.

"Someday," he said, "one of us will die."

"Oh?" she said, raising a thin green eyebrow.

"One of us," Buckman said, "will outlive the other. And that one will rejoice."

The pol-line phone on the larger desk buzzed. Reflexively, Buckman picked it up. On the screen McNulty's rumpled hyped-up features appeared. "Sorry to bother you, General Buckman, but I just got a call from one of my staff. There's no record in Omaha of a birth certificate ever being issued for a Jason Taverner."

Patiently, Buckman said, "Then it's an alias."

"We took fingerprints, voiceprints, footprints, EEG prints. We sent them to One Central, to the overall data bank in Detroit. No match-up. Such fingerprints, footprints, voiceprints, EEG prints, don't exist in any data banks on earth." McNulty tugged himself upright and wheezed apologetically, "Jason Taverner doesn't exist."

8

Jason Taverner did not, at the moment, wish to return to Kathy. Nor, he decided, did he want to try Heather Hart once again. He tapped his coat pocket; he still had his money, and, because of the police pass, he could feel free to travel anywhere. A pol-pass was a passport to the entire planet; until they APB-ed on him he could travel as far as he wanted, including unimproved areas such as specific, acceptable jungle-infested islands in the South Pacific. There they might not find him for months, not with what his money would buy in an open-area spot such as that.

I've got three things going for me, he realized. I've got money, good looks, and personality. Four things: I also have forty-two years of experience as a six.

An apartment.

But, he thought, if I rent an apartment, the rotive manager will be required by law to take my fingerprints; they'll be routinely mailed to Pol-Dat Central . . . and when the police have discovered that my ID cards are fakes, they'll find they have a direct line to me. So there goes that.

What I need, he said to himself, *is to find someone who already has an apartment. In their name, with their prints.*

And that means another girl.

Where do I find such a one? he asked himself, and had the answer already on his tongue: at a first-rate cocktail

lounge. The kind many women go to, with a three-man combo playing fob jazzy, preferably blacks. Well dressed.

Am I well enough dressed, though? he wondered, and took a good look at his silk suit under the steady white-and-red light of a huge AAMCO sign. Not his best but nearly so . . . but wrinkled. Well, in the gloom of a cocktail lounge it wouldn't show.

He hailed a cab, and presently found himself quibbling toward the more acceptable part of the city to which he was accustomed—accustomed, at least, during the most recent years of his life, his career When he had reached the very top.

A club, he thought, where I've appeared. A club I really know. Know the maître d', the hatcheck girl, the flower girl . . . unless they, like me, are somehow now changed.

But as yet it appeared that nothing but himself had changed. *His* circumstances. Not theirs.

The Blue Fox Room of the Hayette Hotel in Reno. He had played there a number of times; he knew the layout and the staff backward and forward.

To the cab he said, "Reno."

Beautifully, the cab peeled off in a great swooping right-hand motion; he felt himself going with it, and enjoyed it. The cab picked up speed: they had entered a virtually unused air corridor, and the upper velocity limit was perhaps as high as twelve hundred m.p.h.

"I'd like to use the phone," Jason said.

The left wall of the cab opened and a picphone slid out, cord twisted in a baroque loop.

He knew the number of the Blue Fox Room by heart; he dialed it, waited, heard a click and then a mature male voice saying, "Blue Fox Room, where Freddy Hydrocephalic is appearing in two shows nightly, at eight and at twelve; only thirty dollars' cover charge and girls provided while you watch. May I help you?"

"Is this good old Jumpy Mike?" Jason said. "Good old Jumpy Mike himself?"

"Yes, this certainly is." The formality of the voice ebbed. "Who am I speaking to, may I ask?" A warm chuckle.

Taking a deep breath, Jason said, "This is Jason Taverner."

"I'm sorry, Mr. Taverner." Jumpy Mike sounded puzzled. "Right now at the moment I can't quite—"

"It's been a long time," Jason interrupted. "Can you give me a table toward the front of the room—"

"The Blue Fox Room is completely sold out, Mr. Taverner," Jumpy Mike rumbled in his fat way. "I'm very sorry."

"No table at all?" Jason said. "At any price?"

"Sorry, Mr. Taverner, none." The voice faded in the direction of remoteness. "Try us in two weeks." Good old Jumpy Mike hung up.

Silence.

Jesus shit Christ, Jason said to himself. "God," he said aloud. "God damn it." His teeth ground against one another, sending sheets of pain through his trigeminal nerve.

"New instructions, big fellow?" the cab asked tonelessly.

"Make it Las Vegas," Jason grated. I'll try the Nellie Melba Room of the Drake's Arms, he decided. Not too long ago he had had good luck there, at a time when Heather Hart had been fulfilling an engagement in Sweden. A reasonable number of reasonably high class chicks hung out there, gambling, drinking, listening to the entertainment, getting it on. It was worth a try, if the Blue Fox Room—and the others like it—were closed to him. After all, what could he lose?

Half an hour later the cab deposited him on the roof field of the Drake's Arms. Shivering in the chill night air, Jason made his way to the royal descent carpet; a moment later he had stepped from it into the warmth-color-light-movement of the Nellie Melba Room.

The time: seven-thirty. The first show would begin soon. He glanced at the notice; Freddy Hydrocephalic was appearing here, too, but doing a lesser tape at lower prices. Maybe he'll remember me, Jason thought. Probably not. And then, as he thought more deeply on it, he thought, No chance at all.

If Heather Hart didn't remember him no one would.

He seated himself at the crowded bar—on the only stool

left—and, when the bartender at last noticed him, ordered scotch and honey, mulled. A pat of butter floated in it.

"That'll be three dollars," the bartender said.

"Put it on my—" Jason began and then gave up. He brought out a five.

And then he noticed her.

Seated several seats down. She had been his mistress years ago; he had not seen her in a hell of a while. But she still has a good figure, he observed, even though she's gotten a lot older. Ruth Rae. Of all people.

One thing about Ruth Rae: she was smart enough not to let her skin become too tanned. Nothing aged a woman's skin faster than tanning, and few somen seemed to know it. For a woman Ruth's age—he guessed she was now thirty-eight or -nine—tanning would have turned her skin into wrinkled leather.

And, too, she dressed well. She showed off her excellent figure. If only time had avoided its constant series of appointments with her face . . . anyhow, Ruth still had beautiful black hair, all coiled in an upsweep at the back of her head. Featherplastic eyelashes, brilliant purple streaks across her cheek, as if she had been seared by psychedelic tiger claws.

Dressed in a colorful sari, barefoot—as usual she had kicked off her high-heeled shoes somewhere—and not wearing her glasses, she did not strike him as bad-looking. Ruth Rae, he mused. Sews her own clothes. Bifocals which she never wears when anyone's around . . . excluding me. Does she still read the Book-of-the-Month selection? Does she still get off reading those endless dull novels about sexual misdeeds in weird, small, but apparently normal Midwestern towns?

That was one factor about Ruth Rae: her obsession with sex. One year that he recalled she had laid sixty men, not including him: he had entered and left earlier, when the stats were not so high.

And she had always liked his music. Ruth Rae liked sexy vocalists, pop ballads and sweet—sickeningly sweet—strings.

In her New York apartment at one time she had set up a huge quad system and more or less lived inside it, eating dietetic sandwiches and drinking fake frosty slime drinks made out of nothing. Listening forty-eight hours at a stretch to disc after disc by the Purple People Strings, which he abominated.

Because her general taste appalled him, it annoyed him that he himself constituted one of her favorites. It was an anomaly which he had never been able to take apart.

What else did he remember about her? Tablespoons of oily yellow fluid every morning: vitamin E. Strangely enough it did not seem to be a shuck in her case; her erotic stamina increased with each spoonful. Lust virtually leaked out of her.

And as he recalled she hated animals. This made him think about Kathy and her cat Domenico. Ruth and Kathy would never groove, he said to himself. But that doesn't matter; they'll never meet.

Sliding from his stool he carried his drink down the bar until he stood before Ruth Rae. He did not expect her to know him, but, at one time, she had found him unable to avoid . . . why wouldn't that be true now? No one was a better judge of sexual opportunity than Ruth.

"Hi," he said.

Foggily—because she did not have on her glasses—Ruth Rae lifted her head, scrutinized him. "Hi," she rasped in her bourbon-bounded voice. "Who are you?"

Jason said, "We met a few years ago in New York. I was doing a walk-on in an episode of *The Phantom Baller* . . . as I recall it, you had charge of costumes."

"The episode," Ruth Rae rasped, "where the Phantom Baller was set upon by pirate queers from another time-period." She laughed, smiled up at him. "What's your name?" she inquired, jiggling her wire-supported exposed boobs.

"Jason Taverner," he said.

"Do you remember my name?"

"Oh yes," he said. "Ruth Rae."

"It's Ruth Gomen now," she rasped. "Sit down." She glanced around her, saw no vacant stools. "Table over there." She stepped supercarefully from her stool and careened in the direction of a vacant table; he took her arm, guided her along. Presently, after a moment of difficult navigation, he had her seated, with himself close beside her.

"You look every bit as beautiful—" he began, but she cut him off brusquely.

"I'm old," she rasped. "I'm thirty-nine."

"That's not old," Jason said. "I'm forty-two."

"It's all right for a man. Not for a woman." Blearily she stared into her half-raised martini. "Do you know what Bob does? Bob Gomen? He raises dogs. Big, loud, pushy dogs with long hair. It gets into the refrigerator." She sipped moodily at her martini; then, all at once, her face glowed with animation; she turned toward him and said, "You don't look forty-two. You look all *right*! Do you know what I think? You ought to be in TV or the movies."

Jason said cautiously, "I have been in TV. A little."

"Oh, like the *Phantom Baller Show*." She nodded. "Well, let's face it; neither of us made it."

"I'll drink to that," he said, ironically amused; he sipped at his mulled scotch and honey. The pat of butter had melted.

"I believe I do remember you," Ruth Rae said. "Didn't you have some blueprints for a house out on the Pacific, a thousand miles away from Australia? Was that you?"

"That was me," he said, lying.

"And you drove a Rolls-Royce flyship."

"Yes," he said. That part was true.

Ruth Rae said, smiling, "Do you know what I'm doing here? Do you have any idea? I'm trying to get to see, to meet, Freddy Hydrocephalic. I'm in love with him." She laughed the throaty laugh he remembered from the old days. "I keep sending him notes reading 'I love you,' and he writes *typed* notes back saying 'I don't want to get involved; I have personal problems.'" She laughed again, and finished her drink.

"Another?" Jason said, rising.

"No." Ruth Rae shook her head. "I don't drink anymore. There was a period"—she paused, her face troubled—"I wonder if anything like that has ever happened to you. I wouldn't think so, to look at you."

"What happened?"

Ruth Rae said, fooling with her empty glass, "I drank *all* the time. Starting at nine o'clock in the morning. And you know what it did for me? It made me look older. I looked fifty. Goddamn booze. Whatever you fear will happen to you, booze will make it happen. In my opinion booze is the great enemy of life. Do you agree?"

"I'm not sure," Jason said. "I think life has worse enemies than booze."

"I guess so. Like the forced-labor camps. Do you know they tried to send me to one last year? I really had a terrible time; I had no money—I hadn't met Bob Gomen yet—and I worked for a savings-and-loan company. One day a deposit *in cash* came in . . . fifty-dollar-bill stuff, three or four of them." She introspected for a time. "Anyhow, I took them and put the deposit slip and envelope into the shredder. But they caught me. Entrapment—a setup."

"Oh," he said.

"But—see, I had a thing going with my boss. The pols wanted to drag me off to a forced-labor camp—one in Georgia—where I'd be gangbanged to death by rednecks, but he protected me. I still don't know how he did it, but they let me go. I owe that man a lot, and I never see him anymore. You never see the ones who really love you and help you; you're always involved with strangers."

"Do you consider me a stranger?" Jason asked. He thought to himself, I remember one more thing about you, Ruth Rae. She always maintained an impressively expensive apartment. No matter who she happened to be married to: she always lived well.

Ruth Rae eyed him questioningly. "No. I consider you a friend."

"Thanks." Reaching, he took hold of her dry hand and held it a second, letting go at exactly the right time.

9

Ruth Rae's apartment appalled Jason Taverner with its luxury. It must cost her, he reasoned, at least four hundred dollars a day. Bob Gomen must be in good financial shape, he decided. Or anyhow was.

"You didn't have to buy that fifth of Vat 69," Ruth said as she took his coat, carrying it and her own to a self-opening closet. "I have Cutty Sark and Hiram Walker's bourbon—"

She had learned a great deal since he had last slept with her: it was true. Emptied, he lay naked on the blankets of the waterbed, rubbing a broken-out spot at the rim of his nose. Ruth Rae, or rather Mrs. Ruth Gomen now, sat on the carpeted floor, smoking a Pall Mall. Neither of them had spoken for some time; the room had become quiet. And, he thought, as drained as I am. Isn't there some principle of thermodynamics, he thought, that says heat can't be destroyed, it can only be transferred? But there's also entropy.

I feel the weight of entropy on me now, he decided. I have discharged myself into a vacuum, and I will never get back what I have given out. I goes only one way. Yes, he thought, I'm sure that is one of the fundamental laws of thermodynamics.

"Do you have an encyclopedia machine?" he asked the woman.

"Hell, no." Worry appeared on her prunelike face. Prune-like—he withdrew the image; it did not seem fair. Her weath-ered face, he decided. That was more like it.

"What are you thinking?" he asked her.

"No, you tell me what you're thinking," Ruth said. "What's on that big alpha-consciousness-type supersecret brain of yours?"

"Do you remember a girl named Monica Buff?" Jason asked.

" 'Remember' her! Monica Buff was my sister-in-law for six years. In all that time she never washed her hair once. Tangled, messy, dark-brown ooze of dog fur hanging around her pasty face and dirty short neck."

"I didn't realize you disliked her."

"Jason, she used to *steal*. If you left your purse around she'd rip you off; not just the paper scrip but all the coins as well. She had the brain of a magpie and the voice of a crow, when she talked, which thank God wasn't often. Do you know that that chick used to go six or seven—some-times, one time in particular—eight days without saying a word? Just huddled up in a corner like a fractured spider strumming on that five-dollar guitar she owned and never learned the chords for. Okay, she did look pretty in an un-kempt messy sort of way. I'll concede that. If you like gross tail."

"How'd she stay alive?" Jason asked. He had known Mon-ica Buff only briefly, and by way of Ruth. But during that time he and she had had a short, mind-blowing affair.

"Shoplifting," Ruth Rae said. "She had that big wicker bag she got in Baja California . . . she used to stuff stuff into that and then go cruising out of the store big as life."

"Why didn't she get caught?"

"She did. They fined her and her brother came up with the bread, so there she was again, out on the street, strolling along barefoot—I mean it!—down Shrewsbury Avenue in Boston, tweaking all the peaches in the grocery-store pro-duce sections. She used to spend ten hours a day in what she called shopping." Glaring at him, Ruth said, "You know what she did that she never got caught at?" Ruth lowered her voice. "She used to feed escaped students."

"And they never busted her for that?" Feeding or sheltering an escaped student meant two years in an FLC—the first time. The second time the sentence was five years.

"No, they never busted her. If she thought a pol team was about to run a spot check she'd quickly phone Pol Central and say a man was trying to break into her house. And then she'd maneuver the student outside and then lock him out, and the pols would come and there he'd be, beating on the door exactly as she said. So they'd cart him off and leave her free." Ruth chuckled, "I heard her make one of those phone calls to Pol Central once. The way she told it, the man—"

Jason said, "Monica was my old lady for three weeks. Five years ago, roughly."

"Did you ever see her wash her hair during that time?"

"No," he admitted.

"And she didn't wear underpants," Ruth said. "Why would a good-looking man like you want to have an affair with a dirty, stringy, mangy freak like Monica Buff? You couldn't have been able to take her anywhere; she smelled. She never bathed."

"Hebephrenia," Jason said.

"Yes." Ruth nodded. "That was the diagnosis. I don't know if you know this but finally she just wandered off, during one of her shopping trips, and never came back; we never saw her again. By now she's probably dead. Still clutching that wicker shopping bag she got in Baja. That was the big moment in her life, that trip to Mexico. She *bathed* for the occasion, and I fixed up her hair—after I washed it half a dozen times. What did you ever see in her? How could you stand her?"

Jason said, "I liked her sense of humor."

It's unfair, he thought, comparing Ruth with a nineteen-year-old girl. Or even with Monica Buff. But—the comparison remained there, in his mind. Making it impossible for him to feel attraction toward Ruth Rae. As good—as experienced, anyhow—as she was in bed.

I am using her, he thought. As Kathy used me. As McNulty used Kathy.

McNulty. Isn't there a microtrans on me somewhere?

Rapidly, Jason Taverner grabbed up his clothing, swiftly carried it to the bathroom. There, seated on the edge of the tub, he began to inspect each article.

It took him half an hour. But he did, at last, locate it. Small as it was. He flushed it down the toilet; shaken, he made his way back into the bedroom. So they know where I am after all, he realized. I can't stay here after all.

And I've jeopardized Ruth Rae's life for nothing.

"Wait," he said aloud.

"Yes?" Ruth said, leaning wearily against the wall of the bathroom, arms folded under her breasts.

"Microtransmitters," Jason said slowly, "only give approximate locations. Unless something actually tracks back to them locked on their signal." Until then—

He could not be sure. After all, McNulty had been waiting in Kathy's apartment. But had McNulty come there in response to the microtransmitter, or because he knew that Kathy lived there? Befuddled by too much anxiety, sex, and scotch, he could not remember; he sat on the tub edge rubbing his forehead, straining to think, to recall exactly what had been said when he and Kathy entered her room to find McNulty waiting for them.

Ed, he thought. They said that Ed planted the microtrans on me. So it did locate me. But—

Still, maybe it only told them the general area. And they assumed, correctly, that it would be Kathy's pad.

To Ruth Rae he said, his voice breaking, "God damn it, I hope I haven't got the pols oinking their asses after you; that would be too much, too goddamn much." He shook his head, trying to clear it. "Do you have any coffee that's super-hot?"

"I'll go punch the stove-console." Ruth Rae skittered barefoot, wearing only a box bangle, from the bathroom into the kitchen. A moment later she returned with a big plastic mug of coffee, marked KEEP ON TRUCKIN'. He accepted it, drank down the steaming coffee.

"I can't stay," he said, "any longer. And anyhow, you're too old."

She stared at him, ludicrously, like a warped, stomped doll. And then she ran off into the kitchen. Why did I say that? he asked himself. The pressure; my fears. He started after her.

In the kitchen doorway Ruth appeared, holding up a stoneware platter marked SOUVENIR OF KNOTTS BERRY FARM. She ran blindly at him and brought it down on his head, her mouth twisting like newborn things just now alive. At that last instant he managed to lift his left elbow and take the blow there; the stoneware platter broke into three jagged pieces, and, down his elbow, blood spurted. He gazed at the blood, the shattered pieces of platter on the carpet, then at her.

"I'm sorry," she said, whispering it faintly. Barely forming the words. The newborn snakes twisted continually, in apology.

Jason said, "I'm sorry."

"I'll put a Band-Aid on it." She started for the bathroom.

"No," he said, "I'm leaving. It's a clean cut; it won't get infected."

"Why did you say that to me?" Ruth said hoarsely.

"Because," he said, "of my own fears of age. Because they're wearing me down, what's left of me. I virtually have no energy left. Even for an orgasm."

"You did really well."

"But it was the last," he said. He made his way into the bathroom; there he washed the blood from his arm, kept cold water flowing on the gash until coagulation began. Five minutes, fifty; he could not tell. He merely stood there, holding his elbow under the faucet. Ruth Rae had gone God knew where. Probably to nark to the pols, he said wearily to himself; he was too exhausted to care.

Hell, he thought. After what I said to her I wouldn't blame her.

10

"No," Police General Felix Buckman said, shaking his head rigidly. "Jason Taverner does exist. He's somehow managed to get the data out of all the matrix banks." The police general pondered. "You're sure you can lay your hands on him if you have to?"

"A downer about that, Mr. Buckman," McNulty said. "He's found the microtrans and snuffed it. So we don't know if he's still in Vegas. If he has any sense he's hustled on. Which he almost certainly has."

Buckman said, "You had better come back here. If he can lift data, prime source material like that, out of our banks, he's involved in effective activity that's probably major. How precise is your fix on him?"

"He is—was—located in one apartment of eighty-five in one wing of a complex of six hundred units, all expensive and fashionable in the West Fireflash District, a place called Copperfield II."

"Better ask Vegas to go through the eighty-five units until they find him. And when you get him, have him air-mailed directly to me. But I still want you at your desk. Take a couple of uppers, forget your hyped-out nap, and get down here."

"Yes, Mr. Buckman," McNulty said, with a trace of pain. He grimaced.

"You don't think we're going to find him in Vegas," Buckman said.

"No, sir."

"Maybe we will. By snuffing the microtrans he may rationalize that he's safe, now."

"I beg to differ," McNulty said. "By finding it he'd know we had bugged him to there in West Fireflash. He'd split. Fast."

Buckman said, "He would if people acted rationally. But they don't. Or haven't you noticed that, McNulty? Mostly they function in a chaotic fashion." Which, he mediated, probably serves them in good stead . . . it makes them less predictable.

"I've noticed that—"

"Be at your desk in half an hour," Buckman said, and broke the connection. McNulty's pedantic foppery, and the fogged-up lethargy of a hype after dark, irritated him always.

Alys, observing everything, said, "A man who's unexisted himself. Has that ever happened before?"

"No," Buckman said. "And it hasn't happened this time. Somewhere, some obscure place, he's overlooked a microdocument of a minor nature. We'll keep searching until we find it. Sooner or later we'll match up a voiceprint or an EEG print and then we'll know who he really is."

"Maybe he's exactly who he says he is." Alys had been examining McNulty's grotesque notes. "Subject belongs to musicians' union. Says he's a singer. Maybe a voiceprint would be your—"

"Get out of my office," Buckman said to her.

"I'm just speculating. Maybe he recorded that new pornochord hit, 'Go Down, Moses' that—"

"I'll tell you what," Buckman said. "Go home and look in the study, in a glassine envelope in the center drawer of my maple desk. You'll find a lightly canceled perfectly centered copy of the one-dollar black U.S. Trans-Mississippi issue. I got it for my own collection but you can have it for

yours; I'll get another. *Just go.* Go and get the damn stamp
and put it away in your album in your safe forever. Don't
ever even look at it again; just have it. And leave me alone
at work. Is that a deal?"

"Jesus," Alys said, her eyes alive with light. "Where'd you
get it?"

"From a political prisoner on his way to a forced-labor
camp. He traded it for his freedom. I thought it was an
equitable arrangement. Don't you?"

Alys said, "The most beautifully engraved stamp ever issued. At any time. By any country."

"Do you want it?" he said.

"Yes." She moved from the office, out into the corridor.
"I'll see you tomorrow. But you don't have to give me something like that to make me go; I want to go home and take
a shower and change my clothes and go to bed for a few
hours. On the other hand, if you want to—"

"I want to," Buckman said, and to himself he added, Because I'm so goddamn afraid of you, so basically, ontologi-
cally scared of everything about you, even your willingness
to leave. I'm even afraid of that!

Why? he asked himself as he watched her head for the
secluded prison ascent tube at the far end of his suite of
offices. I've known her as a child and I feared her then.
Because, I think, in some fundamental way that I don't comprehend, she doesn't play by the rules. We all have rules;
they differ, but we all play by them. For example, he conjectured, we don't murder a man who has just done us a
favor. Even in this, a police state—even *we* observe *that* rule.
And we don't deliberately destroy objects precious to us. But
Alys is capable of going home, finding the one-dollar black,
and setting fire to it with her cigarette. I know that and yet
I gave it to her; I'm still praying that underneath or eventually
or whatever she'll come back and shoot marbles the way the
rest of us do.

But she never will.

He thought, And the reason I offered her the one-dollar

black was because, simply, I hoped to beguile her, tempt her, into returning to rules that we can understand. Rules the rest of us can apply. I'm bribing her, and it's a waste of time— if not much much more—and I know it and she knows it. Yes, he thought. She probably will set fire to the one-dollar black, the finest stamp ever issued, a philatelic item I have never seen for sale during my lifetime. Even at auctions. And when I get home tonight she'll show me the ashes. Maybe she'll leave a corner of it unburned, to prove she really did it.

And I'll believe it. And I'll be even more afraid.

Moodily, General Buckman opened the third drawer of the large desk and placed a tape-reel in the small transport he kept there. Dowland aires for four voices . . . he stood listening to one which he enjoyed very much, among all the songs in Dowland's lute books.

> . . . *For now left and forlorn*
> *I sit, I sigh, I weep, I faint, I die*
> *In deadly pain and endless misery.*

The first man, Buckman mused, to write a piece of abstract music. He removed the tape, put in the lute one, and stood listening to the "Lachrimae Antiquae Pavan." From this, he said to himself, came, at last, the Beethoven final quartets. And everything else. Except for Wagner.

He detested Wagner. Wagner and those like him, such as Berlioz, had set music back three centuries. Until Karlheinz Stockhausen in his "Gesang der Jünglinge" had once more brought music up to date.

Standing by the desk, he gazed down for a moment at the recent 4-D photo of Jason Taverner—the photograph taken by Katharine Nelson. What a damn good-looking man, he thought. Almost professionally good-looking. Well, he's a singer; it fits. He's in show business.

Touching the 4-D photo, he listened to it say, "How now,

brown cow?" And smiled. And, listening once more to the "Lachrimae Antiquae Pavan," thought:

Flow, my tears . . .

Do I really have pol-karma? he asked himself. Loving words and music like this? Yes, he thought, I make a superb pol because I *don't think like a pol.* I don't, for example, think like McNulty, who will always be—what did they used to say?—a pig all his life. I think, not like the people we're trying to apprehend, but like the *important* people we're trying to apprehend. Like this man, he thought, this Jason Taverner. I have a hunch, an irrational but beautifully functional intuition, that he's still in Vegas. We will trap him *there,* and not where McNulty thinks: rationally and logically somewhere farther on.

I am like Byron, he thought, fighting for freedom, giving up his life to fight for Greece. Except that I am not fighting for freedom; I am fighting for a coherent society.

Is that actually true? he asked himself. Is that why I do what I do? To create order, structure, harmony? Rules. Yes, he thought; rules are goddamn important to me, and that is why Alys threatens me; that's why I can cope with so much else but not with her.

Thank God they're not all like her, he said to himself. Thank God, in fact, that she's one of a kind.

Pressing a button on his desk intercom he said, "Herb, will you come in here, please?"

Herbert Maime entered the office, a stack of computer cards in his hands; he looked harried.

"You want to buy a bet, Herb?" Buckman said. "That Jason Taverner is in Las Vegas?"

"Why are you concerning yourself with such a funky little chickenshit matter?" Herb said. "It's on McNulty's level, not yours."

Seating himself, Buckman began an idle colortone game with the picphone; he flashed the flags of various extinct nations. "Look at what this man has done. Somehow he's managed to get all data pertaining to him out of every data bank on the planet *and* the lunar *and* Martian colonies . . . McNulty even tried there. Think for a minute what it would take to do that. Money? Huge sums. Bribes. Astronomical. If Taverner has used that kind of heavy bread he's playing for big stakes. Influence? Same conclusion: he's got a lot of power and we must consider him a major figure. It's who he represents that concerns me most; I think some group, somewhere on earth, is backing him, but I have no idea what for or why. All right; so they expunge all data concerning him; Jason Taverner is the man who doesn't exist. But, having done that, what have they achieved?"

Herb pondered.

"I can't make it out," Buckman said. "It has no sense to it. But, if they're interested in doing it, it must signify something. Otherwise, they wouldn't expend so much"—he gestured—"whatever they've expended. Money, time, influence, whatever. Maybe all three. Plus large slabs of effort."

"I see," Herb said, nodding.

Buckman said, "Sometimes you catch big fish by hooking one small fish. That's what you never know: will the next small fish you catch be the link with something giant or"— he shrugged—"just more small fry to be tossed into the labor pool. Which, perhaps, is all Jason Taverner is. I may be completely wrong. But I'm interested."

"Which," Herb said, "is too bad for Taverner."

"Yes." Buckman nodded. "Now consider this." He paused a moment to quietly fart, then continued, "Taverner made his way to an ID forger, a run-of-the-mill forger operating behind an abandoned restaurant. He had no contacts; he worked through, for God's sake, the desk clerk at the hotel he was staying at. So he must have been desperate for ident cards. All right, where were his powerful backers then? Why couldn't they supply him with excellent forged ID cards, if they could do all this else? Good Christ; they sent him out into the street, into the urban cesspool jungle, right to a pol informant. They jeopardized everything!"

"Yes," Herb said, nodding. "Something screwed up."

"Right. *Something went wrong.* All of a sudden there he was, in the middle of the city, with no ID. Everything he had on him Kathy Nelson forged. How did that come to happen? How did they manage to fuck up and send him groping desperately for forged ID cards, so he could walk three blocks on the street? You see my point."

"But that's how we get them."

"Pardon?" Buckman said. He turned down the lute music on the tape player.

Herb said, "If they didn't make mistakes like that we wouldn't have a chance. They'd remain a metaphysical entity to us, never glimpsed or suspected. Mistakes like that are what we live on. I don't see that it's important *why* they made a mistake; all that matters is that they did. And we should be damn glad of it."

I am, Buckman thought to himself. Leaning, he dialed McNulty's extension. No answer. McNulty wasn't back in the building yet. Buckman consulted his watch. Another fifteen or so minutes.

He dialed central clearing Blue. "What's the story on the Las Vegas operation in the Fireflash District?" he asked the chick operators who sat perched on high stools at the map board pushing little plastic representations with long cue sticks. "The netpull of the individual calling himself Jason Taverner."

A whirr and click of computers as the operator deftly punched buttons. "I'll tie you in with the captain in charge of that detail." On Buckman's pic a uniformed type appeared, looking idiotically placid. "Yes, General Buckman?"

"Have you got Taverner?"

"Not yet, sir. We've hit roughly thirty of the rental units in—"

"When you have him," Buckman said, "call me direct." He gave the nerdish pol type his extension code and rang off, feeling vaguely defeated.

"It takes time," Herb said.

"Like good beer," Buckman murmured, staring emptily ahead, his mind working. But working without results.

"You and your intuitions in the Jungian sense," Herb said. "That's what you are in the Jungian typology: an intuitive, thinking personality, with intuition your main function-mode and thinking—"

"Balls." He wadded up a page of McNulty's coarse notations and tossed it into the shredder.

"Haven't you read Jung?"

"Sure. When I got my master's at Berkeley—the whole poli sci department had to read Jung. I learned everything you learned and a lot more." He heard the irritability in his voice and disliked it. "They're probably conducting their hits like garbage collectors. Banging and clanking . . . Taverner will hear them long before they reach the apartment he's in."

"Do you think you'll net anyone with Taverner? Someone who's his higher-up in the—"

"He wouldn't be with anyone crucial. Not with his ID cards in the local precinct stationhouse. Not with us as close to him as he knows we are. I expect nothing. Nothing but Taverner himself."

Herb said, "I'll make you a bet."

"Okay."

"I'll bet you five quinques, gold ones, that when you get him you get nothing."

Startled, Buckman sat bolt upright. It sounded like his own style of intuition: no facts, no data to base it on, just pure hunch.

"Want to make the bet?" Herb said.

"I'll tell you what I'll do," Buckman said. He got out his wallet, counted the money in it. "I'll bet you one thousand paper dollars that when we net Taverner we enter one of the most important areas we've ever gotten involved with."

Herb said, "I won't bet that kind of money."

"Do you think I'm right?"

The phone buzzed; Buckman picked up the receiver. On the screen the features of the nerdish Las Vegas functionary captain formed. "Our thermo-radex shows a male of Taverner's weight and height and general body structure in one of the as yet unapproached remaining apartments. We're moving in very cautiously, getting everyone else out of the other nearby units."

"Don't kill him," Buckman said.

"Absolutely not, Mr. Buckman."

"Keep your line to me open," Buckman said. "I want to sit in on this from here on in."

"Yes, sir."

Buckman said to Herb Maime, "They've really already got him." He smiled, chuckling with delight.

11

When Jason Taverner went to get his clothes he found Ruth Rae seated in the semi-darkness of the bedroom on the rumpled, still-warm bed, fully dressed and smoking her customary tobacco cigarette. Gray nocturnal light filtered in through the windows. The coal of the cigarette glowed its high, nervous temperature.

"Those things will kill you," he said. "There's a reason why they're rationed out one pack to a person a week."

"Fuck off," Ruth Rae said, and smoked on.

"But you get them on the black market," he said. Once he had gone with her to buy a full carton. Even on his income the price had appalled him. But she had not seemed to mind. Obviously she expected it; she knew the cost of her habit.

"I get them." She stubbed out the far-too-long cigarette in a lung-shaped ceramic ashtray.

"You're wasting it."

"Did you love Monica Buff?" Ruth asked.

"Sure."

"I don't see how you could."

Jason said, "There are different kinds of love."

"Like Emily Fusselman's rabbit." She glanced up at him. "A woman I knew, married, with three kids; she had two kittens and then she got one of those big gray Belgian rabbits that go lipperty lipperty lipperty on those huge hind legs. For the first month the rabbit was afraid to come out of his cage. It was a he, we think, as best we could tell. Then after a month he would come out of his cage and hop around the living room. After too months he learned to climb the stairs and scratch on Emily's bedroom door to wake her up in the morning. He started playing with the cats, and there the trouble began because he wasn't as smart as a cat."

"Rabbits have smaller brains," Jason said.

Ruth Rae said, "Hard by. Anyhow, he adored the cats and tried to do everything they did. He even learned to use the catbox most of the time. Using tufts of hair he pulled from his chest, he made a nest behind the couch and wanted the kittens to get into it. But they never would. The end of it all—nearly—came when he tried to play Gotcha with a German shepherd that some lady brought over. You see, the rabbit learned to play this game with the cats and with Emily Fusselman and the children where he'd hide behind the couch and then come running out, running very fast in circles, and everyone tried to catch him, but they usually couldn't and then he'd run back to safety behind the couch, where no one was supposed to follow. But the dog didn't know the rules of the game and when the rabbit ran back behind the couch the dog went after him and snapped its jaws around the rabbit's rear end. Emily managed to pry the dog's jaws open and she got the dog outside, but the rabbit was badly hurt. He recovered, but after that he was terrified of dogs and ran away if he saw one even through the window. And the part of him the dog bit, he kept that part hidden behind the drapes because he had no hair there and was ashamed. But what was so touching about him was his pushing against the limits of his—what would you say?—physiology? His limitations as a rabbit, trying to become a more evolved life form, like the cats. Wanting all the time to be with them and play with them as an equal. That's all there is to it, really. The kittens wouldn't stay in the nest he built for them, and the dog didn't know the rules and got him. He lived several years. But who would have thought that a rabbit could develop such a complex personality? And when you were sitting on the couch and he wanted you to get off, so he could lie down, he'd nudge you and then if you didn't move he'd bite you. But look at the aspirations of that rabbit and look at his failing. A little life trying. And all the time it was hopeless. But the rabbit didn't know that. Or maybe he did know and kept trying anyhow. But I think he didn't understand. He just wanted to do it so badly. It was his whole life, because he loved the cats."

"I thought you didn't like animals," Jason said.

"Not anymore. Not after so many defeats and wipeouts. Like the rabbit; he eventually, of course, died. Emily Fusselman cried for days. A week. I could see what it had done to her and I didn't want to get involved."

"But stopping loving animals entirely so that you—"

"Their lives are so short. Just so fucking goddamn short. Okay, some people lose a creature they love and then go on and transfer that love to another one. But it hurts; it hurts."

"Then why is love so good?" He had brooded about that, in and out of his own relationships, all his long adult life. He brooded about it acutely now. Through what had recently happened to him, up to Emily Fusselman's rabbit. This moment of painfulness. "You love someone and they leave. They come home one day and start packing their things and you say, 'What's happening?' and they say, 'I got a better offer someplace else,' and there they go, out of your life forever, and after that until you're dead you're carrying around this huge hunk of love with no one to give it to. And if you do find someone to give it to, the same thing happens all over. Or you call them up on the phone one day and say, 'This is Jason,' and they say, 'Who?' and then you know you've had it. They don't know who the hell you are. So I guess they never did know; you never had them in the first place."

Ruth said, "Love isn't just wanting another person the way you want to own an object you see in a store. That's just desire. You want to have it around, take it home and set it up somewhere in the apartment like a lamp. Love is"—she paused, reflecting—"like a father saving his children from a burning house, getting them out and dying himself. When you love you cease to live for yourself; you live for another person."

"And that's good?" It did not sound so good to him.

"It overcomes instinct. Instincts push us into fighting for survival. Like the pols ringing all the campuses. Survival of ourselves at the expense of others; each of us claws his way up. I can give you a good example. My twenty-first husband, Frank. We were married six months. During that time he stopped loving me and became horribly unhappy. *I* still loved him; I wanted to remain with him, but it was hurting him. So I let him go. You see? It was better for him, and because I loved him that's what counted. See?"

Jason said, "But why is it good to go against the instinct for self-survival?"

"You don't think I can say."

"No," he said.

"Because the instinct for survival loses in the end. With every living creature, mole, bat, human, frog. Even frogs who smoke cigars and play chess. You can never accomplish what your survival instinct sets out to do, so ultimately your striving ends in failure and you succumb to death, and that ends it. But if you love you can fade out and watch—"

"I'm not ready to fade out," Jason said.

"—you can fade out and watch with happiness, and with cool, mellow, alpha contentment, the highest form of contentment, the living on of one of those you love."

"But they die, too."

"True." Ruth Rae chewed on her lip.

"It's better not to love so that never happens to you. Even a pet, a dog or a cat. As you pointed out—you love them and they perish. If the death of a rabbit is bad—" He had, then, a glimpse of horror: the crushed bones and hair of a girl, held and leaking blood, in the jaws of a dimly-seen enemy outlooming any dog.

"But you can grieve," Ruth said, anxiously studying his

face. "Jason! Grief is the most powerful emotion a man or child or animal can feel. It's a *good* feeling."

"In what fucking way?" he said harshly.

"Grief causes you to leave yourself. You step outside your narrow little pelt. And you can't feel grief unless you've had love before it—grief is the final outcome of love, because it's love lost. You do understand; I know you do. But you just don't want to think about it. It's the cycle of love completed: to love, to lose, to feel grief, to leave, and then to love again. Jason, grief is awareness that you will have to be alone, and there is nothing beyond that because being alone is the ultimate final destiny of each individual living creature. That's what death is, the great loneliness. I remember once when I first smoked pot from a waterpipe rather than a joint. It, the smoke, was cool, and I didn't realize how much I had inhaled. All of a sudden I died. For a little instant, but several seconds long. The world, every sensation, including even the awareness of my own body, of even having a body, faded out. And it didn't like leave me in isolation in the usual sense because when you're alone in the usual sense you still have sense data coming in even if it's only from your own body. But even the darkness went away. Everything just ceased. Silence. Nothing. Alone."

"They must have soaked it in one of those toxic shit things. That used to burn out so many people back then."

"Yes, I'm lucky I ever got my head back. A freak thing— I had smoked pot a lot of times before and that never happened. That's why I do tobacco, now, after that. Anyhow, it wasn't like fainting; I didn't feel I was going to fall, because I had nothing to fall with, no body . . . and there was no down to fall toward. Everything, including myself, just"— she gestured—"expired. Like the last drop out of a bottle. And then, presently, they rolled the film again. The feature we call reality." She paused, puffing on her tobacco cigarette. "I never told anyone about it before."

"Were you frightened about it?"

She nodded. "Consciousness of unconsciousness, if you

dig what I mean. When we do die we won't feel it because that's what dying is, the loss of all that. So, for example, I'm not at all scared of dying anymore, not after that pot bad trip. But to grieve; it's to die and be alive at the same time. The most absolute, overpowering experience you can feel, therefore. Sometimes I swear we weren't constructed to go through such a thing; it's too much—your body damn near self-destructs with all that heaving and surging. But I *want* to feel grief. To have tears."

"Why?" He couldn't grasp it; to him it was something to be avoided. When you felt that you got the hell out fast.

Ruth said, "Grief reunites you with what you've lost. It's a merging; you go with the loved thing or person that's going away. In some fashion you split with yourself and accompany it, go part of the way with it on its journey. You follow it as far as you can go. I remember one time when I had this dog I loved. I was roughly seventeen or eighteen—just around the age of consent, that's how I remember. The dog got sick and we took him to the vet's. They said he had eaten rat poison and was nothing more than a sack of blood inside and the next twenty-four hours would determine if he'd survive. I went home and waited and then around eleven P.M. I crashed. The vet was going to phone me in the morning when he got there to tell me if Hank had lived through the night. I got up at eight-thirty and tried to get it all together in my head, waiting for the call. I went into the bathroom—I wanted to brush my teeth—and I saw Hank, at the bottom left part of the room; he was slowly in a very measured dignified fashion climbing invisible stairs. I watched him go upward diagonally as he trudged and then at the top right margin of the bathroom he disappeared, still climbing. He didn't look back once. I knew he had died. And then the phone rang and the vet told me that Hank was dead. But I saw him going upward. And of course I felt terrible over-whelming grief, and as I did so, I lost myself and followed along with him, up the fucking stairs."

Both of them stayed silent for a time.

"But finally," Ruth said, clearing her throat, "the grief goes away and you phase back into this world. Without him."

"And you can accept that."

"What the hell choice is there? You cry, you continue to cry, because you don't ever completely come back from where you went with him—a fragment broken off your pulsing, pumping heart is there still. A nick out of it. A cut that never heals. And if, when it happens to you over and over again in life, too much of your heart does finally go away, then you can't feel grief any more. And then you yourself are ready to die. You'll walk up the inclined ladder and someone else will remain behind grieving for you."

"There are no cuts in my heart," Jason said.

"If you split now," Ruth said huskily, but with composure unusual for her, "that's the way it'll be for me right then and there."

"I'll stay until tomorrow," he said. It would take at least until then for the pol lab to discern the spuriousness of his ID cards.

Did Kathy save me? he wondered. Or destroy me? He really did not know. Kathy, he thought, who used me, who at nineteen knows more than you and I put together. More than we will find out in the totality of our lives, all the way to the graveyard.

Like a good encounter-group leader she had torn him down—for what? To rebuild him again, stronger than before? He doubted it. But it remained a possibility. It should not be forgotten. He felt toward Kathy a certain strange cynical trust, both absolute and unconvincing; one half of his brain saw her as reliable beyond the power of the telling of it, and the other half saw her as debased, for sale, and fucking up right and left. He could not put it together into one view. The two images of Kathy remained superimposed in his head.

Maybe I can resolve my parallel conceptions of Kathy before I leave here, he thought. Before morning. But maybe he could stay even one day after that . . . it would be stretching it, however. How good really are the police? he asked himself. They managed to get my name wrong; they pulled the wrong file on me. Isn't it possible they'll fuck up all down the line? Maybe. But maybe not.

He had mutually opposing conceptions of the police, too. And could not resolve those either. And so, like a rabbit, like Emily Fusselman's rabbit, froze where he was. Hoping as he did so that everyone understood the rules: you do not destroy a creature that does not know what to do.

12

The four gray-wrapped pols clustered in the light of the candlelike outdoor fixture made of black iron and cone of perpetual fake flame flickering in the night dark.

"Just two left," the corporal said almost soundlessly; he let his fingers speak for him as he drew them across the rental lists. "A Mrs. Ruth Gomen in two eleven and an Allen Mufi in two twelve. Which'll we hit first?"

"The Mufi man's," one of the uniformed officers said; he smacked his plastic and shot nightstick against his fingers, eager in the dim light to finish it up, now that the end had at last come into sight.

"Two twelve it is," the corporal said, and reached to stroke the door chimes. But then it occurred to him to try the doorknob.

Good. One chance out of several, a minor possibility but suddenly, usefully true. The door was unlocked. He signaled silence, grinned briefly, then pushed the door open.

They saw into a dark living room with empty and nearly empty drink glasses placed here and there, some on the floor. And a great variety of ashtrays overfilled with crushed cigarette packages and ground-out butts.

A cigarette party, the corporal decided. Broken up, now. Everyone went home. With the exception perhaps of Mr. Mufi.

He entered, shone his light here and there, shone it at last toward the far door leading deeper into the over-priced apartment. No sound. No motion. Except the dim, distant, muted chatter of a radio talk show at minimal volume.

He trod across the wall-to-wall carpet, which depicted in gold Richard M. Nixon's final ascent into heaven amid joyous singing above and wails of misery below. At the far door he trod on God, who was smiling a lot as He received his Second Only Begotten Son back into His bosom, and pushed open the bedroom door.

In the big double bed, pulpy-soft, a man asleep, shoulders and arms bare. His clothes heaped on a handy chair. Mr. Allen Mufi, of course. Safe and home in his own private double bed. But—Mr. Mufi was not alone in his very own private bed. Involved with the pastel sheets and blankets a second indistinct shape lay curled up, asleep. Mrs. Mufi, the corporal thought, and shone his light toward her, with mannish curiosity.

All at once Allen Mufi—assuming it was he—stirred. He opened his eyes. And instantly sat bolt upright, staring fixedly at the pols. At the light of the flashlight.

"What?" he said, and he rasped with fear, a deep, convulsive release of shaking breath. "No," Mufi said, and then snatched for some object on the table beside his bed; he dove into the darkness, white and hairy and naked, for something invisible but precious to him. Desperately. He sat back up then, panting, clutching it. A pair of scissors.

"What's that for?" the corporal asked, shining the light into the metal of the scissors.

"I'll kill myself," Mufi said. "If you don't go away and—leave us alone." He stuck the closed blades of the scissors against his hair-darkened chest, near his heart.

"Then it isn't Mrs. Mufi," the corporal said. He returned the circle of light to the other, huddled up, sheet-covered shape. "A wham-bam-thank-you-ma'am one-time gang-bang? Turning your foxy apartment into a motel room?" The corporal walked to the bed, took hold of the top sheet and blankets, then yanked them back.

In the bed beside Mr. Mufi lay a boy, slender, young, naked, with long golden hair.

"I'll be darned," the corporal said.

One of his men said, "I've got the scissors." He tossed them onto the floor by the corporal's right foot.

To Mr. Mufi, who sat trembling and panting, his eyes startled with terror, the corporal said, "How old is this boy?"

The boy had awakened now; he gazed fixedly up but did not stir. No expression appeared on his soft, vaguely formed face.

"Thirteen," Mr. Mufi said croakingly, almost pleadingly. "Legal age of consent."

To the boy the corporal said, "Can you prove it?" He felt intense revulsion now. Acute physical revulsion, making him want to barf. The bed was stained and damp with half-dried sweat and genital secretions.

"ID," Mufi panted. "In his wallet. In his pants on the chair."

One of the team of pols said to the corporal, "You mean if this juve's thirteen there's no crime involved?"

"Hell," another pol said indignantly. "It's obviously a crime, a perverted crime. Let's run them both in."

"Wait a minute. Okay?" The corporal found the boy's pants, rummaged, found the wallet, got it out, inspected the identification. Sure enough. Thirteen years old. He shut the wallet and put it back in the pocket. "No," he said, still half enjoying the situation, amused by Mufi's naked shame but becoming each moment more and more revolted by the man's cowardly horror at being disclosed. "The new revision of the Penal Code, 640.3, has it that twelve is the age of consent for a minor to engage in a sexual act either with another child of either sex or an adult also of either sex but with only one at a time."

"But it's goddamn sick," one of his pols protested.

"That's your opinion," Mufi said, more bravely now.

"Why isn't it a bust, a hell of a big bust?" the pols standing beside him persisted.

"They're systematically taking all victimless crimes off the books," the corporal said. "That's been the process for ten years."

"*This? This* is victimless?"

To Mufi, the corporal said, "What do you find about young boys that you like? Let me in on it; I've always wondered about scans like you."

" 'Scans,' " Mufi echoed, his mouth twisting with discomfort. "So that's what I am."

"It's a category," the corporal said. "Those who prey on minors for homosexual purposes. Legal but still abhorred. What do you do during the day?"

"I'm a used-quibble salesman."

"And if they, your employers, knew you were a scan they wouldn't want you handling their quibbles. Not after what those hairy white hands have been handling outside the workday. Right, Mr. Mufi? Even a used-quibble salesman can't get away morally with being a scan. Even if it's no longer on the books."

Mufi said, "It was my mother's fault. She dominated my father, who was a weak man."

"How many little boys have you induced to go down on you during the last twelve months?" the corporal inquired. "I'm serious. Are these all one-night stands, is that it?"

"I love Ben," Mufi said, staring fixedly ahead, his mouth barely moving. "Later on, when I'm better off financially and can provide, I intend to marry him."

To the boy Ben, the corporal said, "Do you want us to take you out of here? Return you to your parents?"

"He lives here," Mufi said, grinning a little.

"Yeah, I'll stay here," the boy said sullenly. He shivered. "Cripes, could you give me the covers back?" He reached irritably for the top blanket.

"Just keep the noise level down in here," the corporal said, moving away wearily. "Christ. And they took it off the books."

"Probably," Mufi said, with confidence now that the pols were beginning to depart from his bedroom, "because some of those big overweight old police marshals are screwing kids themselves and don't want to get sent up. They couldn't stand the scandal." His grin grew into an insinuating leer.

"I hope," the corporal said, "that someday you do commit a statute violation of some kind, and they haul you in, and I'm on duty the day it happens. So I can book you personally." He hawked, then spat on Mr. Mufi. Spat into his hairy, empty face.

Silently, the team of pols made their way through the living room of cigarette butts, ashes, twisted-up packs, half-filled drink glasses, to the corridor and porchway outside. The corporal yanked the door shut, shivered, stood for a moment, feeling the bleakness of his mind, its withdrawal, for a moment, from the environment around him. He then said, "Two eleven. Mrs. Ruth Gomen. Where the Taverner suspect has to be, if he's anywhere around here at all, it being the last one." Finally, he thought.

He knocked on the front door of 211. And stood waiting with his plastic and shot nightstick gripped at ready, terribly and completely all at once not caring shit about his job. "We've seen Mufi," he said, half to himself. "Now let's see what Mrs. Gomen is like. You think she'll be any better? Let's hope so. I can't take much more of that tonight."

"Anything would be better," one of the pols beside him said somberly. They all nodded and shuffled about, preparing themselves for slow footsteps beyond the door.

13

In the living room of Ruth Rae's lavish, lovely, newly built apartment in the Fireflash District of Las Vegas, Jason Taverner said, "I'm reasonably sure I can count on forty-eight hours on the outside and twenty-four on the inside. So I feel fairly certain that I don't have to get out of here immediately." And if our revolutionary new principle is correct, he thought, then this assumption will modify the situation to my advantage. I will be safe.

THE THEORY CHANGES—

"I'm glad," Ruth said wanly, "that you're able to remain here with me in a civilized way so we can rap a little longer. You want anything more to drink? Scotch and Coke, maybe?"

THE THEORY CHANGES THE REALITY IT DESCRIBES. "No," he said, and prowled about the living room, listening . . . to what he did not know. Perhaps the *absence* of sounds. No TV sets muttering, no thump of feet against the floor above their heads. Not even a pornochord somewhere, blasting out from a quad. "Are the walls fairly thick in these apartments?" he asked Ruth sharply.

"I never hear anything."

"Does anything seem strange to you? Out of the ordinary?"

"No." Ruth shook her head.

"You damn dumb floogle," he said savagely. She gaped at

him in injured perplexity. "I know," he grated, "that they have me. *Now*. *Here*. In this room."

The doorbell bonged.

"Let's ignore it," Ruth said rapidly, stammering and afraid. "I just want to sit and rap with you, about the mellow things in life you've seen and what you want to achieve that you haven't achieved already . . ." Her voice died into silence as he went to the door. "It's probably the man from upstairs. He borrows things. Weird things. Like two fifths of an onion."

Jason opened the door. Three pols in gray uniforms filled the doorway, with weapon tubes and nightsticks aimed at him. "Mr. Taverner?" the pol with the stripes said.

"Yes."

"You are being taken into protective custody for your own protection and welfare, effective immediately, so please come with us and do not turn back or in any way remove yourself physically from contact with us. Your possessions if any will be picked up for you later and transferred to wherever you will be at the time."

"Okay," he said, and felt very little.

Behind him, Ruth Rae emitted a muffled shriek.

"You also, miss," the pol with the stripes said, motioning toward her with his nightstick.

"Can I get my coat?" she asked timidly.

"Come on." The pol stepped briskly past Jason, grabbed Ruth Rae by the arm, and dragged her out the apartment door onto the walkway.

"Do what he says," Jason said harshly to her.

Ruth Rae sniveled, "They're going to put me in a forced-labor camp."

"No," Jason said. "They'll probably kill you."

"You're really a nice guy," one of the pols—without stripes—commented as he and his companions herded Jason and Ruth Rae down the wrought-iron staircase to the ground floor. Parked in one of the slots was a police van, with several pols standing idly around it, weapons held loosely. They looked inert and bored.

"Show me your ID," the pol with stripes said to Jason; he extended his hand, waiting.

"I've got a seven-day police pass," Jason said. His hands shaking, he fished it out, gave it to the pol officer.

Scrutinizing the pass the officer said, "You admit freely of your own volition that you are Jason Taverner?"

"Yes," he said.

Two of the pols expertly searched him for arms. He complied silently, still feeling very little. Only a half-assed hopeless wish that he had done what he knew he should have done: moved on. Left Vegas. Headed anywhere.

"Mr. Taverner," the pol officer said, "the Los Angeles Police Bureau has asked us to take you into protective custody for your own protection and welfare and to transport you safely and with due care to the Police Academy in downtown L.A., which we will now do. Do you have any complaints as to the manner in which you have been treated?"

"No," he said. "Not yet."

"Enter the rear section of the quibble van," the officer said, pointing at the open doors.

Jason did so.

Ruth Rae, stuffed in beside him, whimpered to herself in the darkness as the doors slammed shut and locked. He put his arm around her, kissed her on the forehead. "What did you do?" she whimpered raspingly in her bourbon voice, "that they're going to kill us for?"

A pol, getting into the rear of the van with them from the front cab, said, "We aren't going to snuff you, miss. We're transporting you both back to L.A. That's all. Calm down."

"I don't like Los Angeles," Ruth Rae whimpered. "I haven't been there in years. I *hate* L.A." She peered wildly around.

"So do I," the pol said as he locked the rear compartment off from the cab and dropped the key through a slot to the pols outside. "But we must learn to live with it: it's there."

"They're probably going all through my apartment," Ruth Rae whimpered. "Picking through everything, breaking everything."

"Absolutely," Jason said tonelessly. His head ached, now, and he felt nauseated. And tired. "Who are we going to be taken to?" he asked the pol. "To Inspector McNulty?"

"Most likely no," the pol said conversationally as the quibble van rose noisily into the sky. "The drinkers of intoxicating liquor have made you the subject of their songs and those sitting in the gate are concerning themselves about you, and according to them Police General Felix Buckman wants to interrogate you." He explained, "That was from Psalm Sixty-nine. I sit here by you as a Witness to Jehovah Reborn, who is in this very hour creating new heavens and a new earth, and the former things will not be called to mind, neither will they come up into the heart. Isaiah 65:13, 17."

"A police general?" Jason said, numbed.

"So they say," the obliging young Jesus-freak pol answered. "I don't know what you folks did, but you sure did it right."

Ruth Rae sobbed to herself in the darkness.

"All flesh is like grass," the Jesus-freak pol intoned. "Like low-grade roachweed most likely. Unto us a child is born, unto us a hit is given. The crooked shall be made straight and the straight loaded."

"Do you have a joint?" Jason asked him.

"No, I've run out." The Jesus-freak pol rapped on the forward metal wall. "Hey, Ralf, can you lay a joint on this brother?"

"Here." A crushed pack of Goldies appeared by way of a gray-sleeved hand and arm.

"Thanks," Jason said as he lit up. "You want one?" he asked Ruth Rae.

"I want Bob," she whimpered. "I want my husband."

Silently, Jason sat hunched over, smoking and meditating.

"Don't give up," the Jesus-freak pol crammed in beside him said, in the darkness.

"Why not?" Jason said.

"The forced-labor camps aren't that bad. In Basic Orientation they took us through one; there're showers, and beds with mattresses, and recreation such as volleyball, and arts and hobbies; you know—crafts, like making candles. By hand. And your family can send you packages and once a month they or your friends can visit you." He added, "And you get to worship at the church of your choice."

Jason said sardonically, "The church of my choice is the free, open world."

After that there was silence, except for the noisy clatter of the quibble's engine, and Ruth Rae's whimpering.

14

Twenty minutes later the police quibble van landed on the roof of the Los Angeles Police Academy building.

Stiffly, Jason Taverner stepped out, looked warily around, smelled smog-saturated foul air, saw above him once again the yellowness of the largest city in North America . . . he turned to help Ruth Rae out, but the friendly young Jesus-freak pol had done that already.

Around them a group of Los Angeles pols gathered, interested. They seemed relaxed, curious, and cheerful. Jason saw no malice in any of them and he thought, When they have you they are kind. It is only in netting you that they are venomous and cruel. Because then there is the possibility that you might get away. And here, now, there is no such possibility.

"Did he make any suicide tries?" a L.A. sergeant asked the Jesus-freak pol.

"No, sir."

So that was why he had ridden there.

It hadn't even occurred to Jason, and probably not to Ruth Rae either . . . except perhaps as a heavy, shucky gesture, thought of but never really considered.

"Okay," the L.A. sergeant said to the Las Vegas pol team. "From here on in we'll formally take over custody of the two suspects."

The Las Vegas pols hopped back into their van and it zoomed off into the sky, back to Nevada.

"This way," the sergeant said, with a sharp motion of his hand in the direction of the descent sphincter tube. The L.A. pols seemed to Jason a little grosser, a little tougher and older, than the Las Vegas ones. Or perhaps it was his imagination; perhaps it meant only an increase in his own fear.

What do you say to a police general? Jason wondered. Especially when all your theories and explanations about yourself have worn out, when you know nothing, believe nothing, and the rest is obscure. Aw, the hell with it, he decided wearily, and allowed himself to drop virtually weightlessly down the tube, along with the pols and Ruth Rae.

At the fourteenth floor they exited from the tube.

A man stood facing them, well dressed, with rimless glasses, a topcoat over his arm, pointed leather Oxfords, and, Jason noted, two gold-capped teeth. A man, he guessed, in his mid-fifties. A tall, gray-haired, upright man, with an expression of authentic warmth on his excellently proportioned aristocratic face. He did not look like a pol.

"You are Jason Taverner?" the man inquired. He extended his hand; reflexively, Jason accepted it and shook. To Ruth, the police general said, "You may go downstairs. I'll interview you later. Right now it's Mr. Taverner I want to talk to."

The pols led Ruth off; he could hear her complaining her way out of sight. He now found himself facing the police general and no one else. No one armed.

"I'm Felix Buckman," the police general said. He indicated the open door and hallway behind him. "Come into the office." Turning, he ushered Jason ahead of him, into a vast pastel blue-and-gray suite; Jason blinked: he had never seen this aspect of a police agency before. He had never imagined that quality like this existed.

With incredulity, Jason a moment later found himself seated in a leather-covered chair, leaning back into the softness of styroflex. Buckman, however, did not sit down behind his top-heavy, almost clumsily bulky oak desk; instead he busied himself at a closet, putting away his topcoat.

"I intended to meet you on the roof," he explained. "But the Santana wind blows like hell up there this time of night. It affects my sinus passages." He turned, then, to face Jason. "I see something about you that didn't show up in your 4-D photo. It never does. It's always a complete surprise, at least to me. You're a six, aren't you?"

Waking to full alertness, Jason half rose, said, "You're also a six, General?"

Smiling, showing his gold-capped teeth—an expensive anachronism—Felix Buckman held up seven fingers.

15

In his career as a police official, Felix Buckman had used this shuck each time he had come up against a six. He relied on it especially when, as with this, the encounter was sudden. There had been four of them. All, eventually, had believed him. This he found amusing. The sixes, eugenic experiments themselves, and secret ones, seemed unusually gullible when confronted with the assertion that there existed an additional project as classified as their own.

Without this shuck he would be, to a six, merely an "ordinary." He could not properly handle a six under such a disadvantage. Hence the ploy. Through it his relationship to a six inverted itself. And, under such recreated conditions, he could deal successfully with an otherwise unmanageable human being.

The actual psychological superiority over him which a six possessed was abolished by an unreal fact. He liked this very much.

Once, in an off moment, he had said to Alys, "I can outthink a six for roughly ten to fifteen minutes. But if it goes on any longer—" He had made a gesture, crumpling up a black-market cigarette package. With two cigarettes in it. "After that their overamped field wins out. What I need is a pry bar by which I can jack open their haughty damn minds." And, at last, he had found it.

"Why a 'seven'?" Alys had said. "As long as you're shucking them why not say eight or thirty-eight?"

"The sin of vainglory. Reaching too far." He had not wanted to make that legendary mistake. "I will tell them," he had told her grimly, "what I think they'll believe." And, in the end, he had proved out right.

"They won't believe you," Alys had said.

"Oh, hell, will they!" he had retorted. "It's their secret fear, their bête noire. They're the sixth in a line of DNA reconstruction systems and they know that if it could be done to them it could be done to others in a more advanced degree."

Alys, uninterested, had said faintly, "You should be an announcer on TV selling soap." And that constituted the totality of her reaction. If Alys did not give a damn about something, that something, for her, ceased to exist. Probably she should not have gotten away with it for as long as she had . . . but sometime, he had often thought, the retribution will come: *reality denied comes back to haunt.* To overtake the person without warning and make him insane.

And Alys, he had a number of times thought, was in some odd sense, in some unusual clinical way, pathological.

He sensed it but could not pin it down. However, many of his hunches were like that. It did not bother him, as much as he loved her. He knew he was right.

Now, facing Jason Taverner, a six, he developed his shuck ploy.

"There were very few of us," Buckman said, now seating himself at his oversize oak desk. "Only four in all. One is already dead, so that leaves three. I don't have the slightest idea where they are; we retain even less contact among ourselves than do you sixes. Which is little enough."

"Who was your muter?" Jason asked.

"Dill-Temko. Same as yours. He controlled groups five through seven and then he retired. As you certainly know, he's dead now."

"Yes," Jason said. "It shocked us all."

"Us, too," Buckman said, in his most somber voice. "Dill-

Temko was our parent. Our *only* parent. Did you know that at the time of his death he had begun to prepare schema on an eighth group?"

"What would they have been like?"

"Only Dill-Temko knew," Buckman said, and felt his superiority over the six facing him grow. And yet—how fragile his psychological edge. One wrong statement, one statement too much, and it would vanish. Once lost, he would never regain it.

It was the risk he took. But he enjoyed it; he had always liked betting against the odds, gambling in the dark. He had in him, at times like this, a great sense of his own ability. And he did not consider it imagined . . . despite what a six that knew him to be an ordinary would say. That did not bother him one bit.

Touching a button, he said, "Peggy, bring us a pot of coffee, cream and the rest. Thanks." He then leaned back with studied leisure. And surveyed Jason Taverner.

Anyone who had met a six would recognize Taverner. The strong torso, the massive confirmation of his arms and back. His powerful, ramlike head. But most ordinaries had never knowingly come up against a six. They did not have his experience. Nor his carefully synthesized knowledge of them.

To Alys he had once said, "They will never take over and run *my* world."

"You don't have a world. You have an office."

At that point he terminated the discussion.

"Mr. Taverner," he said bluntly, "how have you managed to get documents, cards, microfilm, even complete files out of data banks all over the planet? I've tried to imagine how it could be done, but I come up with a blank." He fixed his attention on the handsome—but aging—face of the six and waited.

16

What can I tell him? Jason Taverner asked himself as he sat mutely facing the police general. The total reality as I know it? That is hard to do, he realized, because I really do not comprehend it myself.

But perhaps a seven could—well, God knew what it could do. I'll opt, he decided, on a complete explanation.

But when he started to answer, something blocked his speech. *I don't want to tell him anything,* he realized. There is no theoretical limit to what he can do to me; he has his generalship, his authority, and if he's a seven . . . for him, the sky may be the limit. At least for my self-preservation if for nothing else I ought to operate on that assumption.

"Your being a six," Buckman said, after an interval of silence, "makes me see this in a different light. It's other sixes that you're working with, is it?" He kept his eyes rigidly fixed on Jason's face; Jason found it uncomfortable and disconcerting. "I think what we have here," Buckman said, "is the first concrete evidence that sixes are—"

"No," Jason said.

" 'No'?" Buckman continued to stare fixedly at him. "You're not involved with other sixes in this?"

Jason said, "I know one other six. Heather Hart. And she considers me a twerp fan." He ground out the words bitterly.

That interested Buckman; he had not been aware that the

well-known singer Heather Hart was a six. But, thinking about it, it seemed reasonable. He had never, however, come up against a female six in his career; his contacts with them were just not that frequent.

"If Miss Hart is a six," Buckman said aloud, "maybe we should ask her to come in too and consult with us." A police euphemism that rolled easily off his tongue.

"Do that," Jason said. "Put her through the wringer." His tone had become savage. "Bust her. Put her in a forced-labor camp."

You sixes, Buckman said to himself, have little loyalty to one another. He had discovered this already, but it always surprised him. An elite group, bred out of aristocratic prior circles to set and maintain the mores of the world, who had in practice drizzled off into nothingness because they could not stand one another. To himself he laughed, letting his face show, at least, a smile.

"You're amused?" Jason said. "Don't you believe me?"

"It doesn't matter." Buckman brought a box of Cuesta Rey cigars from a drawer of his desk, used his little knife to cut off the end of one. The little steel knife made for that purpose alone.

Across from him Jason Taverner watched with fascination.

"A cigar?" Buckman inquired. He held the box toward Jason.

"I have never smoked a good cigar," Jason said. "If it got out that I—" He broke off.

" 'Got out'?" Buckman asked, his mental ears pricking up. "Got out to whom? The police?"

Jason said nothing. But he had clenched his fist and his breathing had become labored.

"Are there strata in which you're well known?" Buckman said. "For example, among intellectuals in forced-labor camps. You know—the ones who circulate mimeographed manuscripts."

"No," Jason said.

"Musical strata, then?"

Jason said tightly, "Not anymore."

"Have you ever made phonograph records?"

"Not here."

Buckman continued to scrutinize him unblinkingly; over long years he had mastered the ability. "Then where?" he asked, in a voice barely over the threshold of audibility. A voice deliberately sought for: its tone lulled, interfered with identification of the words' meaning.

But Jason Taverner let it slide by; he failed to respond. These damn bastard sixes, Buckman thought, angered—mostly at himself. *I can't play funky games with a six.* It just plain does not work. And, at any minute, he could cancel my statement out of his mind, my claim to superior genetic heritage.

He pressed a stud on his intercom. "Have a Miss Katharine Nelson brought in here," he instructed Herb Maime. "A police informant down in the Watts District, that ex-black area. I think I should talk to her."

"Half hour."

"Thanks."

Jason Taverner said hoarsely, "Why bring her into this?"

"She forged your papers."

"All she knows about me is what I had her put on the ID cards."

"And that was spurious?"

After a pause Jason shook his head no.

"So you do exist."

"Not—here."

"Where?"

"I don't know."

"Tell me how you got those data deleted from all the banks."

"I never did that."

Hearing that, Buckman felt an enormous hunch overwhelm him; it gripped him with paws of iron. "You haven't been taking material out of the data banks; you've been trying to put material in. *There were no data there in the first place.*"

Finally, Jason Taverner nodded.

"Okay," Buckman said; he felt the glow of discovery lurking inside him, now, revealing itself in a cluster of comprehensions. "You took nothing out. But there's some reason why the data weren't there in the first place. Why not? Do you know?"

"I know," Jason Taverner said, staring down at the table; his face had twisted into a gross mirror-thing. "I don't exist."

"But you once did."

"Yes," Taverner said, nodding unwillingly. Painfully.

"Where?"

"I don't know!"

It always comes back to that, Buckman said to himself. I don't know. Well, Buckman thought, maybe he doesn't. But he did make his way from L.A. to Vegas; he did shack up with that skinny, wrinkled broad the Vegas pols loaded into the van with him. Maybe, he thought, I can get something from her. But his hunch registered a no.

"Have you had dinner?" Buckman inquired.

"Yes," Jason Taverner said.

"But you'll join me in the munchies. I'll have them bring something in to us." Once more he made use of the intercom. "Peggy—it's so late now . . . get us two breakfasts at that new place down the street. Not the one we used to go to, but the new one with the sign showing the dog with the girl's head. Barfy's."

"Yes, Mr. Buckman," Peggy said and rang off.

"Why don't they call you 'General'?" Jason Taverner asked.

Buckman said, "When they call me 'General' I feel I ought to have written a book on how to invade France while staying out of a two-front war."

"So you're just plain 'Mister'."

"That's right."

"And they let you do it?"

"For me," Buckman said, "there is no 'they.' Except for five police marshals here and there in the world, and they call themselves 'Mister,' too." And how they would like to demote me further, he thought. Because of all that I did.

"But there's the Director."

Buckman said, "The Director has never seen me. He never will. Nor will he see you either, Mr. Taverner. But nobody can see you, because, as you pointed out, you don't exist."

Presently a gray uniformed pol woman entered the office, carrying a tray of food. "What you usually order this time of night," she said as he set the tray down on Buckman's desk. "One short stack of hots with a side order of ham; one short stack of hots with a side order of sausage."

"Which would you like?" Buckman asked Jason Taverner.

"Is the sausage well cooked?" Jason Taverner asked, peering to see. "I guess it is. I'll take it."

"That's ten dollars and one gold quinque," the pol woman said. "Which of you is going to pay for it?"

Buckman dug into his pockets, fished out the bills and change. "Thanks." The woman departed. "Do you have any children?" he asked Taverner.

"No."

"I have a child," General Buckman said. "I'll show you a little 3-D pic of him that I received." He reached into his desk, brought out a palpitating square of three-dimensional but nonmoving colors. Accepting the picture, Jason held it properly in the light, saw outlined statically a young boy in shorts and sweater, barefoot, running across a field, tugging on the string of a kite. Like the police general, the boy had light short hair and a strong and impressive wide jaw. Already.

"Nice," Jason said. He returned the pic.

Buckman said, "He never got the kite off the ground. Too young, perhaps. Or afraid. Our little boy has a lot of anxiety. I think because he sees so little of me and his mother; he's at a school in Florida and we're here, which is not a good thing. You say you have no children?"

"Not that I know of," Jason said.

" 'Not that you know of'?" Buckman raised an eyebrow. "Does that mean you don't go into the matter? You've never tried to find out? By law, you know, you as the father are required to support your children in or out of wedlock."

Jason nodded.

"Well," General Buckman said, as he put the pic away in his desk, "everyone to his own. But consider what you've left out of your life. Haven't you ever loved a child? It hurts your heart, the innermost part of you, where you can easily die."

"I didn't know that," Jason said.

"Oh, yes. My wife says you can forget any kind of love except what you've felt toward children. That only goes one way; it never reverts. And if something comes between you and a child—such as death or a terrible calamity such as a divorce—you never recover."

"Well, hell, then"—Jason gestured with a forkful of sausage—"then it would be better not to feel that kind of love."

"I don't agree," Buckman said. "You should always love, and especially a child, because that's the strongest form of love."

"I see," Jason said.

"No, you don't see. Sixes never see; they don't understand. It's not worth discussing." He shuffled a pile of papers on his desk, scowling, puzzled, and nettled. But gradually he calmed down, became his cool assured self once more. But he could not understand Jason Taverner's attitude. But he, his child, was all-important; it, plus his love of course for the boy's mother—this was the pivot of his life.

They ate for a time without speaking, with, suddenly, no bridge connecting them one to the other.

"There's a cafeteria in the building," Buckman said at last, as he drank down a glass of imitation Tang. "But the food there is poisoned. All the help must have relatives in forced-labor camps. They're getting back at us." He laughed. Jason Taverner did not. "Mr. Taverner," Buckman said, dabbing at his mouth with his napkin, "I am going to let you go. I'm not holding you."

Staring at him, Jason said, "Why?"

"Because you haven't done anything."

Jason said hoarsely, "Getting forged ID cards. A felony."

"I have the authority to cancel any felony charge I wish," Buckman said. "I consider that you were forced into doing that by some situation you found yourself in, a situation which you refuse to tell me about, but of which I have gotten a slight glimpse."

After a pause Jason said, "Thanks."

"But," Buckman said, "you will be electronically monitored wherever you go. You will never be alone except for your own thoughts in your own mind and perhaps not even there. Everyone you contact or reach or see will be brought in for questioning eventually . . . just as we're bringing in the Nelson girl right now." He leaned toward Jason Taverner, speaking slowly and intently so that Taverner would listen and understand. "I believe you took no data from any data banks, public or private. I believe you don't understand your own situation. But"—he let his voice rise perceptibly—"sooner or later you will understand your situation and when that happens we want to be in on it. So—we will always be with you. Fair enough?"

Jason Taverner rose to his feet. "Do all you sevens think this way?"

"What way?"

"Making strong, vital, instant decisions. The way you do. The way you ask questions, listen—God, how you listen!—and then make up your mind absolutely."

Truthfully, Buckman said, "I don't know because I have so little contact with other sevens."

"Thanks," Jason said. He held out his hand; they shook. "Thanks for the meal." He seemed calm now. In control of himself. And very much relieved. "Do I just wander out of here? How do I get onto the street?"

"We'll have to hold you until morning," Buckman said. "It's a fixed policy; suspects are never released at night. Too much goes on in the streets after dark. We'll provide you a cot and a room; you'll have to sleep in your clothes . . . and at eight o'clock tomorrow morning I'll have Peggy escort you to the main entrance of the academy." Pressing the stud on his intercom, Buckman said, "Peg, take Mr. Taverner to detention for now; take him out again at eight A.M. sharp. Understood?"

"Yes, Mr. Buckman."

Spreading his hands, smiling, General Buckman said, "So that's it. There is no more."

17

"Mr. Taverner," Peggy was saying insistently. "Come along with me; put your clothes on and follow me to the outside office. I'll meet you there. Just go through the blue-and-white doors."

Standing off to one side, General Buckman listened to the girl's voice; pretty and fresh, it sounded good to him, and he guessed that it sounded that way to Taverner, too.

"One more thing," Buckman said, stopping the sloppily dressed, sleepy Taverner as he started to make his way toward the blue-and-white doors. "I can't renew your police pass if someone down the line voids it. Do you understand? What you've got to do is apply to us, exactly following legal lines, for a total set of ID cards. It'll mean intensive interrogation, but"—he thumped Jason Taverner on the arm—"a six can take it."

"Okay," Jason Taverner said. He left the office, closing the blue-and-white doors behind him.

Into his intercom Buckman said, "Herb, make sure they put both a microtrans and a heterostatic class eighty warhead on him. So we can follow him and if it's necessary at any time we can destroy him."

"You want a voice tap, too?" Herb said.

"Yes, if you can get it onto his throat without him noticing."

"I'll have Peg do it," Herb said, and signed off.

Could a Mutt and Jeff, say, between me and McNulty, have brought any more information out? he asked himself. No, he decided. Because the man himself simply doesn't know. What we must do is wait for him to figure it out . . . and be there with him, either physically or electronically, when it happens. As in fact I pointed out to him.

But it still strikes me, he realized, that we very well may have blundered onto something the sixes are doing as a group—despite their usual mutual animosity.

Again pressing the button of his intercom he said, "Herb, have a twenty-four-hour surveillance put on that pop singer Heather Hart or whatever she calls herself. And get from Data Central the files of all what they call 'sixes.' You understand?"

"Are the cards punched for that?" Herb said.

"Probably not," Buckman said drearily. "Probably nobody thought to do it ten years ago when Dill-Temko was alive, thinking up more and weirder life forms to shamble about." Like us sevens, he thought wryly. "And they certainly wouldn't think of it these days, now that the sixes have failed politically. Do you agree?"

"I agree," Herb said, "but I'll try for it anyhow."

Buckman said, "If the cards *are* punched for that, I want a twenty-four-hour surveillance on all sixes. And even if we can't roust them all out we can at least put tails on the ones we know."

"Will do, Mr. Buckman." Herb clicked off.

18

"Goodbye and good luck, Mr. Taverner," the pol chick named Peg said to him at the wide entrance to the great gray academy building.

"Thanks," Jason said. He inhaled a deep sum of morning air, smog-infested as it was. I got out, he said to himself. They could have hung a thousand busts on me but they didn't.

A female voice, very throaty, said from close by, "How now, little man?"

Never in his life had he been called "little man"; he stood over six feet tall. Turning, he started to say something in answer, then made out the creature who had addressed him.

She too stood a full six feet in height; they matched in that department. But in contrast to him she wore tight black pants, a leather shirt, red, with tassle fringes, gold hooped earrings, and a belt made of chain. And spike heeled shoes. Jesus Christ, he thought, appalled. Where's her whip?

"Were you talking to me?" he said.

"Yes." She smiled, showing teeth ornamented with gold signs of the zodiac. "They put three items on you before you got out of there; I thought you ought to know."

"I know," Jason said, wondering who or what she was.

"One of them," the girl said, "is a miniaturized H-bomb. It can be detonated by a radio signal emitted from this building. Did you know about that?"

Presently he said, "No. I didn't."

"It's the way he works things," the girl said. "My brother . . . he raps mellow and nice to you, civilizedly, and then he has one of his staff—he has a huge staff—plant that garbage on you before you can walk out the door of the building."

"Your brother," Jason said. "General Buckman." He could see, now, the resemblance between them. The thin, elongated nose, the high cheekbones, the neck, like a Modigliani, tapered beautifully. Very patrician, he thought. They, both of them, impressed him.

So she must be a seven, too, he said to himself. He felt himself become wary, again; the hackles on his neck burned as he confronted her.

"I'll get them off you," she said, still smiling, like General Buckman, a gold-toothed smile.

"Good enough," Jason said.

"Come over to my quibble." She started off lithely; he loped clumsily after her.

A moment later they sat together in the front bucket seats of her quibble.

"Alys is my name," she said.

He said, "I'm Jason Taverner, the singer and TV personality."

"Oh, really? I haven't watched a TV program since I was nine."

"You haven't missed much," he said. He did not know if he meant it ironically; frankly, he thought, I'm too tired to care.

"This little bomb is the size of a seed," Alys said. "And it's embedded, like a tick, in your skin. Normally, even if you knew it was there someplace on you, you still could never find it. But I borrowed this from the academy." She held up a tubelike light. "This glows when you get it near a seed bomb." She began at once, efficiently and nearly professionally, to move the light across his body.

At his left wrist the light glowed.

"I also have the kit they use to remove a seed bomb," Alys

said. From her mailpouch purse she brought a shallow tin, which she at once opened. "The sooner it's cut out of you the better," she said, as she lifted a cutting tool from the kit.

For two minutes she cut expertly, meanwhile spraying an analgesic compound on the wound. And then—it lay in her hand. As she had said, the size of a seed.

"Thanks," he said. "For removing the thorn from my paw."

Alys laughed gaily; she replaced the cutting tool in the kit, shut the lid, returned it to her huge purse. "You see," she said, "he never does it himself; it's always one of his staff. So he can remain ethical and aloof, as if it has nothing to do with him. I think I hate that the most about him." She pondered. "I really hate him."

"Is there anything else you can cut or tear off me?" Jason inquired.

"They tried—Peg, who is a police technician expert at it, tried—to stick a voice tap on your gullet. But I don't think she got it to stick." Cautiously, she explored his neck. "No, it didn't catch; it fell off. Fine. That takes care of that. You do have a microtrans on you somewhere; we'll need a strobe light to pick up its flux." She fished in the glove compartment of the quibble and came up with a battery-operated strobe disc. "I think I can find it," she said, setting the strobe light into activity.

The microtrans turned out to be in residence in the cuff of his left sleeve. Alys pushed a pin through it, and that was that.

"Is there anything else?" Jason asked her.

"Possibly a minicam. A very small camera transmitting a TV image back to academy monitors. But I didn't see them wind one into you; I think we can take a chance and forget that." She turned, then, to scrutinize him. "Who are you?" she asked. "By the way."

Jason said, "An unperson."

"Meaning what?"

"Meaning that I don't exist."

"Physically?"

"I don't know," —he said, truthfully. Maybe, he thought,

if I had been more open with her brother the police general . . . maybe he could have worked it out. After all, Felix Buckman was a seven. Whatever that meant.

But still—Buckman had probed in the right direction; he had brought out a good deal. And in a very short time—a period punctuated by a late-night breakfast and a cigar.

The girl said, "So you're Jason Taverner. The man McNulty was trying to pin down and couldn't. The man with no data on him anywhere in the world. No birth certificate; no school records; no—"

"How is it you know all this?" Jason said.

"I looked over McNulty's report." Her tone was blithe. "In Felix's office. It interested me."

"Then why did you ask me who I am?"

Alys said, "I wondered if you knew. I had heard from McNulty; this time I wanted your side of it. The antipol side, as they call it."

"I can't add anything to what McNulty knows," Jason said.

"That's not true." She had begun to interrogate him now, precisely in the manner her brother had a short time ago. A low, informal tone of voice, as if something merely casual were being discussed, then the intense focus on his face, the graceful motions of her arms and hands, as if, while talking to him, she danced a little. With herself. Beauty dancing on beauty, he thought; he found her physically, sexually exciting. And he had had enough of sex, God knew, for the next several days.

"Okay," he conceded. "I know more."

"More than you told Felix?"

He hesitated. And, in doing so, answered.

"Yes," Alys said.

He shrugged. It had become obvious.

"Tell you what," Alys said briskly. "Would you like to see how a police general lives? His home? His billion-dollar castle?"

"You'd let me in there?" he said, incredulous. "If he found out—" He paused. Where is this woman leading me? he asked himself. Into terrible danger; everything in him sensed it, became at once wary and alert. He felt his own cunning course through him, infusing every part of his somatic being. His body knew that here, more than at any other time, he had to be careful. "You have legal access to his home?" he said, calming himself; he made his voice natural, devoid of any unusual tension.

"Hell," Alys said, "I live with him. We're twins; we're very close. Incestuously close."

Jason said, "I don't want to walk into a setup hammered out between you and General Buckman."

"A setup between Felix and me?" She laughed sharply. "Felix and I couldn't collaborate in painting Easter eggs. Come on; let's shoot over to the house. Between us we have a good deal of interesting objects. Medieval wooden chess sets, old bone-china cups from England. Some beautiful early U.S. stamps printed by the National Banknote Company. Do stamps interest you?"

"No," he said.

"Guns?"

He hesitated. "To some extent." He remembered his own gun; this was the second time in twenty-four hours that he had had reason to remember it.

Eying him, Alys said, "You know, for a small man you're not bad-looking. And you're older than I like . . . but not much so. You're a six, aren't you?"

He nodded.

"Well?" Alys said. "Do you want to see a police general's castle?"

Jason said, "Okay." They would find him wherever he went, whenever they wanted him. With or without a micro-trans pinned on his cuff.

Turning on the engine of her quibble, Alys Buckman spun the wheel, pressed down on the pedal; the quibble shot up at a ninety-degree angle to the street. A police engine, he realized. Twice the horsepower of domestic models.

"There is one thing," Alys said as she steered through traffic, "that I want you to get clear in your mind." She glanced over at him to be sure he was listening. "Don't make any sexual advances toward me. If you do I'll kill you." She tapped her belt and he saw, tucked within it, a police-model weapon tube; it glinted blue and black in the morning sun.

"Noticed and attended to," he said, and felt uneasy. He already did not like the leather and iron costume she wore; fetishistic qualities were profoundly involved, and he had never cared for them. And now this ultimatum. Where was her head sexually? With other lesbians? Was that it?

In answer to his unspoken question, Alys said calmly, "All my libido, my sexuality, is tied up with Felix."

"Your *brother*?" He felt cold, frightened incredulity. "How?"

"We've lived an incestuous relationship for five years," Alys said, adroitly maneuvering her quibble in the heavy morning Los Angeles traffic. "We have a child, three years old. He's kept by a housekeeper and nurse down in Key West, Florida. Barney is his name."

"And you're telling me this?" he said, amazed beyond belief. "Someone you don't even know?"

"Oh, I know you very well, Jason Taverner," Alys said; she lifted the quibble up into a higher lane, increased velocity. The traffic, now, had thinned; they were leaving greater L.A. "I've been a fan of yours, of your Tuesday night TV show, for years. And I have records of yours, and once I heard you sing live at the Orchid Room at the Hotel St. Francis in San Francisco." She smiled briefly at him. "Felix and I, we're both collectors . . . and one of the things I collect is Jason Taverner records." Her darting, frenetic smile increased. "Over the years I've collected all nine."

Jason said huskily, his voice shaking, "Ten. I've put out ten LPs. The last few with light-show projection tracks."

"Then I missed one," Alys said, agreeably. "Here. Turn around and look in the back seat."

Twisting about, he saw in the rear seat his earliest album: *Taverner and the Blue, Blue Blues.* "Yes," he said, seizing it and bringing it forward onto his lap.

"There's another one there," Alys said. "My favorite out of all of them."

He saw, then, a dog-eared copy of *There'll Be a Good Time with Taverner Tonight*. "Yes," he said. "That's the best one I ever did."

"You see?" Alys said. The quibble dipped now, spiraling down in a helical pattern toward a cluster of large estates, tree- and grass-surrounded, below. "Here's the house."

19

Its blades vertical now, the quibble sank to an asphalt spot in the center of the great lawn of the house. Jason barely noticed the house: three story, Spanish style with black iron railings on the balconies, red-tile roof, adobe or stucco walls; he could not tell. A large house, with beautiful oak trees surrounding it; the house had been built into the landscape without destroying it. The house blended and seemed a part of the trees and grass, an extension into the realm of the manmade.

Alys shut off the quibble, kicked open a balky door. "Leave the records in the car and come along," she said to him as she slid from the quibble and upright, onto the lawn.

Reluctantly, he placed the record albums back on the seat and followed her, hurrying to catch up with her; the girl's long black-sheathed legs carried her rapidly toward the huge front gate of the house.

"We even have pieces of broken glass bottles embedded in the top of the walls. To repel bandits . . . in this day and age. The house once belonged to the great Ernie Till, the Western actor." She pressed a button mounted on the front gate before the house and there appeared a brown-uniformed private pol, who scrutinized her, nodded, released the power surge that slid the gate aside.

To Alys, Jason said, "What do you know? You know I'm—"

"You're fabulous," Alys said matter-of-factly. "I've known it for years."

"But you've been where I was. Where I always am. Not here."

Taking his arm, Alys guided him down an adobe-and-slate corridor and then down a flight of five brick steps, into a sunken living room, an ancient place in this day, but beautiful.

He did not, however, give a damn; he wanted to talk to her, to find out what and how she knew. And what it signified.

"Do you remember this place?" Alys said.

"No," he said.

"You should. You've been here before."

"I haven't," he said, guardedly; she had thoroughly trapped his credulity by producing the two records. *I've got to have them,* he said to himself. To show to— yes, he thought; to whom? To General Buckman? And if I do show him, what will it get me?

"A cap of mescaline?" Alys said, going to a drug case, a large hand-oiled walnut cabinet at the end of the leather and brass bar on the far side of the living room.

"A little," he said. But then his response surprised him; he blinked. "I want to keep my head clear," he amended.

She brought him a tiny enameled drug tray on which rested a crystal tumbler of water and a white capsule. "Very good stuff. Harvey's Yellow Number One, imported from Switzerland in bulk, capsuled on Bond Street." She added, "And not strong at all. Color stuff."

"Thanks." He accepted the glass and the white capsule; he drank the mescaline down, placed the glass back on the tray. "Aren't you having any?" he asked her, feeling—belatedly—wary.

"I'm already spaced," Alys said genially, smiling her gold baroque tooth smile. "Can't you tell? I guess not; you've never seen me any other way."

"Did you know I'd be brought to the L.A. Police Academy?" he asked. You must have, he thought, *because you had the two records of mine with you.* Had you not known, the chances of your having them alone are zero out of a billion, virtually.

"I monitored some of their transmissions," Alys said; turning, she roamed restlessly off, tapping on the small enameled tray with one long fingernail. "I happened to pick up the official traffic between Vegas and Felix. I like to listen to him now and then during the time he's on duty. Not always, but"—she pointed toward a room beyond an open corridor at the near side—"I want to look at something; I'll show it to you, if it's as good as Felix said."

He followed, the buzz of questions in his mind dinning at him as he walked. If she can get across, he thought, go back and forth, as she seems to have done—

"He said the center drawer of his maple desk," Alys said reflectively as she stood in the center of the house's library; leather-bound books rose up in cases mounted to the high ceiling of the chamber. Several desks, a glass case of tiny cups, various early chess sets, two ancient Tarot card decks . . . Alys wandered over to a New England desk, opened a drawer, peered within. "Ah," she said, and brought out a glassine envelope.

"Alys—" Jason began, but she cut him off with a brusque snap of her fingers.

"Be quiet while I look at this." From the surface of the desk she took a large magnifying glass; she scrutinized the envelope. "A stamp," she explained, then, glancing up. "I'll take it out so you can look at it." Finding a pair of philatelic tongs she carefully drew the stamp from its envelope and set it down on the felt pad at the front edge of the desk.

Obediently, Jason peeped through the magnifying lens at the stamp. It seemed to him a stamp like any other stamp, except that unlike modern stamps it had been printed in only one color.

"Look at the engraving on the animals," Alys said. "The herd of steer. It's absolutely perfect; every line is exact. This stamp has never been—" She stopped his hand as he started to touch the stamp. "Oh no," she said. "Don't ever touch a stamp with your fingers; always use tongs."

"Is it valuable?" he asked.

"Not really. But they're almost never sold. I'll explain it to you someday. This is a present to me from Felix, because he loves me. Because, he says, I'm good in bed."

"It's a nice stamp," Jason said, disconcerted. He handed the magnifying glass back to her.

"Felix told me the truth; it's a good copy. Perfectly centered, light cancellation that doesn't mar the center picture, and—" Deftly, with the tongs, she flipped the stamp over on its back, allowed it to lie on the felt pad face down. All at once her expression changed; her face glowed hotly and she said, "That motherfucker."

"What's the matter?" he said.

"A thin spot." She touched a corner of the stamp's back side with the tongs. "Well, you can't tell from the front. But that's Felix. Hell, it's probably counterfeit anyhow. Except that Felix always somehow manages not to buy counterfeits. Okay, Felix; that's one for you." Thoughtfully, she said, "I wonder if he's got another one in his own collection. I could switch them." Going to a wall safe, she twiddled for a time with the dials, opened the safe at last, and brought out a huge and heavy album, which she lugged to the desk. "Felix," she said, "does not know I know the combination to that safe. So don't tell him." She cautiously turned heavy-gauge pages, came to one on which four stamps rested. "No one-dollar black," she said. "But he may have hidden it elsewhere. He may even have it down at the academy." Closing the album, she restored it to the wall safe.

"The mescaline," Jason said, "is beginning to affect me." His legs ached: for him that was always a sign that mescaline was beginning to act in his system. "I'll sit down," he said, and managed to locate a leather-covered easy chair before his legs gave way. Or *seemed* to give way; actually they never did: it was a drug-instigated illusion. But all the same it felt real.

"Would you like to see a collection of chaste and ornate snuffboxes?" Alys inquired. "Felix has a terribly fine collection. All antiques, in gold, silver, alloys, with cameo engravings, hunting scenes—no?" She seated herself opposite him, crossed her long, black-sheathed legs; her high-heeled shoe dangled as she swung it back and forth. "One time Felix bought an old snuffbox at an auction, paid a lot for it, brought it home. He cleaned the old snuff out of it and found a spring-operated level mounted at the bottom of the box, or what seemed to be the bottom. The lever operated when you screwed down a tiny screw. It took him all day to find a tool small enough to rotate the screw. But at least he got it." She laughed.

"What happened?" Jason said.

"The bottom of the box—a false bottom with a tin plate concealed in it. He got the plate out." She laughed again, her gold tooth ornamentation sparkling. "It turned out to be a two-hundred-year-old dirty picture. Of a chick copulating with a Shetland pony. Tinted, too, in eight colors. Worth, oh, say, five thousand dollars—not much, but it genuinely delighted us. The dealer, of course, didn't know it was there."

"I see," Jason said.

"You don't have any interest in snuffboxes," Alys said, still smiling.

"I'd like—to see it," he said. And then he said. "Alys, you know about me; you know who I am. *Why doesn't anybody else know?*"

"Because they've never been there."

"*Where?*"

Alys massaged her temples, twisted her tongue, stared blankly ahead, as if lost in thought. As if barely hearing him. "You know," she said, sounding bored and a little irritable. "Christ, man, you lived there forty-two years. What can I tell you about that place that you don't already know?" She glanced up, then, her heavy lips curling mischievously; she grinned at him.

"How did I get here?" he said.

"You—" She hesitated. "I'm not sure I should tell you."

Loudly, he said, *"Why not?"*

"Let it come in time." She made a damping motion with her hand. "In time, in time. Look, man; you've already been hit by a lot; you almost got shipped to a labor camp, and you know what kind, today. Thanks to that asshole McNulty and my dear brother. My brother the police general." Her face had become ugly with revulsion, but then she smiled her provocative smile once again. Her lazy, gold-toothed, inviting smile.

Jason said, "I want to know where I am."

"You're in my study in my house. You're perfectly safe; we got all the insects off you. And no one's going to break in here. Do you know what?" She sprang from her chair, bounding to her feet like a superlithe animal; involuntarily he drew back. "Have you ever made it by phone?" she demanded, bright-eyed and eager.

"Made what?"

"The grid," Alys said. "Don't you know about the phone grid?"

"No," he admitted. But he had heard of it.

"Your—everybody's—sexual aspects are linked electronically, and amplified, to as much as you can endure. It's addictive, because it's electronically enhanced. People, some of them, get so deep into it they can't pull out; their whole lives revolve around the weekly—or, hell, even daily!—setting up of the network of phone lines. It's regular picturephones, which you activate by credit card, so it's free at the time you do it; the sponsors bill you once a month and if you don't pay they cut your phone out of the grid."

"How many people," he asked, "are involved in this?"

"Thousands."

"At one time?"

Alys nodded. "Most of them have been doing it two, three years. And they've deteriorated physically—and mentally—from it. Because the part of the brain where the orgasm is experienced is gradually burned out. But don't put down the people; some of the finest and most sensitive minds on earth are involved. For them it's a sacred, holy communion. Except you can spot a gridder when you see one; they look debauched, old, fat, listless— the latter always *between* the phone-line orgies, of course."

"And you do this?" She did not look debauched, old, fat, or listless to him.

"Now and then. But I never get hooked; I cut myself out of the grid just in time. Do you want to try it?"

"No," he said.

"Okay," Alys said reasonably, undaunted. "What would you like to do? We have a good collection of Rilke and Brecht in interlinear translation discs. The other day Felix came home with a quad-and-light set of all seven Sibelius symphonies; it's very good. For dinner Emma is preparing frog's legs . . . Felix loves both frog's legs and escargot. He eats out in good French and Basque restaurants most of the time but tonight—"

"I want to know," Jason interrupted, "where I am."

"Can't you simply be happy?"

He rose to his feet—with difficulty—and confronted her. Silently.

20

The mescaline had furiously begun to affect him; the room grew lit up with colors, and the perspective factor altered so that the ceiling seemed a million miles high. And, gazing at Alys, he saw her hair come alive . . . like Medusa's, he thought, and felt fear.

Ignoring him, Alys continued, "Felix especially likes Basque cuisine, but they cook with so much butter that it gives him pyloric spasms. He also has a good collection of *Weird Tales,* and he loves baseball. And—let's see." She wandered off, a finger tapping against her lips as she reflected. "He's interested in the occult. Do you—"

"I feel something," Jason said.

"What do you feel?"

Jason said, "I can't get away."

"It's the mes. Take it easy."

"I—" He pondered; a giant weight lay on his brain, but all throughout the weight streaks of light, of satori-like insight, shot here and there.

"What I collect," Alys said, "is in the next room, what we call the library. This is the study. In the library Felix has all his law books . . . did you know he's a lawyer, as well as a police general? And he has done some good things; I have to admit it. Do you now what he did once?"

He could not answer; he could only stand. Inert, hearing the sounds but not the meaning. Of it.

"For a year Felix was legally in charge of one-fourth of Terra's forced-labor camps. He discovered that by virtue of an obscure law passed years ago when the forced-labor camps were more like death camps—with a lot of blacks in them—anyhow, he discovered that this statute permitted the camps to operate only during the Second Civil War. And he had the power to close any and all camps at any time he felt it to be in the public interest. And those blacks and the students who'd been working in the camps are damn tough and strong, from years of heavy manual labor. They're not like the effete, pale, clammy students living beneath the campus areas. And then he researched and discovered another obscure statute. Any camp that isn't operating at a profit *has* to be—or rather had to be—closed. So Felix changed the amount of money—very little, of course—paid to the detainees. So all he had to do was jack up their pay, show red ink in the books, and bam; he could shut down the camps." She laughed.

He tried to speak but couldn't. Inside him his mind churned like a tattered rubber ball, sinking and rising, slowing down, speeding up, fading and then flaring brilliantly; the shafts of light scampered all through him, piercing every part of his body.

"But the big thing Felix did," Alys said, "had to do with the student kibbutzim under the burned-out campuses. A lot of them are desperate for food and water; you know how it is: the students try to make it into town, foraging for supplies, ripping off and looting. Well, the police maintain a lot of agents among the students agitating for a final shootout with the police . . . which the police and nats are hopefully waiting for. Do you see?"

"I see," he said, "a hat."

"But Felix tried to keep off any sort of shootout. But to do it he had to get supplies to the students; do you see?"

"The hat is red," Jason said. "Like your ears."

"Because of his position as marshal in the pol hierarchy,

Felix had access to informant reports as to the condition of each student kibbutz. He knew which ones were failing and which were making it. It was his job to boil out of the horde of abstracts the ultimately important facts: which kibbutzim were going under and which were not. Once he had listed those in trouble, other high police officers met with him to decide how to apply pressure which would hasten the end. Defeatist agitation by police finks, sabotage of food and water supplies. Desperate—actually hopeless—forays out of the campus area in search of help—for instance, at Columbia one time they had a plan of getting to the Harry S Truman Labor Camp and liberating the detainees and arming them, but at that even Felix had to say 'Intervene!' But anyhow it was Felix's job to determine the tactic for each kibbutz under scrutiny. Many, many times he advised no action at all. For this, of course, the hardhats criticized him, demanded his removal from his position." Alys paused. "He was a full police marshal, then, you have to realize."

"Your red," Jason said, "is fantidulous."

"I know." Alys's lips turned down. "Can't you hold your hit, man? I'm trying to tell you something. Felix got *demoted,* from police marshal to police general, because he saw to it, when he could, that in the kibbutzim the students were bathed, fed, their medical supplies looked after, cots provided. Like he did for the forced-labor camps under his jurisdiction. So now he's just a general. But they leave him alone. They've done all they can to him for now and he still holds a high office."

"But your incest," Jason said. "What if?" He paused; he could not remember the rest of his sentence. "If," he said, and that seemed to be it; he felt a furious glow, arising from the fact that he had managed to convey his message to her. "If," he said again, and the inner glow became wild with happy fury. He exclaimed aloud.

"You mean what if the marshals knew that Felix and I have a son? What would they do?"

"They would do," Jason said. "Can we hear some music?

Or give me—" His words ceased; none more entered his brain. "Gee," he said. "My mother wouldn't be here. Death."

Alys inhaled deeply, sighed. "Okay, Jason," she said. "I'll give up trying to rap with you. Until your head is back."

"Talk," he said.

"Would you like to see my bondage cartoons?"

"What," he said, "that's?"

"Drawings, very stylized, of chicks tied up, and men—"

"Can I lie down?" he said. "My legs won't work. I think my right leg extends to the moon. In other words"—he considered—"I broke it standing up."

"Come here." She led him, step by step, from the study and back into the living room. "Lie down on the couch," she told him. With agonizing difficulty he did so. "I'll go get you some Thorazine; it'll counteract the mes."

"This is a mess," he said.

"Let's see . . . where the hell did I put that? I rarely if ever have to use it, but I keep it in case something like this . . . God damn it, can't you drop a single cap of mes and *be* something? I take five at once."

"But you're vast," Jason said.

"I'll be back; I'm going upstairs." Alys strode off, toward a door located several distances away; for a long, long time he watched her dwindle—how did she accomplish it? It seemed incredible that she could shrink down to almost nothing—and then she vanished. He felt, at that, terrible fear. He knew that he had become alone, without help. Who will help me? he asked himself. I have to get away from these stamps and cups and snuffboxes and bondage cartoons and phone grids and frog's legs I've got to get to that quibble I've got to fly away and back to where I know back in town maybe with Ruth Rae if they've let her go or even back to Kathy Nelson this woman is too much for me so is her brother them and their incest child in Florida named what?

He rose unsteadily, groped his way across a rug that sprang a million leaks of pure pigment as he trod on it, crushing it with his ponderous shoes, and then, at last, he stumbled against the front door of the unsteady room.

Sunlight. He had gotten outside.

The quibble.

He hobbled to it.

Inside he sat at the controls, bewildered by legions of knobs, levers, wheels, pedals, dials. "Why doesn't it go?" he said aloud. "Get going!" he told it, rocking back and forth in the driver's seat. "Won't she let me go?" he asked the quibble.

The keys. Of course he couldn't fly it no keys.

Her coat in the back seat; he had witnessed it. And also her large mailpouch purse. There, the keys in her purse. There.

The two record albums. *Taverner and the Blue, Blue Blues.* And the best of them all: *There'll be a Good Time.* He groped, managed somehow to lift *both* record albums up, conveyed them to the empty seat beside him. I have the proof here, he realized. It's here in these records and it's here in the house. With her. I've got to find it here if I'm going to. Find it. Nowhere else. Even General Mr. Felix What-Is-He-Named? he won't find it. He doesn't know. As much as me.

Carrying the enormous record albums he ran back to the house—around him the landscape flowed, with whip, tall, tree-like organisms gulping in air out of the sweet blue sky, organisms which absorbed water and light, ate the hue into the sky . . . he reached the gate, pushed against it. The gate did not budge. Button.

He found no.

Step by step. Feel each inch with fingers. Like in the dark. Yes, he thought. I'm in darkness. He set down the much-too-big record albums, stood against the wall beside the gate, slowly massaged the rubberlike surface of the wall. Nothing. Nothing.

The button.

He pressed it, grabbed up the record albums, stood in front of the gate as it incredibly slowly creaked its noisy protesting way open.

A brown-uniformed man carrying a gun appeared. Jason said, "I had to go back to the quibble for something."

"Perfectly all right, sir," the man in the brown uniform said. "I saw you leave and I knew you'd be back."

"Is she insane?" Jason asked him.

"I'm not in a position to know, sir," the man in the brown uniform said, and he backed away, touching his visored cap.

The front door of the house hung open as he had left it. He scrambled through, descended brick steps, found himself once more in the radically irregular living room with its million-mile-high ceiling. "Alys!" he said. Was she in the room? He carefully looked in all directions; as he had done when searching for the button he phased his way through every visible inch of the room. The bar at the far end with the handsome walnut drug cabinet . . . couch, chairs. Pictures on the walls. A face in one of the pictures jeered at him but he did not care; it could not leave the wall. The quad phonograph . . .

His records. Play them.

He lifted at the lid of the phonograph but it wouldn't open. Why? he asked. Locked? No, it slid out. He slid it out, with a terrible noise, as if he had destroyed it. Tone arm. Spindle. He got one of his records out of its sleeve and placed in on the spindle. I can work these things, he said, and turned on the amplifiers, setting the mode to *phono*. Switch that activated the changer. He twisted it. The tone arm lifted; the turntable began to spin, agonizingly slowly. What was the matter with it? Wrong speed? No; he checked. Thirty-three and a third. The mechanism of the spindle heaved and the record dropped.

Loud noise of the needle hitting the lead-in groove. Crackles of dust, clicks. Typical of old quad records. Easily misused and damaged; all you had to do was breathe on them.

Background hiss. More crackles.

No music.

Lifting the tone arm, he set it farther in. Great roaring crash as the stylus struck the surface; he winced, sought the volume control to turn it down. Still no music. No sound of himself singing.

The strength the mescaline had over him began now to waver; he felt coldly, keenly sober. The other record. Swiftly he got it from its jacket and sleeve, placed it on the spindle, rejected the first record.

Sound of the needle touching plastic surface. Background hiss and the inevitable crackles and clicks. Still no music.

The records were blank.

PART THREE

Never may my woes be relieved,
Since pity is fled;
And tears and sighs and groans my weary days
Of all joys have deprived.

21

"Alys!" Jason Taverner called loudly. No answer. Is it the mescaline? he asked himself. He made his way clumsily from the phonograph toward the door through which Alys had gone. A long hallway, deep-pile wool carpet. At the far end stairs with a black iron railing, leading up to the second floor.

He strode as quickly as possible up the hall, to the stairs, and then, step by step, up the stairs.

The second floor. A foyer, with an antique Hepplewhite table off to one side, piled high with *Box* magazines. That, weirdly, caught his attention; who, Felix or Alys, or both, read a low-class mass-circulation pornographic magazine like *Box*? He passed on then, still—because of the mescaline, certainly—seeing small details. The bathroom; that was where he would find her.

"Alys," he said grimly; perspiration trickled from his forehead down his nose and cheeks; his armpits had become steamy and damp with the emotions cascading through his body. "God damn it," he said, speaking to her although he could not see her. "There's no music on those records, no me. They're fakes. Aren't they?" Or is it the mescaline? he asked himself. "I've got to know!" he said. "Make them play if they're okay. Is the phonograph broken, is that it? Needle point or stylus or whatever you call them broken off?" It happens, he thought. Maybe it's riding on the tops of the grooves.

A half-open door; he pushed it wide. A bedroom, with the bed unmade. And on the floor a mattress with a sleeping bag thrown onto it. A little pile of men's supplies: shaving cream, deodorant, razor, aftershave, comb . . . a guest, he thought, here before but now gone.

"Is anybody here?" he yelled.

Silence.

Ahead he saw the bathroom; past the partially opened door he caught sight of an amazingly old tub on painted lion's legs. An antique, he thought, even down to their bathtub. He loped haltingly down the hall, past other doors, to the bathroom; reaching it, he pushed the door aside.

And saw, on the floor, a skeleton.

It wore black shiny pants, leather shirt, chain belt with wrought-iron buckle. The foot bones had cast aside the high-heeled shoes. A few tufts of hair clung to the skull, but outside of that, there remained nothing: the eyes had gone, all the flesh had gone. And the skeleton itself had become yellow.

"God," Jason said, swaying; he felt his vision fail and his sense of gravity shift: his middle ear fluctuated in its pressures so that the room caromed around him, silently in perpetual ball motion. Like a pourout of Ferris wheel at a child's circus.

He shut his eyes, hung on to the wall, then, finally, looked again.

She has died, he thought. But when? A hundred thousand years ago? A few minutes ago?

Why has she died? he asked himself.

Is it the mescaline? That I took? *Is this real?*

It's real.

Bending, he touched the leather fringed shirt. The leather felt soft and smooth; it hadn't decayed. Time hadn't touched her clothing; that meant something but he did not comprehend what. Just her, he thought. Everything else in this house is the same as it was. So it can't be the mescaline affecting me. But I can't be sure, he thought.

Downstairs. Get out of here.

He loped erratically back down the hall, still in the process of scrambling to his feet, so that he ran bent over like an ape of some unusual kind. He seized the black iron railing, descended two, three steps at once, stumbled and fell, caught himself and hauled himself back up to a standing position. In his chest his heart labored, and his lungs, overtaxed, inflated and emptied like a bellows.

In an instant he had sped across the living room to the front door—then, for reasons obscure to him but somehow important, he snatched up the two records from the phonograph, stuffed them into their jackets, carried them with him through the front door of the house, out into the bright warm sun of midday.

"Leaving, sir?" the brown-uniformed private cop asked, noticing him standing there, his chest heaving.

"I'm sick," Jason said.

"Sorry to hear that, sir. Can I get you anything?"

"The keys to the quibble."

"Miss Buckman usually leaves the keys in the ignition," the cop said.

"I looked," Jason said, panting.

The cop said, "I'll go ask Miss Buckman for you."

"No," Jason said, and then thought, But if it's the mescaline it's okay. Isn't it?

" 'No'?" the cop said, and all at once his expression changed. "Stay where you are," he said. "Don't head toward that quibble." Spinning, he dashed into the house.

Jason sprinted across the grass, to the asphalt square and the parked quibble. The keys; were they in the ignition? No. Her purse. He seized it and dumped everything out on the seats. A thousand objects, but no keys. And then, crushing him, a hoarse scream.

At the front gate of the house the cop appeared, his face distorted. He stood sideways, reflexively, lifted his gun, held it with both hands, and fired at Jason. But the gun wavered; the cop was trembling too badly.

Crawling out of the far side of the quibble, Jason lurched

across the thick moist lawn, toward the nearby oak trees.

Again the cop fired. Again he missed. Jason heard him curse; the cop started to run toward him, trying to get closer to him; then all at once the cop spun and sped back into the house.

Jason reached the trees. He crashed through dry underbrush, limbs of bushes snapping as he forced his way through. A high adobe wall . . . and what had Alys said? Broken bottles cemented on top? He crawled along the base of the wall, fighting the thick underbrush, then abruptly found himself facing a broken wooden door; it hung partially open, and beyond it he saw other houses and a street.

It was not the mescaline, he realized. The cop saw it, too. Her lying there. The ancient skeleton. As if dead all these years.

On the far side of the street a woman, with an armload of packages, was unlocking the door of her flipflap.

Jason made his way across the street, forcing his mind to work, forcing the dregs of the mescaline away. "Miss," he said, gasping.

Startled, the woman looked up. Young, heavy-set, but with beautiful auburn hair. "Yes?" she said nervously, surveying him.

"I've been given a toxic dose of some drug," Jason said, trying to keep his voice steady. "Will you drive me to a hospital?"

Silence. She continued to stare at him wide-eyed; he said nothing—he merely stood panting, waiting. Yes or no; it had to be one or the other.

The heavy-set girl with the auburn hair said, "I—I'm not a very good driver. I just got my license last week."

"I'll drive," Jason said.

"But I won't come along." She backed away, clutching her armload of badly-wrapped brown-paper parcels. Probably she had been on her way to the post office.

"Can I have the keys?" he said; he extended his hand. Waited.

"But you might pass out and then my flipflap—"

"Come with me then," he said.

She handed him the keys and crept into the rear seat of the flipflap. Jason, his heart pulsing with relief, got in behind the wheel, stuck the key into the ignition, turned the motor on, and, in a moment, sent the flipflap flipflapping up into the sky, at its maximum speed of forty knots an hour. It was, he noted for some odd reason, a very inexpensive model flipflap: a Ford Greyhound. An economy flipflap. And not new.

"Are you in great pain?" the girl asked anxiously; her face, in his rear-view mirror, still showed nervousness, even panic. The situation was too much for her.

"No," he said.

"What was the drug?"

"They didn't say." The mescaline had virtually worn off, now; thank God his six physiology had the strength to combat it: he did not relish the idea of piloting a slow-moving flipflap through the midday Los Angeles traffic while on a hit of mescaline. And, he thought savagely, a big hit. Despite what she said.

She. Alys. Why are the records blank? he asked silently. The records—where were they? He peered about, stricken. Oh. On the seat beside him; automatically he had thrust them in as he himself got into the flipflap. So they're okay. I can try to play them again on another phonograph.

"The nearest hospital," the heavy-set girl said, "is St. Martin's at Thirty-fifth and Webster. It's small, but I went there to have a wart removed from my hand, and they seemed very conscientious and kind."

"We'll go there," Jason said.

"Are you feeling worse or better?"

"Better," he said.

"Did you come from the Buckman's house?"

"Yes." He nodded.

The girl said, "Is it true that they're brother and sister, Mr. and Mrs. Buckman? I mean—"

"Twins," he said.

"I understand that," the girl said. "But you know, it's

strange; when you see them together it's as if they're husband and wife. They kiss and hold hands, and he's very deferential to her and then sometimes they have terrible fights.'' The girl remained silent a moment and then leaning forward said, "My name is Mary Anne Dominic. What is your name?''

"Jason Taverner," he informed her. Not that it meant anything. After all. After what had seemed for a moment—but then the girl's voice broke into his thoughts.

"I'm a potter," she said shyly. "These are pots I'm taking to the post office to mail to stores in northern California, especially to Gump's in San Francisco and Frazer's in Berkeley.''

"Do you do good work?'' he asked; almost all of his mind, his faculties, remained fixed in time, fixed at the instant he had opened the bathroom door and seen her—it—on the floor. He barely heard Miss Dominic's voice.

"I try to. But you never know. Anyhow, they sell.''

"You have strong hands," he said, for want of anything better to say; his words still emerged semireflexively, as if he were uttering them with only a fragment of his mind.

"Thank you," Mary Anne Dominic said.

Silence.

"You passed the hospital," Mary Anne Dominic said. "It's back a little way and to the left.'' Her original anxiety had now crawled back into her voice. "Are you really going there or is this some—''

"Don't be scared," he said, and this time he paid attention to what he said; he used all his ability to make his tone kind and reassuring. "I'm not an escaped student. Nor am I an escapee from a forced-labor camp.'' He turned his head and looked directly into her face. "But I am in trouble.''

"Then you didn't take a toxic drug.'' Her voice wavered. It was as if that which she had most feared throughout her whole life had finally overtaken her.

"I'll land us," he said. "To make you feel safer. This is far enough for me. Please don't freak; I won't hurt you.'' But the girl sat rigid and stricken, waiting for—well, neither of them knew.

At an intersection, a busy one, he landed at the curb, quickly opened the door. But then, on impulse, he remained within the flipflap for a moment, turned still in the girl's direction.

"Please get out," she quavered. "I don't mean to be impolite, but I'm really scared. You hear about hunger-crazed students who somehow get through the barricades around the campuses—"

"Listen to me," he said sharply, breaking into her flow of speech.

"Okay." She composed herself, hands on her lapful of packages, dutifully—and fearfully—waiting.

Jason said, "You shouldn't be frightened so easily. Or life is going to be too much for you."

"I see." She nodded humbly, listening, paying attention as if she were at a college classroom lecture.

"Are you always afraid of strangers?" he asked her.

"I guess so." Again she nodded; this time she hung her head as if he had admonished her. And in a fashion he had.

"Fear," Jason said, "can make you do more wrong than hate or jealousy. If you're afraid you don't commit yourself to life completely; fear makes you always, always hold something back."

"I think I know what you mean," Mary Anne Dominic said. "One day about a year ago there was this dreadful pounding on my door, and I ran into the bathroom and locked myself in and pretended I wasn't there, because I thought somebody was trying to break in . . . and then later I found out that the woman upstairs had got her hand caught in the drain of her sink—she has one of those Disposall things—and a knife had gotten down into it and she reached her hand down to get it and got caught. And it was her little boy at the door—"

"So you do understand what I mean," Jason interrupted.

"Yes. I wish I wasn't that way. I really do. But I still am."

Jason said, "How old are you?"

"Thirty-two."

That surprised him; she seemed much younger. Evidently

she had not ever really grown up. He felt sympathy for her; how hard it must have been for her to let him take over her flipflap. And her fears had been correct in one respect: he had not been asking for help for the reason he claimed.

He said to her, "You're a very nice person."

"Thank you," she said dutifully. Humbly.

"See that coffee shop over there?" he said, pointing to a modern, well-patronized cafe. "Let's go over there. I want to talk to you." I have to talk to someone, anyone, he thought, or six or not I am going to lose my mind.

"But," she protested anxiously, "I have to get my packages into the post office before two so they'll get the midafternoon pickup for the Bay Area."

"We'll do that first, then," he said. Reaching for the ignition switch, he pulled out the key, handed it back to Mary Anne Dominic. "You drive. As slowly as you want."

"Mr.—Taverner," she said. "I just want to be let alone."

"No," he said. "You shouldn't be alone. It's killing you; it's undermining you. All the time, every day, you should be somewhere with people."

Silence. And then Mary Anne said, "The post office is at Forty-ninth and Fulton. Could you drive? I'm sort of nervous."

It seemed to him a great moral victory; he felt pleased.

He took back the key, and shortly, they were on their way to Forty-ninth and Fulton.

22

Later, they sat in a booth at a coffee shop, a clean and attractive place with young waitresses and a reasonably loose patronage. The jukebox drummed out Louis Panda's "Memory of Your Nose." Jason ordered coffee only; Miss Dominic had a fruit salad and iced tea.

"What are those two records you're carrying?" she asked.

He handed them to her.

"Why, they're by you. If you're Jason Taverner. Are you?"

"Yes." He was certain of that, at least.

"I don't think I've ever heard you sing," Mary Anne Dominic said. "I'd love to, but I don't usually like pop music; I like those great old-time folk singers out of the past, like Buffy St. Marie. There's nobody now who could sing like Buffy."

"I agree," he said somberly, his mind still returning to the house, the bathroom, the escape from the frantic brown-uniformed private cop. *It wasn't the mescaline,* he told himself once again. Because the cop saw it, too.

Or saw *something*.

"Maybe he didn't see what I saw," he said aloud. "Maybe he just saw her lying there. Maybe she fell. Maybe—" He thought, Maybe I should go back.

"Who didn't see what?" Mary Anne Dominic asked, and then flushed bright scarlet. "I didn't mean to poke into your life; you said you're in trouble and I can see you have something weighty and heavy on your mind that's obsessing you."

"I have to be sure," he said, "what actually happened. Everything is there in that house." And on these records, he thought.

Alys Buckman knew about my TV program. She knew about my records. She knew which one was the big hit; she owned it. But—

There had been no music on the records. Broken stylus, hell—some kind of sound, distorted perhaps, should have come out. He had handled records too long and phonographs too long not to know that.

"You're a moody person," Mary Anne Dominic said. From her small cloth purse she had brought a pair of glasses; she now laboriously read the bio material on the back of the record jackets.

"What's happened to me," Jason said briefly, "has made me moody."

"It says here that you have a TV program."

"Right." He nodded. "At nine on Tuesday night. On NBC."

"Then you're really famous. I'm sitting here talking to a famous person that I ought to know about. How does it make you feel—I mean, my not recognizing who you are when you told me your name?"

He shrugged. And felt ironically amused.

"Would the jukebox have any songs by you?" She pointed to the multicolored Babylonian Gothic structure in the far corner.

"Maybe," he said. It was a good question.

"I'll go look." Miss Dominic fished a half quinque from her pocket, slid from the booth, and crossed the coffee shop to stare down at the titles and artists of the jukebox's listing.

When she gets back she is going to be less impressed by me, Jason mused. He knew the effect of one ellipsis: unless he manifested himself everywhere, from every radio and phonograph, jukebox and sheet-music shop, TV screen, in the universe, the magic spell collapsed.

She returned smiling. " 'Nowhere Nuthin' Fuck-up,' " she said, reseating herself. He saw then that the half quinque was gone. "It should play next."

Instantly he was on his feet and across the coffee shop to the jukebox.

She was right. Selection B4. His most recent hit, "Nowhere Nuthin' Fuck-up," a sentimental number. And already the mechanism of the jukebox had begun to process the disc.

A moment later his voice, mellowed by quad sound points and echo chambers, filled the coffee shop.

Dazed, he returned to the booth.

"You sound superwonderful," Mary Anne said, politely, perhaps, given her taste, when the disc had ended.

"Thanks." It had been him, all right. The grooves on *that* record hadn't been blank.

"You're really far out," Mary Anne said enthusiastically, all smiles and twinkly glasses.

Jason said simply, "I've been at it a long time." She had sounded as if she meant it.

"Do you feel bad that I hadn't heard of you?"

"No." He shook his head, still dazed. Certainly she was not alone in that, as the events of the past two days—two days? had it only been that?—had shown.

"Can—I order something more?" Mary Anne asked. She hesitated. "I spent all my money on stamps; I—"

"I'm picking up the tab," Jason said.

"How do you think the strawberry cheesecake would be?"

"Outstanding," he said, momentarily amused by her. The woman's earnestness, her anxieties . . . does she have any boy friends of any kind? he wondered. Probably not . . . she lived in a world of pots, clay, brown wrapping paper, troubles with her little old Ford Greyhound, and, in the background, the stereo-only voices of the old-time greats: Judy Collins and Joan Baez.

"Ever listened to Heather Hart?" he asked. Gently.

Her forehead wrinkled. "I—don't recall for sure. Is she a folk singer or—" Her voice trailed off; she looked sad. As if she sensed that she was failing to be what she ought to be, failing to know what every reasonable person knew. He felt sympathy for her.

"Ballads," Jason said. "Like what I do."

"Could we hear your record again?"

He obligingly returned to the jukebox, scheduled it for replay.

This time Mary Anne did not seem to enjoy it.

"What's the matter?" he asked.

"Oh," she said, "I always tell myself I'm creative; I make pots and like that. But I don't know if they're actually any good. I don't know how to tell. People say to me—"

"People tell you everything. From that you're worthless to priceless. The worst and the best. You're always reaching somebody here"—he tapped the salt shaker—"and not reaching somebody there." He tapped her fruit-salad bowl.

"But there has to be some way—"

"There are experts. You can listen to them, to their theories. They always have theories. They write long articles and discuss your stuff back to the first record you cut nineteen years ago. They compare recordings you don't even remember having cut. And the TV critics—"

"But to be noticed." Again, briefly, her eyes shone.

"I'm sorry," he said, rising to his feet once more. He could wait no longer. "I have to make a phone call. Hopefully I'll be right back. If I'm not"—he put his hand on her shoulder, on her knitted white sweater, which she had probably made herself—"it's been nice meeting you."

Puzzled, she watched him in her wan, obedient way as he elbowed a path to the back of the crowded coffee shop, to the phone booth.

Shut up inside the phone booth, he read off the number of the Los Angeles Police Academy from the emergency listings and, after dropping in his coin, dialed.

"I'd like to speak to Police General Felix Buckman," he said, and, without surprise, heard his voice shake. Psychologically I've had it, he realized. Everything that's happened . . . up to the record on the jukebox—it's too

goddamn much for me. I am just plain scared. And disoriented. So maybe, he thought, the mescaline has not worn completely off after all. But I did drive the little flipflap okay; that indicates something. Fucking dope, he thought. You can always tell when it hits you but never when it unhits, if it ever does. It impairs you forever or you think so; you can't be sure. Maybe it never leaves. And they say, Hey, man, your brain's burned out, and you say, Maybe so. You can't be sure and you can't not be sure. And all because you dropped a cap or one cap too many that somebody said, Hey this'll get you off.

"This is Miss Beason," a female voice sounded in his ear. "Mr. Buckman's assistant. May I help you?"

"Peggy Beason," he said. He took a deep, unsteady breath and said, "This is Jason Taverner."

"Oh yes, Mr. Taverner. What did you want? Did you leave anything behind?"

Jason said, "I want to talk to General Buckman."

"I'm afraid Mr. Buckman—"

"It has to do with Alys," Jason said.

Silence. And then: "Just a moment please, Mr. Taverner," Peggy Beason said. "I'll ring Mr. Buckman and see if he can free himself a moment."

Clicks. Pause. More silence. Then a line opened.

"Mr. Taverner?" It was not General Buckman. "This is Herbert Maime, Mr. Buckman's chief of staff. I understand you told Miss Beason that it has to do with Mr. Buckman's sister, Miss Alys Buckman. Frankly I'd like to ask just what are the circumstances under which you happen to know Miss—"

Jason hung up the phone. And walked sightlessly back to the booth, where Mary Anne Dominic sat eating her strawberry cheesecake.

"You did come back after all," she said cheerfully.

"How," he said, "is the cheesecake?"

"A little too rich." She added, "But good."

He grimly reseated himself. Well, he had done his best to get through to Felix Buckman. To tell him about Alys. But—

what would he have been able to say, after all? The futility of everything, the perpetual impotence of his efforts and intentions . . . weakened even more, he thought, by what she gave me, that cap of mescaline.

If it had been mescaline.

That presented a new possibility. He had no proof, no evidence, that Alys had actually given him mescaline. It could have been anything. What, for example, was mescaline doing coming from Switzerland? That made no sense; that sounded synthetic, not organic: a product of a lab. Maybe a new multi-ingredient cultish drug. Or something stolen from police labs.

The record of "Nowhere Nuthin' Fuck-up." Suppose the drug had made him hear it. And see the listing on the jukebox. But Mary Anne Dominic had heard it, too; in fact she had discovered it.

But the two blank records. What about them?

As he sat pondering, an adolescent boy in a T-shirt and jeans bent over him and mumbled, "Hey, you're Jason Taverner, aren't you?" He extended a ballpoint pen and piece of paper. "Could I have your autograph, sir?"

Behind him a pretty little red-haired teenybopper, bra-less, in white shorts, smiled excitedly and said, "We always catch you on Tuesday night. You're fantastic. And you look in real life, you look just like on the screen, except that in real life you're more, you know, tanned." Her friendly nipples jiggled.

Numbly, by habit, he signed his name. "Thanks, guys," he said to them; there were four of them in all now.

Chattering to themselves, the four kids departed. Now people in nearby booths were watching Jason and muttering interestedly to one another. As always, he said to himself. This is how it's been up to the other day. *My reality is leaking back.* He felt uncontrollably, wildly elated. This was what he knew; this was his life-style. He had lost it for a short time but now—finally, he thought, I'm starting to get it back!

Heather Hart. He thought, I can call her now. And get through to her. She won't think I'm a twerp fan.

Maybe I only exist so long as I take the drug. That drug, whatever it is, that Alys gave me.

Then my career, he thought, the whole twenty years, is nothing but a retroactive hallucination created by the drug.

What happened, Jason Taverner thought, *is that the drug wore off.* She—somebody—stopped giving it to me and I woke up to reality, there in that shabby, broken-down hotel room with the cracked mirror and the bug-infested mattress. And I stayed that way until now, until Alys gave me another dose.

He thought, No wonder she knew about me, about my Tuesday-night TV show. Through her drug she created it. And those two record albums—props which she kept to reinforce the hallucination.

Jesus Christ, he thought, is that it?

But, he thought, the money I woke up with in the hotel room, this whole wad of it. Reflexively he tapped his chest, felt its thick existence, still there. If in real life I doled out my days in fleabag hotels in the Watts area, where did I get that money?

And I would have been listed in the police files, and in all the other data banks throughout the world. I wouldn't be listed as a famous entertainer, but I'd be there as a shabby bum who never amounted to anything, whose only highs came from a pill bottle. For God knows how long. I may have been taking the drug for years.

Alys, he remembered, said I had been to the house before.

And apparently, he decided, it's true. I had. To get my doses of the drug.

Maybe I am only one of a great number of people leading synthetic lives of popularity, money, power, by means of a capsule. While living actually, meanwhile, in bug-infested, ratty old hotel rooms. On skid row. Derelicts, nobodies. Amounting to zero. But, meanwhile, dreaming.

"You certainly are deep in a brown study," Mary Anne said. She had finished her cheesecake; she looked satiated, now. And happy.

"Listen," he said hoarsely. "Is my record really in that jukebox?"

Her eyes widened as she tried to understand. "How do you mean? We listened to it. And the little thingy, where it tells the selections, that's there. Jukeboxes never made mistakes."

He fished out a coin. "Go play it again. Set it up for three plays."

Obediently, she surged from her seat, into the aisle, and bustled over to the jukebox, her lovely long hair bouncing against her ample shoulders. Presently he heard it, heard his big hit song. And the people in the booths and at the counter were nodding and smiling at him in recognition; they knew it was he who was singing. His audience.

When the song ended there was a smattering of applause from the patrons of the coffee shop. Grinning reflexively, professionally in return he acknowledged their recognition and approval.

"It's there," he said, as the song replayed. Savagely, he clenched his fist, struck the plastic table separating him from Mary Anne Dominic. "God damn it, *it's there.*"

With some odd twist of deep, intuitive, female desire to help him Mary Anne said, "And I'm here, too."

"I'm not in a run-down hotel room, lying on a cot dreaming," he said huskily.

"No, you're not." Her tone was tender, anxious. She clearly felt concern for him. For his alarm.

"Again I'm real," he said. "But if it could happen once, for two days—" To come and go like this, to fade in and out—

"Maybe we should leave," Mary Anne said apprehensively.

That cleared his mind. "Sorry," he said, wanting to reassure her.

"I just mean that people are listening."

"It won't hurt them," he said. "Let them listen; let them see how you carry your worries and troubles with you even when you're a world-famous star." He rose to his feet, however. "Where do you want to go?" he asked her. "To your apartment?" It meant doubling back, but he felt optimistic enough to take the risk.

"My apartment?" she faltered.

"Do you think I'd hurt you?" he said.

For an interval she sat nervously pondering. "N-no," she said at last.

"Do you have a phonograph?" he asked. "At your apartment?"

"Yes, but not a very good one; it's just stereo. But it works."

"Okay," he said, herding her up the aisle toward the cash register. "Let's go."

23

Mary Anne Dominic had decorated the walls and ceiling of her apartment herself. Beautiful, strong, rich colors; he gazed about, impressed. And the few art objects in the living room had a powerful beauty about them. Ceramic pieces. He picked up one lovely blue-glaze vase, studied it.

"I made that," Mary Anne said.

"This vase," he said, "will be featured on my show."

Mary Anne gazed at him in wonder.

"I'm going to have this vase with me very soon. In fact"— he could visualize it—"a big production number in which I emerge from the vase singing, like the magic spirit of the vase." He held the blue vase up high, in one hand, revolving it. " 'Nowhere Nuthin' Fuck-up,' " he said. "And your career is launched."

"Maybe you should hold it with both hands," Mary Anne said uneasily.

" 'Nowhere Nuthin' Fuck-up,' the song that brought us more recognition—" The vase slid from between his fingers and dropped to the floor. Mary Anne leaped forward, but too late. The vase broke into three pieces and lay there beside Jason's shoe, rough unglazed edges pale and irregular and without artistic merit.

A long silence passed.

"I think I can fix it," Mary Anne said.

He could think of nothing to say.

"The most embarrassing thing that ever happened to me," Mary Anne said, "was one time with my mother. You see, my mother had a progressive kidney ailment called Bright's disease; she was always going to the hospital for it when I was a kid growing up and she was forever working it into the conversation that she was going to die from it and wouldn't I be sorry then—as if it was my fault—and I really believed her, that she would die one day. But then I grew up and moved away from home and she still didn't die. And I sort of forgot about her; I had my own life and things to do. So naturally I forgot about her damn kidney condition. And then one day she came to visit, not here but at the apartment I had before this, and she really bugged me, sitting around narrating all her aches and complaints on and on . . . I finally said, 'I've got to go shopping for dinner,' and I split for the store. My mother limped along with me and on the way she laid the news on me that now both her kidneys were so far gone that they would have to be removed and she would be going in for that and so forth and they'd try to install an artificial kidney but it probably wouldn't work. So she was telling me this, how it really had come now; she really was going to die finally, like she'd always said . . . and all of a sudden I looked up and realized I was in the supermarket, at the meat counter, and this real nice clerk that I liked was coming over to say hello, and he said, 'What would you like today, miss?' and I said, 'I'd like a kidney pie for dinner.' It was embarrassing. 'A great big kidney pie,' I said, 'all flaky and tender and steaming and full of nice juices.' 'To serve how many?' he asked. My mother sort of kept staring at me with this creepy look. I really didn't know how to get out of it once I was in it. Finally I did buy a kidney pie, but I had to go to the delicatessen section; it was in a sealed can, from England. I paid I think four dollars for it. It tasted very good."

"I'll pay for the vase," Jason said. "How much do you want for it?"

Hesitating, she said, "Well, there's the wholesale price I

get when I sell to stores. But I'd have to charge you retail prices because you don't have a wholesale number, so—"

He got out his money. "Retail," he said.

"Twenty dollars."

"I can work you in another way," he said. "All we need is an angle. How about this—we can show the audience a priceless vase from antiquity, say from fifth-century China, and a museum expert will step out, in uniform, and certify its authenticity. And then you'll have your wheel there— you'll make a vase before the audience's very eyes, and we'll show them that your vase is better."

"It wouldn't be. Early Chinese pottery is—"

"We'll show them; we'll make them believe. I know my audience. Those thirty million people take their clue from my reaction; there'll be a pan up on my face, showing my response."

In a low voice Mary Anne said, "I can't go up there on stage with those TV cameras looking at me; I'm so—overweight. People would laugh."

"The exposure you'll get. The sales. Museums and stores will know your name, your stuff, buyers will be coming out of the woodwork."

Mary Anne said quietly, "Leave me alone, please. I'm very happy. I know I'm a good potter; I know that the stores, the good ones, like what I do. Does everything have to be on a great scale with a cast of thousands? Can't I lead my little life the way I want to?" She glared at him, her voice almost inaudible. "I don't see what all your exposure and fame have done for you— back at the coffee shop you said to me, 'Is my record really on that jukebox?' You were afraid it wasn't; you were a lot more insecure than I'll ever be."

"Speaking of that," Jason said, "I'd like to play these two records on your phonograph. Before I go."

"You'd better let me put them on," Mary Anne said. "My set is tricky." She took the two albums, and the twenty dollars; Jason stood where he was, by the broken pieces of vase.

As he waited there he heard familiar music. His biggest-selling album. The grooves of the record were no longer blank.

"You can keep the records," he said. "I'll be going." Now, he thought, I have no further need for them; I'll probably be able to buy them in any record shop.

"It's not the sort of music I like . . . I don't think I'd really be playing them all that much."

"I'll leave them anyhow," he said.

Mary Anne said, "For your twenty dollars I'm giving you another vase. Just a moment." She hurried off; he heard the noises of paper and labored activity. Presently the girl reappeared, holding another blue-glaze vase. This one had more to it; the intuition came to him that she considered it one of her best.

"Thank you," he said.

"I'll wrap it and box it, so it won't get broken like the other." She did so, working with feverish intensity mixed with care. "I found it very thrilling," she said as she presented him with the tied-up box, "to have had lunch with a famous man. I'm extremely glad I met you and I'll remember it a long time. And I hope your troubles work out; I mean, I hope what's worrying you turns out okay."

Jason Taverner reached into his inside coat pocket, brought forth his little initialed leather card case. From it he extracted one of his embossed multicolored business cards and passed it to Mary Anne. "Call me at the studio any time. If you change your mind and want to appear on the program. I'm sure we can fit you in. By the way—this has my private number."

"Goodbye," she said, opening the front door for him.

"Goodbye." He paused, wanting to say more. But there remained nothing to say. "We failed," he said, then. "We absolutely failed. Both of us."

She blinked. "How do you mean?"

"Take care of yourself," he said, and walked out of the apartment, onto the midafternoon sidewalk. Into the hot sun of full day.

24

Kneeling over Alys Buckman's body, the police coroner said, "I can only tell you at this point that she died from an overdose of a toxic or semitoxic drug. It'll be twenty-four hours before we can tell what specifically the drug was."

Felix Buckman said, "It had to happen. Eventually." He did not, surprisingly, feel very much. In fact, in a way, on some level, he experienced deep relief to have learned from Tim Chancer, their guard, that Alys had been found dead in their second-floor bathroom.

"I thought that guy Taverner did something to her," Chancer repeated, over and over again, trying to get Buckman's attention. "He was acting funny; I knew something was wrong. I took a couple of shots at him but he got away. I guess maybe it's a good thing I didn't get him, if he wasn't responsible. Or maybe he felt guilty because he got her to take the drug; could that be?"

"No one had to make Alys take a drug," Buckman said bitingly. He walked from the bathroom, out into the hall. Two gray-clad pols stood at attention, waiting to be told what to do. "She didn't need Taverner or anyone else to administer it to her." He felt, now, physically sick. God, he thought. What will the effect be on Barney? That was the bad part. For reasons obscure to him, their child adored his mother. Well, Buckman thought, there's no accounting for other people's tastes.

And yet he, himself—he loved her. She had a powerful quality, he reflected. I'll miss it. She filled up a good deal of space.

And a good part of his life. For better or worse.

White-face, Herb Maime climbed the stairs two steps at a time, peering up at Buckman. "I got here as quickly as I could," Herb said, holding out his hand to Buckman. They shook. "What was it?" Herb said. He lowered his voice. "An overdose of something?"

"Apparently," Buckman said.

"I got a call earlier today from Taverner," Herb said. "He wanted to talk to you; he said it had something to do with Alys."

Buckman said, "He wanted to tell me about Alys's death. He was here at the time."

"Why? How did he know her?"

"I don't know," Buckman said. But at the moment it did not seem to matter to him much. He saw no reason to blame Taverner . . . given Alys's temperament and habits, she had probably instigated his coming here. Perhaps when Taverner left the academy building she had nailed him, carted him off in her souped-up quibble. To the house. After all, Taverner was a six. And Alys liked sixes. Male and female both.

Especially female.

"They may have been having an orgy," Buckman said.

"Just the two of them? Or do you mean other people were here?"

"Nobody else was here. Chancer would have known. They may have had a phone orgy; that's what I meant. She's come so damn close so many times to burning out her brain with those goddamn phone orgies—I wish we could track down the new sponsors, the ones that took over when we shot Bill and Carol and Fred and Jill. Those degenerates." His hand shaking, he lit a cigarette, smoking rapidly. "That reminds me of something Alys said one time, unintentionally funny.

She was talking about having an orgy and she wondered if she should send out formal invitations. 'I'd better,' she said, 'or everyone won't come at the same time.' " He laughed.

"You've told me that before," Herb said.

"She's really dead. Cold, stiff dead." Buckman stubbed out his cigarette in a nearby ashtray. "My wife," he said to Herb Maime. "She was my wife."

Herb, with a shake of his head, indicated the two gray-wrapped pols standing at attention.

"So what?" Buckman said. "Haven't they read the libretto of *Die Walküre*?" Tremblingly, he lit another cigarette. "Sigmund and Siglinde. 'Schwester und Braut.' Sister and bride. And the hell with Hunding." He dropped the cigarette to the carpet; standing there, he watched it smolder, starting the wool on fire. And then, with his boot heel, he ground it out.

"You should sit down," Herb said. "Or lie down. You look terrible."

"It's a terrible thing," Buckman said. "It genuinely is. I disliked a lot about her, but, Christ—how vital she was. She always tried anything new. That's what killed her, probably some new drug she and her fellow witch friends brewed up in their miserable basement labs. Something with film developer in it or Drano or a lot worse."

"I think we should talk to Taverner," Herb said.

"Okay. Pull him in. He's got that microtrans on him, doesn't he?"

"Evidently not. All the insects we placed on him as he was leaving the academy building ceased to function. Except, perhaps, for the seed warhead. But we have no reason to activate it."

Buckman said, "Taverner is a smart bastard. Or else he got help. From someone or ones he's working with. Don't bother to try to detonate the seed warhead; it's undoubtedly been cut out of his pelt by some obliging colleague." Or by Alys, he conjectured. My helpful sister. Assisting the police at every turn. Nice.

"You'd better leave the house for a while," Herb said. "While the coroner's staff does its procedural action."

"Drive me back to the academy," Buckman said. "I don't think I can drive; I'm shaking too bad." He felt something on his face; putting up his hand, he found that his chin was wet. "What's this on me?" he said, amazed.

"You're crying," Herb said.

"Drive me back to the academy and I'll wind up what I have to do there before I can turn it over to you," Buckman said. "And then I want to come back here." Maybe Taverner did give her something, he said to himself. But Taverner is nothing. She did it. And yet . . .

"Come on," Herb said, taking him by the arm and leading him to the staircase.

Buckman, as he descended, said, "Would you ever in Christ's world have thought you'd see me cry?"

"No," Herb said. "But it's understandable. You and she were very close."

"You could say that," Buckman said, with sudden savage anger. "God damn her," he said. "I told her she'd eventually do it. Some of her friends brewed it up for her and made her the guinea pig."

"Don't try to do much at the office," Herb said as they passed through the living room and outside, where their two quibbles sat parked. "Just wind it up enough for me to take over."

"That's what I said," Buckman said. "Nobody listens to me, God damn it."

Herb thumped him on the back and said nothing; the two men walked across the lawn in silence.

On the ride back to the academy building, Herb, at the wheel of the quibble, said, "There're cigarettes in my coat." It was the first thing either of them had said since boarding the quibble.

"Thanks," Buckman said. He had smoked up his own week's ration.

"I want to discuss one matter with you," Herb said. "I wish it could wait but it can't."

"Not even until we get to the office?"

Herb said, "There may be other policy-level personnel there when we get back. Or just plain other people—my staff, for instance."

"Nothing I have to say is—"

"Listen," Herb said. "About Alys. About your marriage to her. Your sister."

"My incest," Buckman said harshly.

"Some of the marshals may know about it. Alys told too many people. You know how she was about it."

"Proud of it," Buckman said, lighting a cigarette with difficulty. He still could not get over the fact that he had found himself crying. I really must have loved her, he said to himself. And all I seemed to feel was fear and dislike. And the sexual drive. How many times, he thought, we discussed it before we did it. All the years. "I never told anybody but you," he said to Herb.

"But Alys."

"Okay. Well, then possibly some of the marshals know, and if he cares, the Director."

"The marshals who are opposed to you," Herb said, "and who know about the"—he hesitated—"the incest—will say that she committed suicide. Out of shame. You can expect that. And they will leak it to the media."

"You think so?" Buckman said. Yes, he thought, it would make quite a story. Police general's marriage to his sister, blessed with a secret child hidden away in Florida. The general and his sister posing as husband and wife in Florida, while they're with the boy. And the boy: product of what must be a deranged genetic heritage.

"What I want you to see," Herb said, "and I'm afraid you're going to have to take a look at it now, which isn't an ideal time with Alys just recently dead and—"

"It's our coroner," Buckman said. "We own him, there at the academy." He did not understand what Herb was getting at. "He'll say it was an overdose of a semitoxic drug, as he already told us."

"But taken deliberately," Herb said. "A suicidal dose."

"What do you want me to do?"

Herb said, "Compel him—order him—to find an inquest verdict of murder."

He saw, then. Later, when he had overcome some of his grief, he would have thought of it himself. But Herb Maime was right: it had to be faced now. Even before they got back to the academy building and their staffs.

"So we can say," Herb said, "that—"

"That elements within the police hierarchy hostile to my campus and labor-camp policies took revenge by murdering my sister," Buckman said tightly. It froze his blood to find himself thinking of such matters already. But—

"Something like that," Herb said. "No one named specifically. No marshals, I mean. Just suggest that *they* hired someone to do it. Or ordered some junior officer eager to rise in the ranks to do it. Don't you agree I'm right? And we must act rapidly; it's got to be declared immediately. As soon as we get back to the academy you should send a memo to all the marshals and the Director, stating that."

I must turn a terrible personal tragedy into an advantage, Buckman realized. Capitalize on the accidental death of my own sister. If it *was* accidental.

"Maybe it's true," he said. Possibly Marshal Holbein, for example, who hated him enormously, had arranged it.

"No," Herb said. "It's not true. But start an inquiry. And you must find someone to pin it on; there must be a trial."

"Yes," he agreed dully. With all the trimmings. Ending in an execution, with many dark hints in media releases that "higher authorities" were involved, but who, because of their positions, could not be touched. And the Director, hopefully, would officially express his sympathy concerning the tragedy, and his hope that the guilty party would be found and punished.

"I'm sorry that I have to bring this up so soon," Herb said.

"But they got you down from marshal to general; if the incest story is publicly believed they might be able to force you to retire. Of course, even if we take the initiative, they may air the incest story. Let's hope you're reasonably well covered."

"I did everything possible," Buckman said.

"Whom should we pin it on?" Herb asked.

"Marshal Holbein and Marshal Ackers." His hatred for them was as great as theirs for him: they had, five years ago, slaughtered over ten thousand students at the Stanford Campus, a final bloody—and needless—atrocity of that atrocity of atrocities, the Second Civil War.

Herb said, "I don't mean who planned it. That's obvious; as you say, Holbein and Ackers and the others. I mean who actually injected her with the drug."

"The small fry," Buckman said. "Some political prisoner in one of the forced-labor camps." It didn't really matter. Any one of a million camp inmates, or any student from a dying kibbutz, would do.

"I would say pin it on somebody higher up," Herb said.

"Why?" Buckman did not follow his thinking. "It's always done that way; the apparatus always picks an unknown, unimportant—"

"Make it one of her friends. Somebody who *could have* been her equal. In fact, make it somebody well known. In fact, make it somebody in the acting field here in this area; she was a celebrity-fucker."

"Why somebody important?"

"To tie Holbein and Ackers in with those gunjy, degenerate phone-orgy bastards she hung out with." Herb sounded genuinely angry, now; Buckman, startled, glanced at him. "The ones who really killed her. Her cult friends. Pick someone as high as you can. And then you'll really have something to pin on the marshals. Think of the scandal that'll make. Holbein part of the phone grid."

Buckman put out his cigarette and lit another. Meanwhile thinking. What I have to do, he realized, is out-scandal them. My story has to be more lurid than theirs.

It would take some story.

25

In his suite of offices at the Los Angeles Police Academy building, Felix Buckman sorted among the memos, letters, and documents on his desk, mechanically selecting the ones that needed Herb Maime's attention and discarding those that could wait. He worked rapidly, with no real interest. As he inspected the various papers, Herb, in his own office, began typing out the first informal statement which Buckman would make public concerning the death of his sister.

Both men finished after a brief interval and met in Buckman's main office, where he kept his crucial activities. At his oversize oak desk.

Seated behind the desk he read over Herb's first draft. "Do we have to do this?" he said, when he had finished reading it.

"Yes," Herb said. "If you weren't so dazed by grief you'd be the first to recognize it. Your being able to see matters of this sort clearly has kept you at policy level; if you hadn't had that faculty they'd have reduced you to training-school major five years ago."

"Then release it," Buckman said. "Wait." He motioned for Herb to come back. "You quote the coroner. Won't the media know that the coroner's investigation couldn't be completed this soon?"

"I'm backdating the time of death. I'm stipulating that it took place yesterday. For that reason."

"Is that necessary?"

Herb said simply, "Our statement has to come first. Before theirs. And they won't wait for the coroner's inquest to be completed."

"All right," Buckman said. "Release it."

Peggy Beason entered his office, carrying several classified police memoranda and a yellow file. "Mr. Buckman," she said, "at a time like this I don't want to bother you, but these—"

"I'll look at them," Buckman said. But that's all, he said to himself. Then I'm going home.

Peggy said, "I knew you were looking for this particular file. So was Inspector McNulty. It just arrived, about ten minutes ago, from Data Central." She placed the file before him on the blotter of his desk. "The Jason Taverner file."

Astonished, Buckman said, "But there is no Jason Taverner file."

"Apparently someone else had it out," Peggy said. "Anyhow they just put it on the wire, so they must have just now gotten it back. There's no note of explanation; Data Central merely—"

"Go away and let me look at it," Buckman said.

Quietly, Peggy Beason left his office, closing the door behind her.

"I shouldn't have talked to her like that," Buckman said to Herb Maime.

"It's understandable."

Opening the Jason Taverner file, Buckman uncovered a glossy eight-by-five publicity still. Clipped to it a memo read: *Courtesy of the Jason Taverner Show, nine o'clock Tuesday nights on NBC.*

"Jesus God," Buckman said. The gods, he thought, are playing with us. Pulling off our wings.

Leaning over, Herb looked to see, too. Together, they

gazed down at the publicity still, wordlessly, until finally Herb said, "Let's see what else there is."

Buckman tossed the eight-by-five photo aside with its memo, read the first page of the file.

"How many viewers?" Herb said.

"Thirty million," Buckman said. Reaching, he picked up his phone. "Peggy," he said, "get the NBC-TV outlet here in L.A. KNBC or whatever it is. Put me through to one of the network executives, the higher the better. Tell them it's us."

"Yes, Mr. Buckman."

A moment later a responsible-looking face appeared on the phone screen and in Buckman's ear a voice said, "Yes, sir. What can we do for you, General?"

"Do you carry the *Jason Taverner Show*?" Buckman said.

"Every Tuesday night for three years. At nine o'clock sharp."

"You've aired it for *three years*?"

"Yes, General."

Buckman hung up the phone.

"Then what was Taverner doing in Watts," Herb Maime said, "buying forged ID cards?"

Buckman said, "We couldn't even get a birth record on him. We worked every data bank that exists, every newspaper file. Have you ever heard of the *Jason Taverner Show* on NBC at nine o'clock Tuesday night?"

"No," Herb said cautiously, hesitating.

"You're not sure?"

"We've talked so much about Taverner—"

"I never heard of it," Buckman said. "And I watch two hours of TV every night. Between eight and ten." He turned to the next page of the file, hurling the first page away; it fell to the floor and Herb retrieved it.

On the second page: a list of the recordings that Jason Taverner had made over the years, giving title, stock number, and date. He stared sightlessly at the list; it went back nineteen years.

Herb said, "He did tell us he's a singer. And one of his ID cards put him in the musicians' union. So that part is true."

"It's all true," Buckman said harshly. He flipped to page three. It disclosed Jason Taverner's financial worth, the sources and amounts of his income. "A lot more than I make," Buckman said, "as a police general. More than you and I make together."

"He had plenty of money when we had him in here. And he gave Kathy Nelson a hell of a lot of money. Remember?"

"Yes, Kathy told McNulty that; I remember it from McNulty's report." Buckman pondered, meanwhile mindlessly dog-earing the edge of the Xerox page. And then ceased. Abruptly.

"What is it?" Herb said.

"This is a Xerox copy. The file at Data Central is never pulled; only copies are sent out."

Herb said, "But it has to be pulled to be Xeroxed."

"A period of five seconds," Buckman said.

"I don't know," Herb said. "Don't ask me to explain it. I don't know how long it takes."

"Sure you do. We all do. We've watched it done a million times. It goes on all day."

"Then the computer erred."

Buckman said, "Okay. He has never had any political affiliations; he's entirely clean. Good for him." He leafed further into the file. "Mixed up with the Syndicate for a while. Carried a gun but had a permit for it. Was sued two years ago by a viewer who said a blackout skit was a takeoff on him. Someone named Artemus Franks living in Des Moines. Taverner's attorneys won." He read here and there, not searching for anything in particular, just marveling. "His forty-five record, 'Nowhere Nuthin' Fuck-up,' which is his latest, has sold over two million copies. Ever heard of it?"

"I don't know," Herb said.

Buckman gazed up at him for a time. "I never heard of it. That's the difference between you and me, Maime. You're not sure. I am."

"You're right," Herb said. "But I really don't know, at this point. I find this very confusing, and we have other business; we have to think about Alys and the coroner's report. We should talk to him as soon as possible. He's probably still at the house; I'll call him and you can—"

"Taverner," Buckman said, "was with her when she died."

"Yes, we know that. Chancer said so. You decided it wasn't important. But I do think just for the record we should haul him in and talk to him. See what he has to say."

"Could Alys have known him before today?" Buckman said. He thought, Yes, she always liked sixes, especially the ones in the entertainment field. Such as Heather Hart. She and the Hart woman had a three-month romance the year before last . . . a relationship which I almost failed to hear about: they did a good job of hushing it up. That was one time Alys kept her mouth shut.

He saw, then, in Jason Taverner's file a mention of Heather Hart; his eyes fixed on it as he thought about her. Heather Hart had been Taverner's mistress for roughly a year.

"After all," Buckman said, "both of them are sixes."

"Taverner and who?"

"Heather Hart. The singer. This file is up to date; it says Heather Hart appeared on Jason Taverner's show this week. His special guest." He tossed the file away from him, rummaged in his coat pocket for his cigarettes.

"Here." Herb extended his own pack.

Buckman rubbed his chin, then said, "Let's have the Hart woman brought in, too. Along with Taverner."

"Okay." Nodding, Herb made a note of that on his customary vest-pocket pad.

"It was Jason Taverner," Buckman said quietly, as if to himself, "who killed Alys. Jealous over Heather Hart. He found out about their relationship."

Herb Maime blinked.

"Isn't that right?" Buckman gazed up at Herb Maime, steadily.

"Okay," Herb Maime said after a time.

"Motive. Opportunity. A witness: Chancer, who can testify

that Taverner came running out apprehensively and tried to get hold of the keys to Alys's quibble. And then when Chancer went in the house to investigate, his suspicions aroused, Taverner ran off and escaped. With Chancer shooting over his head, telling him to stop."

Herb nodded. Silently.

"That's it," Buckman said.

"Want him picked up right away?"

"As soon as possible."

"We'll notify all the checkpoints. Put out an APB. If he's still in Los Angeles we may be able to catch him with an EEG-gram projection from a copter. A match of patterns, as they're beginning to do now in New York. In fact we can have a New York police copter brought in just for this."

Buckman said, "Fine."

"Will we say that Taverner was involved in her orgies?"

"There were no orgies," Buckman said.

"Holbein and those with him will—"

"Let them prove it," Buckman said. "Here in a court in California. Where we have jurisdiction."

Herb said, "Why Taverner?"

"It has to be somebody," Buckman said, half to himself; he intertwined his fingers before him on the surface of his great antique oak desk. With his fingers he pressed convulsively, straining with all the force he possessed, one finger against another. "It always, always," he said, "has to be somebody. And Taverner is somebody important. Just what she liked. In fact that's why he was there; that's the celebrity type she preferred. And"—he glanced up—"why not? He'll do just fine." Yes, why not? he thought, and continued grimly to press his fingers tighter and tighter together on the desk before him.

26

Walking down the sidewalk, away from Mary Anne's apartment, Jason Taverner said to himself, My luck has turned. It's all come back, everything I lost. Thank God!

I'm the happiest man in the whole fucking world, he said to himself. This is the greatest day of my life. He thought, You never appreciate it until you lose it, until all of a sudden you don't have it any more. Well, for two days I lost it and now it's back and now I appreciate it.

Clutching the box containing the pot Mary Anne had made, he hurried out into the street to flag down a passing cab.

"Where to, mister?" the cab asked as it slid open its door.

Panting with fatigue, he climbed inside, shut the door manually. "803 Norden Lane," he said, "in Beverly Hills." Heather Hart's address. He was going back to her at last. And as he really was, not as she had imagined him during the awful last two days.

The cab zoomed up into the sky and he leaned gratefully back, feeling even more weary than he had at Mary Anne's apartment. So much had happened. What about Alys Buckman? he wondered. Should I try to get in touch with General Buckman again? But by now he probably knows. And I should keep out of it. A TV and recording star should not get mixed up in lurid matters, he realized. The gutter press, he reflected, is always ready to play it up for all it's worth.

But I owed her something, he thought. She cut off those electronic devices the pols fastened onto me before I could get out of the Police Academy building.

But they won't be looking for me now. I have my ID back; I'm known to the entire planet. Thirty million viewers can testify to my physical and legal existence.

I will never have to fear a random checkpoint again, he said to himself, and shut his eyes in dozing sleep.

"Here we are, sir," the cab said suddenly. His eyes flew open and he sat upright. Already? Glancing out he saw the apartment complex in which Heather had her West Coast hideaway.

"Oh, yeah," he said, digging into his coat for his roll of paper money. "Thanks." He paid the cab and it opened its door to let him out. Feeling in a good mood again, he said, "If I didn't have the fare wouldn't you open the door?"

The cab did not answer. It had not been programed for that question. But what the hell did he care? He had the money.

He strode up onto the sidewalk, then along the redwood rounds path to the main lobby of the choice ten-story structure that floated, on compressed air jets, a few feet from the ground. The flotation gave its inhabitants a ceaseless sensation of being gently lulled, as if on a giant mother's bosom. He had always enjoyed that. Back East it had not caught on, but out here on the Coast it enjoyed an expensive vogue.

Pressing the stud for her apartment, he stood holding the cardboard box with its vase on the tips of the upraised fingers of his right hand. I better not, he decided; I might drop it like I did before, with the other one. But I'm not going to drop it; my hands are steady now.

I'll give the damn vase to Heather, he decided. A present I picked up for her because I understand her consummate taste.

The viewscreen for Heather's unit lit up and a female face appeared, peering at him. Susie, Heather's maid.

"Oh, Mr. Taverner," Susie said, and at once released the

latch of the door, operated from within regions of vast security. "Come on in. Heather's gone out but she—"

"I'll wait," he said. He skipped across the foyer to the elevator, punched the *up* button, waited.

A moment later Susie stood holding the door of Heather's unit open for him. Dark-skinned, pretty and small, she greeted him as she always had: with warmth. And— familiarity.

"Hi," Jason said, and entered.

"As I was telling you," Susie said, "Heather's out shopping but she should be back by eight o'clock. Today she has a lot of free time and she told me she wanted to make the best use of it because there's a big recording session with RCA scheduled for the latter part of the week."

"I'm not in a hurry," he said candidly. Going into the living room, he placed the cardboard box on the coffee table, dead center, where Heather would be certain to see it. "I'll listen to the quad and crash," he said. "If it's all right."

"Don't you always?" Susie said. "I've got to go out, too; I have a dentist's appointment at four-fifteen and it's all the way on the other side of Hollywood."

He put his arm around her and gripped her firm right boob.

"We're horny today," Susie said, pleased.

"Let's get it on," he said.

"You're too tall for me," Susie said, and moved off to resume whatever she had been doing when he rang.

At the phonograph he sorted through a stack of recently played albums. None of them appealed to him, so he bent down and examined the spines of her full collection. From them he took several of her albums and a couple of his own. These he stacked up on the changer and set it into motion. The tone arm descended, and the sound of *The Heart of Hart* disc, a favorite of his, edged out and echoed through the large living room, with all its drapes beautifully augmenting the natural quad acoust-tones, spotted artfully here and there.

He lay down on the couch, removed his shoes, made himself comfortable. She did a damn good job when she taped this, he said to himself, half out loud. I'm as exhausted as I've ever been in my life, he realized. Mescaline does that to me. I could sleep for a week. Maybe I will. To the sound of Heather's voice and mine. Why haven't we ever done an album together? he asked himself. A good idea. Would sell. Well. He shut his eyes. Twice the sales, and Al could get us promotion from RCA. But I'm under contract to Reprise. Well, it can be worked out. There's work in. Everything. But, he thought, it's worth it.

Eyes shut, he said, "And now the sound of Jason Taverner." The changer dropped the next disc. Already? he asked himself. He sat up, examined his watch. He had dozed through *The Heart of Hart,* had barely heard it. Lying back again he once more shut his eyes. Sleep, he thought, to the sound of me. His voice, enhanced by a two-track overlay of guitars and strings, resonated about him.

Darkness. Eyes open, he sat up, knowing that a great deal of time had passed.

Silence. The changer had played the entire stack, hours' worth. What time was it?

Groping, he found a lamp familiar to him, located the switch, turned it on.

His watch read ten-thirty. Cold and hungry. Where's Heather? he wondered, fumbling with his shoes. My feet cold and damp and my stomach is empty. Maybe I can—

The front door flew open. There stood Heather, in her cheruba coat, holding a copy of the L.A. *Times.* Her face, stark and gray, confronted him like a death mask.

"What is it?" he said, terrified.

Coming toward him, Heather held out the paper. Silently. Silently, he took it. Read it.

**TV PERSONALITY SOUGHT IN CONNECTION WITH DEATH
OF POL GENERAL'S SISTER**

"Did you kill Alys Buckman?" Heather rasped.

"No," he said, reading the article.

Popular television personality Jason Taverner, star of his own hour-long evening variety show, is believed by the Los Angeles Pol Dept to have been deeply involved in what pol experts say is a carefully planned vengeance murder, the Policy Academy announced today. Taverner, 42, is sought by both

He ceased reading, crumpled the newspaper savagely. "Shit," he said, then. Sucking in his breath he shuddered. Violently.

"It gives her age as thirty-two," Heather said. "I know for a fact that she's—was—thirty-four."

"I saw it," Jason said. "I was in the house."

Heather said, "I didn't know you knew her."

"I just met her. Today."

"Today? Just today? I doubt that."

It's true. General Buckman interrogated me at the academy building and she stopped me as I was leaving. They had planted a bunch of electronic tracking devices on me, including—"

"They only do that to students," Heather said.

He finished, "And Alys cut them off. And then she invited me to their house."

"And she died."

"Yes." He nodded. "I saw her body as a withered yellow skeleton and it frightened me; you're damn right it frightened me. I got out of there as quickly as I could. Wouldn't you have?"

"Why did you see her as a skeleton? Had you two taken some sort of dope? She always did, so I suppose you did, too."

"Mescaline," Jason said. "That's what she told me, but I don't think it was." I wish I knew what it was, he said to himself, his fear still freezing his heart. Is this a hallucination brought on by it, as was the sight of her skeleton? Am I living this or am I in that fleabag hotel room? He thought, Good God, *what do I do now?*

"You better turn yourself in," Heather said.

"They can't pin it on me," he said. But he knew better. In the last two days he had learned a great deal about the police who ruled their society. Legacy of the Second Civil War, he thought. From pigs to pols. In one easy jump.

"If you didn't do it they won't charge you. The pols are fair. It's not as if the nats are after you."

He uncrumpled the newspaper, read a little more.

believed to be an overdose of a toxic compound administered by Taverner while Miss Buckman was either sleeping or in a state

"They give the time of the murder as yesterday," Heather said. "Where were you yesterday? I called your apartment and didn't get any answer. And you just now said—"

"It wasn't yesterday. It was earlier today." Everything had become uncanny; he felt weightless, as if floating along with the apartment into a bottomless sky of oblivion. "They backdated it. I had a pol lab expert on my show once and after the show he told me how they—"

"Shut up," Heather said sharply.

He ceased talking. And stood. Helplessly. Waiting.

"There's something about me in the article," Heather said, between clenched teeth. "Look on the back page."

Obediently, he turned to the back page, the continuation of the article.

as a hypothesis pol officials offered the theory that the relationship between Heather Hart, herself also a popular TV and recording personality, and Miss Buckman triggered Taverner's vengeful spree in which

Jason said, "What kind of relationship did you have with Alys? Knowing her—"

"You said you didn't know her. You said you just met her today."

"She was weird. Frankly I think she was a lesbian. Did

you and she have a sexual relationship?" He heard his voice rise; he could not control it. "That's what the article hints at. Isn't that right?"

The force of her blow stung his face; he retreated involuntarily, holding his hands up defensively. He had never been slapped like that before, he realized. It hurt like hell. His ears rang.

"Okay," Heather breathed. "Hit me back."

He drew his arm back, made a fist, then let his arm fall, his fingers relaxing. "I can't," he said. "I wish I could. You're lucky."

"I guess I am. If you killed her you could certainly kill me. What do you have to lose? They'll gas you anyhow."

Jason said, "You don't believe me. That I didn't do it."

"That doesn't matter. They think you did it. Even if you get off it means the end of your goddamn career, and mine, for that matter. We're finished; do you understand? Do you realize what you've done?" She was screaming at him, now; frightened, he moved toward her, then, as the volume of her voice increased, away again. In confusion.

"If I could talk to General Buckman," he said, "I might be able to—"

"Her *brother*? You're going to appeal to him?" Heather strode at him, her fingers writhing clawlike. "He's head of the commission investigating the murder. As soon as the coroner reported that it was homicide, General Buckman announced he personally was taking charge of the incident— can't you manage to read the whole article? I read it ten times on the way back here; I picked it up in Bel Aire after I got my new fall, the one they ordered for me from Belgium. It finally arrived. And now look. What does it matter?"

Reaching, he tried to put his arms around her. Stiffly, she pulled away.

"I'm not going to turn myself in," he said.

"Do whatever you want." Her voice had sunk to a blunted whisper. "I don't care. Just go away. I don't want to have anything more to do with you. I wish you were both dead, you and her. That skinny bitch—all she ever meant to me was trouble. Finally I had to throw her bodily out; she clung to me like a leech."

"Was she good in bed?" he said, and drew back as Heather's hand rose swiftly, fingers groping for his eyes.

For an interval neither of them spoke. They stood close together. Jason could hear her breathing and his own. Rapid, noisy fluctuations of air. In and out, in and out. He shut his eyes.

"You do what you want," Heather said presently. "I'm going to turn myself in at the academy."

"They want you, too?" he said.

"Can't you read the whole article? Can't you just do *that*? They want my testimony. As to how you felt about my relationship with Alys. It was public knowledge that you and I were sleeping together then, for Christ's sake."

"I didn't know about your relationship."

"I'll tell them that. When"—she hesitated, then went on—"when did you find out?"

"From this newspaper," he said. "Just now."

"You didn't know about it yesterday when she was killed?"

At that he gave up; hopeless, he said to himself. Like living in a world made of rubber. Everything bounced. Changed shape as soon as it was touched or even looked at.

"Today, then," Heather said. "If that's what you believe. You would know, if anyone would."

"Goodbye," he said. Sitting down, he fished his shoes out from beneath the couch, put them on, tied the laces, stood up. Then, reaching, he lifted the cardboard box from the coffee table. "For you," he said, and tossed it to her. Heather clutched at it; the box struck her on the chest and then fell to the floor.

"What is it?" she asked.

"By now," he said, "I've forgotten."

Kneeling, Heather picked up the box, opened it, brought forth newspapers and the blue-glazed vase. It had not broken. "Oh," she said softly. Standing up she inspected it; she held it close to the light. "It's incredibly beautiful," she said. "Thank you."

Jason said, "I didn't kill that woman."

Wandering away from him, Heather placed the vase on a high shelf of knickknacks. She said nothing.

"What can I do," he said, "but go?" He waited but still she said nothing. "Can't you speak?" he demanded.

"Call them," Heather said. "And tell them you're here."

He picked up the phone, dialed the operator. "I want to put through a call to the Los Angeles Police Academy," he told the operator. "To General Felix Buckman. Tell him it's Jason Taverner calling." The operator was silent. "Hello?" he said.

"You can dial that direct, sir."

"I want you to do it," Jason said.

"But, sir—"

"Please," he said.

27

Phil Westerburg, the Los Angeles Police Agency chief deputy coroner, said to General Felix Buckman, his superior, "I can explain the drug best this way. You haven't heard of it because it isn't in use yet; she must have ripped it off from the academy's special-activities lab." He sketched on a piece of paper. "Time-binding is a function of the brain. It's a structuralization of perception and orientation."

"Why did it kill her?" Buckman asked. It was late and his head hurt. He wished the day would end; he wished everyone and everything would go away. "An overdose?" he demanded.

"We have no way of determining as yet what would constitute an overdose with KR-3. It's currently being tested on detainee volunteers at the San Bernardino forced-labor camp, but so far"—Westerburg continued to sketch—"anyhow, as I was explaining. Time-binding is a function of the brain and goes on as long as the brain is receiving input. Now, we know that the brain can't function if it can't bind space as well . . . but as to why, we don't know yet. Probably it has to do with the instinct to stabilize reality in such a fashion that sequences can be ordered in terms of before-and-after—that would be time—and, more importantly, space-occupying, as with a three-dimensional object as compared to, say, a drawing of that object."

He showed Buckman his sketch. It meant nothing to Buckman; he stared at it blankly and wondered where, this late at night, he could get some Darvon for his headache. Had Alys had any? She had squirreled so many pills.

Westerburg continued, "Now, one aspect of space is that any given unit of space excludes all other given units; if a thing is there it can't be here. Just as in time if an event comes before, it can't also come after."

Buckman said, "Couldn't this wait until tomorrow? You originally said it would take twenty-four hours to develop a report on the exact toxin involved. Twenty-four hours is satisfactory to me."

"But you requested that we speed up the analysis," Westerburg said. "You wanted the autopsy to begin immediately. At two-ten this afternoon, when I was first officially called in."

"Did I?" Buckman said. Yes, he thought, I did. Before the marshals can get their story together. "Just don't draw pictures," he said. "My eyes hurt. Just tell me."

"The exclusiveness of space, we've learned, is only a function of the brain as it handles perception. It regulates data in terms of mutually restrictive space units. Millions of them. Trillions, theoretically, in fact. But in itself, space is not exclusive. In fact, in itself, space does not exist at all."

"Meaning?"

Westerburg, refraining from sketching, said, "A drug such as KR-3 breaks down the brain's ability to exclude one unit of space out of another. So here versus there is lost as the brain tries to handle perception. It can't tell if an object has gone away or if it's still there. When this occurs the brain can no longer exclude alternative spatial vectors. It opens up the entire range of spatial variation. The brain can no longer tell which objects exist and which are only latent, unspatial possibilities. So as a result, competing spatial corridors are opened, into which the garbled percept system enters, and a whole new universe appears to the brain to be in the process of creation."

"I see," Buckman said. But actually he did not either see

or care. I only want to go home, he thought. And forget this.

"That's very important," Westerburg said earnestly. "KR-3 is a major breakthrough. Anyone affected by it is forced to perceive irreal universes, whether they want to or not. As I said, trillions of possibilities are theoretically all of a sudden real; chance enters and the person's percept system chooses one possibility out of all those presented to it. It *has* to choose, because if it didn't, competing universes would overlap, and the concept of space itself would vanish. Do you follow me?"

Seated a short way off, at his own desk, Herb Maime said, "He means that the brain seizes on the spatial universe nearest at hand."

"Yes," Westerburg said. "You've read the classified lab report on KR-3, have you, Mr. Maime?"

"I read it a little over an hour ago," Herb Maime said. "Most of it was too technical for me to grasp. But I did notice that its effects are transitory. The brain finally reestablishes contact with the actual space-time objects that it formerly perceived."

"Right," Westerburg said, nodding. "But during the interval in which the drug is active the subject exists, or thinks he exists—"

"There's no difference," Herb said, "between the two. That's the way the drug works; it abolishes that distinction."

"Technically," Westerburg said. "But to the subject an actualized environment envelopes him, one which is alien to the former one that he always experienced, and he operates as if he had entered a new world. A world with changed aspects . . . the amount of change being determined by how great the so-to-speak distance is between the space-time world he formerly perceived and the new one he's forced to function in."

"I'm going home," Buckman said. "I can't stand any more of this." He rose to his feet. "Thanks, Westerburg," he said, automatically extending his hand to the chief deputy coroner. They shook. "Put together an abstract for me," he said to

Herb Maime, "and I'll look it over in the morning." He started off, his gray topcoat over his arm. As he always carried it.

"Do you now see what happened to Taverner?" Herb said.

Halting, Buckman said, "No."

"He passed over to a universe in which he didn't exist. And we passed over with him because we're objects of his percept-system. And then when the drug wore off he passed back again. What actually locked him back here was nothing he took or didn't take but her death. So then of course his file came to us from Data Central."

"Good night," Buckman said. He left the office, passed through the great, silent room of spotless metal desks, all alike, all cleared at the end of the day, including McNulty's, and then at last found himself in the ascent tube, rising to the roof.

The night air, cold and clear, made his head ache terribly; he shut his eyes and gritted his teeth. And then he thought, I could get an analgesic from Phil Westerburg. There's probably fifty kinds in the academy's pharmacy, and Westerburg has the keys.

Taking the descent tube he rearrived on the fourteenth floor, returned to his suite of offices, where Westerburg and Herb Maime still sat conferring.

To Buckman, Herb said, "I want to explain one thing I said. About us being objects of his percept system."

"We're not," Buckman said.

Herb said, "We are and we aren't. Taverner wasn't the one who took the KR-3. It was Alys. Taverner, like the rest of us, became a datum in your sister's percept system and got dragged across when she passed into an alternate construct of coordinates. She was very involved with Taverner as a wish-fulfillment performer, evidently, and had run a fantasy number in her head for some time about knowing him as an actual person. But although she did manage to accomplish this by taking the drug, he and we at the same time remained in our own universe. We occupied two space corridors at the same time, one real, one irreal. One is an actuality; one is a latent possibility among many, spatialized temporarily by the KR-3. But just temporarily. For about two days."

"That's long enough," Westerburg said, "to do enormous physical harm to the brain involved. Your sister's brain, Mr. Buckman, was probably not so much destroyed by toxicity but by a high and sustained overload. We may find that the ultimate cause of death was irreversible injury to cortical tissue, a speed-up of normal neurological decay . . . her brain so to speak died of old age over an interval of two days."

"Can I get some Darvon from you?" Buckman said to Westerburg.

"The pharmacy is locked up," Westerburg said.

"But you have the key."

Westerburg said, "I'm not supposed to use it when the pharmacist isn't on duty."

"Make an exception," Herb said sharply. "This time."

Westerburg moved off, sorting among his keys.

"If the pharmacist was there," Buckman said, after a time, "he wouldn't need the key."

"This whole planet," Herb said, "is run by bureaucrats." He eyed Buckman. "You're too sick to take anymore. After he gets you the Darvon, go home."

"I'm not sick," Buckman said. "I just don't feel well."

"But don't stick around here. I'll finish up. You start to leave and then you come back."

"I'm like an animal," Buckman said. "Like a laboratory rat."

The phone on his big oak desk buzzed.

"Is there any chance it's one of the marshals?" Buckman said. "I can't talk to them tonight; it'll have to wait."

Herb picked up the phone. Listened. Then, cupping his hand over the receiver, he said, "It's Taverner. Jason Taverner."

"I'll talk to him." Buckman took the phone from Herb Maime, said into it, "Hello, Taverner. It's late."

In his ear, Taverner said tinnily, "I want to give myself up. I'm at the apartment of Heather Hart. We're waiting here together."

To Herb Maime, Buckman said, "He wants to give himself up."

"Tell him to come down here," Herb said.

"Come down here," Buckman said into the phone. "Why do you want to give up?" he said. "We'll kill you in the end, you miserable murdering motherfucker; you know that. Why don't you run?"

"Where?" Taverner squeaked.

"To one of the campuses. Go to Columbia. They're stabilized; they have food and water for a while."

Taverner said, "I don't want to be hunted anymore."

"To live is to be hunted," Buckman rasped. "Okay, Taverner," he said. "Come down here and we'll book you. Bring the Hart woman with you so we can record her testimony." You goddamn fool, he thought. Giving yourself up. "Cut your testicles off while you're at it. You stupid bastard." His voice shook.

"I want to clear myself," Taverner's voice echoed thinly in Buckman's ear.

"When you show up here," Buckman said, "I'll kill you with my own gun. Resisting arrest, you degenerate. Or whatever we want to call it. We'll call it what we feel like. Anything." He hung up the phone. "He's coming down here to be killed," he said to Herb Maime.

"You picked him. You can unpick him if you want. Clear him. Send him back to his phonograph records and his silly TV show."

"No." Buckman shook his head.

Westerburg appeared with two pink capsules and a paper cup of water. "Darvon compound," he said, presenting them to Buckman.

"Thank you." Buckman swallowed the pills, drank the water, crushed the paper cup and dropped it into his shredder. Quietly, the teeth of the shredder spun, then ceased. Silence.

"Go home," Herb said to him. "Or, better yet, go to a motel, a good downtown motel for the night. Sleep late tomorrow; I'll handle the marshals when they call."

"I have to meet Taverner."

"No you don't. I'll book him. Or a desk sergeant can book him. Like any other criminal."

"Herb," Buckman said, "I intend to kill the guy, as I said on the phone." Going to his desk he unlocked the bottom drawer, got out a cedar box, set it on the desk. He opened the box and from it brought forth a single-shot Derringer twenty-two pistol. He loaded it with a hollow-nosed shell, half cocked it, held it with its muzzle pointed at the ceiling. For safety's sake. Habit.

"Let's see that," Herb said.

Buckman handed it to him. "Made by Colt," he said. "Colt acquired the dies and patents. I forget when."

"This is a nice gun," Herb said, weighing it, balancing it in his hand. "A fine handgun." He gave it back. "But a twenty-two slug is too small. You'd have to get him exactly between the eyes. He'd have to be standing directly in front of you." He placed his hand on Buckman's shoulder. "Use a thirty-eight special or a forty-five," he said. "Okay? Will you do that?"

"You know who owns this gun?" Buckman said. "Alys. She kept it here because she said if she kept it at home she might use it on me sometime during an argument, or late at night when she gets—got—depressed. But it's not a woman's gun. Derringer made women's guns, but this isn't one of them."

"Did you get it for her?"

"No," Buckman said. "She found it in a pawnshop down in the Watts area. Twenty-five bucks she paid for it. Not a bad price, considering its condition." He glanced up, into Herb's face. "We really have to kill him. The marshals will crucify me if we don't hang it on him. And I've got to stay at policy level."

"I'll take care of it," Herb said.

"Okay." Buckman nodded. "I'll go home." He placed the

pistol back in its box, back on its red-velvet cushion, closed the box, then opened it once more and dumped the twenty-two bullet from the barrel. Herb Maime and Phil Westerburg watched. "The barrel breaks to the side in this model," Buckman said. "It's unusual."

"You better get a black-and-gray to take you home," Herb said. "The way you feel and with what's happened you shouldn't be driving."

"I can drive," Buckman said. "I can always drive. What I can't do properly is kill a man with a twenty-two slug who's standing directly in front of me. Somebody has to do it for me."

"Good night," Herb said quietly.

"Good night." Buckman left them, made his way through the various offices, the deserted suites and chambers of the academy, once more to the ascent tube. The Darvon had already begun to lessen the pain in his head; he felt grateful for that. Now I can breathe the night air, he thought. Without suffering.

The door of the ascent tube slid open. There stood Jason Taverner. And, with him, an attractive woman. Both of them looked frightened and pale. Two tall, handsome, nervous people. Obviously sixes. Defeated sixes.

"You are under police arrest," Buckman said. "Here are your rights. Anything you say may be held against you. You have a right to counsel and if you cannot afford an attorney one will be appointed for you. You have a right to be tried by a jury, or you can waive that right and be tried by a judge appointed by the Police Academy of Los Angeles City and County. Do you understand what I have just said?"

"I came here to clear myself," Jason Taverner said.

"My staff will take your depositions," Buckman said. "Go into the blue-colored offices over there where you were taken before." He pointed. "Do you see him in there? The man in the single-breasted suit with the yellow tie?"

"Can I clear myself?" Jason Taverner said. "I admit to being in the house when she died, but I didn't have anything to do with it. I went upstairs and found her in the bathroom.

She was getting some Thorazine for me. To counteract the mescaline she gave me."

"He saw her as a skeleton," the woman—evidently Heather Hart—said. "Because of the mescaline. Can't he get off on the grounds that he was under the influence of a powerful hallucinogenic chemical? Doesn't that legally clear him? He had no control over what he did, and I didn't have anything to do with it at all. I didn't even know she was dead until I read tonight's paper."

"In some states it might," Buckman said.

"But not here," the woman said wanly. Comprehendingly.

Emerging from his office, Herb Maime sized up the situation and declared, "I'll book him and take their statements, Mr. Buckman. You go ahead on home as we agreed."

"Thank you," Buckman said. "Where's my topcoat?" He glanced around for it. "God, it's cold," he said. "They turn the heat off at night," he explained to Taverner and the Hart woman. "I'm sorry."

"Good night," Herb said to him.

Buckman entered the ascent tube and pressed the button that closed the door. He still did not have his topcoat. Maybe I should take a black-and-gray, he said to himself. Get some junior-grade eager cadet type to drive me home, or, like Herb said, go to one of the good downtown motels. Or one of the new soundproof hotels by the airport. But then my quibble would be here and I wouldn't have it to drive to work tomorrow morning.

The cold air and the darkness of the roof made him wince. Even the Darvon can't help me, he thought. Not completely. I can still feel it.

He unlocked the door of his quibble, got inside and slammed the door after him. Colder in here than out there, he thought. Jesus. He started up the engine and turned on the heater. Frigid wind blew up at him from the floor vents. He began to shake. I'll feel better when I can get home, he thought. Looking at his wristwatch, he saw that it was two-thirty. No wonder it's so cold, he thought.

Why did I pick Taverner? he asked himself. Out of a planet

of six billion people . . . this one specific man who never harmed anyone, never did anything except let his file come to the attention of the authorities. That's it right there, he realized. Jason Taverner let himself come to our attention, and, as they say, once come to the authorities' attention, never completely forgotten.

But I can unpick him, he thought, as Herb pointed out.

No. Again it had to be no. The die was cast from the beginning. Before any of us even laid hands on it. Taverner, he thought, you were doomed from the start. From your first act upward.

We play roles, Buckman thought. We occupy positions, some small, some large. Some ordinary, some strange. Some outlandish and bizarre. Some visible, some dim or not visible at all. Jason Taverner's role was large and visible at the end, and it was at the end that the decision had to be made. If he could have stayed as he started out: one small man without proper ID cards, living in a ratty, broken-down, slum hotel—if he could have remained that he might have gotten away . . . or at the very worst wound up in a forced-labor camp. But Taverner did not elect to do that.

Some irrational will within him made him want to appear, to be visible, to be *known*. All right, Jason Taverner, Buckman thought, you are known, again, as you were once before, but better known now, known in a new way. In a way that serves higher ends—ends you know nothing about, but must accept without understanding. As you go to your grave your mouth will be still open, asking the question, "What did I do?" You will be buried that way: with your mouth still open.

And I could never explain it to you, Buckman thought. Except to say: don't come to the attention of the authorities. Don't ever interest us. Don't make us want to know more about you.

Someday your story, the ritual and shape of your downfall, may be made public, at a remote future time when it no longer matters. When there are no more forced-labor camps and no more campuses surrounded by rings of police carrying rapid-fire submachine guns and wearing gas masks that make them look like great-snouted, huge-eyed root-eaters, some kind of noxious lower animal. Someday there may be a post mortem inquiry and it will be learned that you in fact did no harm—did nothing, actually, but become noticed.

The real, ultimate truth is that despite your fame and your great public following you are expendable, he thought. And I am not. That is the difference between the two of us. Therefore you must go and I remain.

His ship floated on, up into the band of nighttime stars. And to himself he sang quietly, seeking to look ahead, to see forward into time, to the world of his home, of music and thought and love, to books, ornate snuffboxes and rare stamps. To the blotting out, for a moment, of the wind that rushed about him as he drove on, a speck nearly lost in the night.

There is beauty which will never be lost, he declared to himself; I will preserve it; I am one of those who cherishes it. And I abide. And that, in the final analysis, is all that matters.

Tunelessly, he hummed to himself. And felt at last some meager heat as, finally, the standard police model quibble heater mounted below his feet began to function.

Something dripped from his nose onto the fabric of his coat. My God, he thought in horror. I'm crying again. He put up his hand and wiped the greaselike wetness from his eyes. Who for? he asked himself. Alys? For Taverner? The Hart woman? Or for all of them?

No, he thought. It's a reflex. From fatigue and worry. It doesn't mean anything. Why does a man cry? he wondered. Not like a woman; not for that. Not for sentiment. A man cries over the loss of something, something alive. A man can cry over a sick animal that he knows won't make it. The death of a child: a man can cry for that. But not because things are sad.

A man, he thought, cries not for the future or the past but for the present. And what is the present, now? They are booking Jason Taverner back at the Police Academy building and he is telling them his story. Like everyone else, he has an account to give, an offering which makes clear his lack of guilt. Jason Taverner, as I fly this craft, is doing that right now.

Turning the steering wheel, he sent his quibble in a long trajectory that brought it at last into an Immelmann; he made the craft fly back the way it had come, at no increase in speed, nor at any loss. He merely flew in the opposite direction. Back toward the academy.

And yet still he cried. His tears became each moment denser and faster and deeper. I'm going the wrong way, he thought. Herb is right; I have to get away from there. All I can do there now is witness something I can no longer control. I am painted on, like a fresco. Dwelling in only two dimensions. I and Jason Taverner are figures in an old child's drawing. Lost in dust.

He pressed his foot down on the accelerator and pulled back on the steering wheel of the quibble; it spluttered up, its engine missing and misfiring. The automatic choke is still closed, he said to himself. I should have revved it up for a while. It's still cold. Once more he changed direction.

Aching, and with fatigue, he at last dropped his home route card into the control turret of the quibble's guiding section and snapped on the automatic pilot. I should rest, he said to himself. Reaching, he activated the sleep circuit above his head; the mechanism hummed and he shut his eyes.

Sleep, artificially induced, came as always at once. He felt himself spiraling down into it and was glad. But then, almost at once, beyond the control of the sleep circuit, a dream came. Very clearly he did not want the dream. But he could not stop it.

The countryside, brown and dry, in summer, where he had lived as a child. He rode a horse, and approaching him on his left a squad of horses nearing slowly. On the horses rode men in shining robes, each a different color; each wore a pointed helmet that sparkled in the sunlight. The slow, solemn knights passed him and as they traveled by he made out the face of one: an ancient marble face, a terribly old man with rippling cascades of white beard. What a strong nose

he had. What noble features. So tired, so serious, so far
beyond ordinary men. Evidently he was a king.

Felix Buckman let them pass; he did not speak to them
and they said nothing to him. Together, they all moved toward
the house from which he had come. A man had sealed himself
up inside the house, a man alone, Jason Taverner, in the
silence and darkness, without windows, by himself from now
on into eternity. Sitting, merely existing, inert. Felix Buckman continued on, out into the open countryside. And then
he heard from behind him one dreadful single shriek. They
had killed Taverner, and seeing them enter, sensing them in
the shadows around him, knowing what they intended to do
with him, Taverner had shrieked.

Within himself Felix Buckman felt absolute and utter des-
olate grief. But in the dream he did not go back nor look
back. There was nothing that could be done. No one could
have stopped the posse of varicolored men in robes; they
could not have been said no to. Anyhow, it was over. Taverner
was dead.

His heaving, disordered brain managed to spike a relay
signal via minute electrodes to the sleep circuit. A voltage
breaker clicked open, and a solid, disturbing tone awakened
Buckman from his sleep and from his dream.

God, he thought, and shivered. How cold it had become.
How empty and alone he felt himself to be.

The great, weeping grief within him, left from the dream,
meandered in his breast, still disturbing him. I've got to land,
he said to himself. See some person. Talk to someone. I can't
stay alone. Just for a second if I could—

Shutting off the automatic pilot he steered the quibble
toward a square of fluorescent light below: an all-night gas
station.

A moment later he bumpily landed before the gas pumps
of the station, rolling to a stop near another quibble, parked
and empty, abandoned. No one in it.

Glare lit up the shape of a middle-aged black man in a
topcoat, neat, colorful tie, his face aristocratic, each feature
starkly outlined. The black man paced about across the oil-

streaked cement, his arms folded, an absent expression on his face. Evidently he waited for the robotrix attendant to finish fueling up his ship. The black man was neither impatient nor resigned; he merely existed, in remoteness and isolation and splendor, strong in his body, standing high, seeing nothing because there was nothing he cared to see.

Parking his quibble, Felix Buckman shut off the motor, activated the door latch and lock, stepped stiffly out into the cold of night. He made his way toward the black man.

The black man did not look at him. He kept his distance. He moved about, calmly, distantly. He did not speak.

Into his coat pocket Felix Buckman reached with cold-shaken fingers; he found his ballpoint pen, plucked it out, groped in his pockets for a square of paper, any paper, a sheet from a memo pad. Finding it, he placed it on the hood of the black man's quibble. In the white, stark light of the service station Buckman drew on the paper a heart pierced by an arrow. Trembling with cold he turned toward the black man pacing and extended the piece of drawn-on paper to him.

His eyes bulging briefly, in surprise, the black man grunted, accepted the piece of paper, held it by the light, examining it. Buckman waited. The black man turned the paper over, saw nothing on the back, one again scrutinized the heart with the arrow piercing it. He frowned, shrugged, then handed the paper back to Buckman and wandered on, his arms once again folded, his large back to the police general. The slip of paper fluttered away, lost.

Silently, Felix Buckman returned to his own quibble, lifted open the door, squeezed inside behind the wheel. He turned on the motor, slammed the door, and flew up into the night sky, his ascent warning bulbs winking red before him and behind. They shut automatically off, then, and he droned along the line of the horizon, thinking nothing.

The tears came once again.

All of a sudden he spun the steering wheel; the quibble popped violently, bucked, leveled out laterally on a descending trajectory; moments later he once again glided to a stop in the hard glare beside the parked, empty quibble, the pacing black man, the fuel pumps. Buckman braked to a stop, shut off his engine, stepped creakingly out.

The black man was looking at him.

Buckman walked toward the black man. The black man did not retreat; he stood where he was. Buckman reached him, held out his arms and seized the black man, enfolded him in them, and hugged him. The black man grunted in surprise. And dismay. Neither man said anything. They stood for an instant and then Buckman let the black man go, turned, walked shakingly back to his quibble.

"Wait," the black man said.

Buckman revolved to face him.

Hesitating, the black man stood shivering and then said, "Do you know how to get to Ventura? Up on air route thirty?" He waited. Buckman said nothing. "It's fifty or so miles north of here," the black man said. Still Buckman said nothing. "Do you have a map of this area?" the black man asked.

"No," Buckman said. "I'm sorry."

"I'll ask the gas station," the black man said, and smiled a little. Sheepishly. "It was—nice meeting you. What's your name?" The black man waited a long moment. "Do you want to tell me?"

"I have no name," Buckman said. "Not right now." He could not really bear to think of it, at this time.

"Are you an official of some kind? Like a greeter? Or from the L.A. Chamber of Commerce? I've had dealings with them and they're all right."

"No," Buckman said. "I'm an individual. Like you."

"Well, I have a name," the black man said. He deftly reached into his inner coat pocket, brought out a small stiff card, which he passed to Buckman. "Montgomery L. Hopkins is the handle. Look at the card. Isn't that a good printing job? I like the letters raised like that. Fifty dollars a thousand it cost me; I got a special price because of an introductory offer not to be repeated." The card had beautiful great embossed black letters on it. "I manufacture inexpensive biofeedback headphones of the analog type. They sell retail for under a hundred dollars."

"Come and visit me," Buckman said.

"Call me," the black man said. Slowly and firmly, but also a little loudly, he said. "These places, these coin-operated robot gas stations, are downers late at night. Sometime later on we can talk more. Where it's friendly. I can sympathize and understand how you're feeling, when it happens that places like this get you on a bummer. A lot of times I get gas on my way home from the factory so I won't have to stop late. I go out on a lot of night calls for several reasons. Yes, I can tell you're feeling down at the mouth—you know, depressed. That's why you handed me that note which I'm afraid I didn't flash on at the time but do now, and then you wanted to put your arms around me, you know, like you did, like a child would, for a second. I've had that sort of inspiration, or rather call it impulse, from time to time during my life. I'm forty-seven now. I understand. You want to not be by yourself late at night, especially when it's unseasonably chilly like it is right now. Yes, I agree completely, and now you don't exactly know what to say because you did something suddenly out of irrational impulse without thinking through to the final consequences. But it's okay; I can dig it. Don't worry about it one damn bit. You must drop over. You'll like my house. It's very mellow. You can meet my wife and our kids. Three in all."

"I will," Buckman said. "I'll keep your card." He got out his wallet, pushed the card into it. "Thank you."

"I see that my quibble's ready," the black man said. "I was low on oil, too." He hesitated, started to move away, then returned and held out his hand. Buckman shook it briefly. "Goodbye," the black man said.

Buckman watched him go; the black man paid the gas station, got into his slightly battered quibble, started it up, and lifted off into the darkness. As he passed above Buckman the black man raised his right hand from the steering wheel and waved in salutation.

Good night, Buckman thought as he silently waved back

with cold-bitten fingers. Then he reentered his own quibble, hesitated, feeling numb, waited, then, seeing nothing, slammed his door abruptly and started up his engine. A moment later he had reached the sky.

Flow, my tears, he thought. The first piece of abstract music ever written. John Dowland in his Second Lute Book in 1600. I'll play it on that big new quad phonograph of mine when I get home. Where it can remind me of Alys and all the rest of them. Where there will be a symphony and a fire and it will all be warm.

I will go get my little boy. Early tomorrow I'll fly down to Florida and pick up Barney. Have him with me from now on. The two of us together. No matter what the consequences. But now there won't be any consequences; it's all over. It's safe. Forever.

His quibble crept across the night sky. Like some wounded, half-dissolved insect. Carrying him home.

PART FOUR

Hark! you shadows that in darkness dwell,
Learn to condemn light.
Happy, happy they that in hell
Feel not the world's despite.

EPILOGUE

The trial of Jason Taverner for the first-degree murder of Alys Buckman mysteriously backfired, ending with a verdict of not guilty, due in part to the excellent legal help NBC and Bill Wolfer provided, but due also to the fact that Taverner had committed no crime. There had in fact been no crime, and the original coroner's finding was reversed—accompanied by the retirement of the coroner and his replacement by a younger man. Jason Taverner's TV ratings, which had dropped to a low point during the trial, rose with the verdict, and Taverner found himself with an audience of thirty-five million, rather than thirty.

The house which Felix Buckman and his sister Alys had owned and occupied drifted along in a nebulous legal status for several years; Alys had willed her part of the equity to a lesbian organization called the Sons of Caribron with headquarters in Lee's Summit, Missouri, and the society wished to make the house into a retreat for their several saints. In March of 2003 Buckman sold his share of the equity to the Sons of Caribron, and, with the money derived, moved himself and all the items of his many collections to Borneo, where living was cheap and the police amiable.

Experiments with the multiple-space-inclusion drug KR-3 were abandoned late in 1992, due to its toxic qualities. However, for several years the police covertly experimented with

it on inmates in forced-labor camps. But ultimately, due to
the general widespread hazards involved, the Director ordered the project abandoned.

Kathy Nelson learned—and accepted—a year later that
her husband Jack had been long dead, as McNulty had told
her. The recognition of this precipitated a blatant psychotic
break in her, and she again was hospitalized, this time for
good at a far less stylish psychiatric hospital than Morningside.

For the fifty-first and final time in her life Ruth Rae married, in this terminal instance, to an elderly, wealthy, pot-
bellied importer of firearms located in lower New Jersey,
barely operating within the limit of the law. In the spring of
1994 she died of an overdose of alcohol taken with a new
tranquilizer, Phrenozine, which acts as a central nervous system depressant, as well as suppressing the vagus nerve. At
the time of her death she weighed ninety-two pounds, the
result of difficult—and chronic—psychological problems. It
never became possible to certify with any clarity the death
as either an accident or a deliberate suicide; after all, the
medication was relatively new. Her husband, Jake Mongo,
at the time of her death had become heavily in debt and
outlasted her barely a year. Jason Taverner attended her fu-
neral and, at the later graveside ceremony, met a girl friend
of Ruth's named Fay Krankheit, with whom he presently
formed a working relationship that lasted two years. From
her Jason learned that Ruth Rae had periodically attached
herself to the phone-grid sex network; learning this, he
understood better why she had become as she had when he
met her in Vegas.

Cynical and aging, Heather Hart gradually abandoned her
singing career and dropped out of sight. After a few tries to
locate her, Jason Taverner gave up and wrote it off as one of
the better successes of his life, despite its dreary ending.

He heard, too, that Mary Anne Dominic had won a major
international prize for her ceramic kitchenware, but he never
bothered to trace her down. Monica Buff, however, showed

up in his life toward the end of 1998, as unkempt as ever but still attractive in her grubby way. Jason dated her a few times and then dumped her. For months she wrote him odd, long letters with cryptic signs drawn over the words, but that, too, stopped at last, and for this he was glad.

In the warrens under the ruins of the great universities the student populations gradually gave up their futile attempts to maintain life as they understood it, and voluntarily—for the most part—entered forced-labor camps. So the dregs of the Second Civil War gradually ebbed away, and in 2004, as a pilot model, Columbia University was rebuilt and a safe, sane student body allowed to attend its police-sanctioned courses.

Toward the end of his life retired Police General Felix Buckman, living in Borneo on his pension, wrote an autobiographical exposé of the planetwide police apparatus, the book soon being circulated illegally throughout the major cities of earth. For this, in the summer of 2017, General Buckman was shot by an assassin, never identified, and no arrests were ever made. His book, *The Law-and-order Mentality,* continued to clandestinely circulate for a number of years after his death, but even that, too, eventually became forgotten. The forced-labor camps dwindled away and at last ceased to exist. The police apparatus became by degrees, over the decades, too cumbersome to threaten anyone, and in 2136 the rank of police marshal was abandoned.

Some of the bondage cartoons that Alys Buckman had collected during her aborted life found their way into museums displaying artifacts of faded-out popular cultures, and ultimately she became officially identified by the *Librarian's Journal Quarterly* as the foremost authority of the late twentieth century in the matter of S-M art. The one-dollar black Trans-Mississippi postage stamp which Felix Buckman had laid on her was bought at auction in 1999 by a dealer from Warsaw, Poland. It disappeared thereupon into the hazy world of philately, never to surface again.

Barney Buckman, the son of Felix and Alys Buckman,

grew eventually into difficult manhood, joined the New York police, and during his second year as a beat cop fell from a substandard fire escape while responding to a report of burglary in a tenement where wealthy blacks had once lived. Paralyzed from the waist down at twenty-three, he began to interest himself in old television commercials, and, before long, owned an impressive library of the most ancient and sought-after items of this sort, which he bought and sold and traded shrewdly. He lived a long life, with only a feeble memory of his father and no memory at all of Alys. By and large Barney Buckman complained little, and continued in particular to absorb himself in old-time Alka-Seltzer plugs, his specialty out of all the rest of such golden trivia.

Someone at the Los Angeles Police Academy stole the twenty-two Derringer pistol which Felix Buckman had kept in his desk, and with this the gun vanished forever. Lead slug weapons had by that time become generally extinct except as collector's pieces, and the inventory clerk at the academy whose job it was to keep track of the Derringer assumed wisely that it had become a prop in the bachelors' quarters of some minor police official, and let the investigation drop there.

In 2047 Jason Taverner, long since retired from the entertainment field, died in an exclusive nursing home of acolic fibrosis, an ailment acquired by Terrans at various Martian colonies privately maintained for dubious enthrallment of the weary rich. His estate consisted of a five-bedroom house in Des Moines, filled mostly with memorabilia, and many shares of stock in a corporation which had tried—and failed—to finance a commercial shuttle service to Proxima Centaurus. His passing was not generally noticed, although small obit squibs appeared in most metropolitan newspapers, ignored by the TV news people but not by Mary Anne Dominic, who, even in her eighties, still considered Jason Taverner a celebrity, and her meeting him an important milestone in her long and successful life.

The blue vase made by Mary Anne Dominic and purchased by Jason Taverner as a gift for Heather Hart wound up in a private collection of modern pottery. It remains there to this day, and is much treasured. And, in fact, by a number of people who know ceramics, openly and genuinely cherished. And loved.